I0823993

SEVEN FOR A SECRET

ALSO BY MARY E. ROACH

Young Adult

Better Left Buried

Adult

We Are the Match

SEVEN FOR A SECRET

MARY E. ROACH

HYPERION
LOS ANGELES NEW YORK

First Edition, September 2025
10 9 8 7 6 5 4 3 2 1
FAC-004510-25198
Printed in the United States of America

This book is set in Adobe Caslon Pro/Adobe
Designed by Phil Buchanan

Library of Congress Cataloging-in-Publication Data
Names: Roach, Mary E., author.
Title: Seven for a secret / by Mary E. Roach.
Other titles: 7 for a secret
Description: Los Angeles; New York: Hyperion, 2025. • Audience term: Teenagers • Audience: Ages 14 and up. • Summary: Seventeen-year-old Nev, the only girl to return from a group home where eight girls disappeared, embarks on a relentless quest for answers, peace, and revenge when the men responsible for the home begin turning up dead.
Identifiers: LCCN 2024056831 • ISBN 9781368114608 (hardcover)
Subjects: CYAC: Mystery and detective stories—Fiction. • Missing persons—Fiction. • LGBTQ+ people—Fiction. • LCGFT: Detective and mystery fiction. • Thrillers (Fiction) • Novels.
Classification: LCC PZ7.1.R57747 Se 2025 • DDC [Fic]—dc23
LC record available at https://lccn.loc.gov/2024056831

Reinforced binding

The authorized representative in the EU for product safety and compliance is Disney Trading B.V., Asterweg 15S, 1031 HL, Amsterdam, The Netherlands
email: DCP.DL-EU.bookscontact@disney.com

Visit www.HyperionTeens.com

Certified Sourcing
www.forests.org
SFI-01681

Logo Applies to Text Stock Only

for my sister,

and for yours

CONTENT WARNING

Some elements in this story may be difficult for some readers, including ableism, murder, implied dismemberment, referenced intimate partner violence, and referenced CSA (sexual assault of a minor). If reading about any of these elements is unsafe or difficult for you, please exercise caution.

BEGINNING

WE KILLED HIM IN THE FOREST WHERE THE GIRLS WENT missing and silence covered up their names.

We stabbed him first, one by one and then over and over again until there was more blood in the moss and the soil than in his body.

And then we dragged his body through the forest as he had dragged ours, night after night, and this time it felt like going home.

There is a small shack in the wild green outside the town where we all see faces in the dark.

It was there we cut him up, limb by limb by limb. We used his saws, the ones our bones once felt, and we wept—but not for him.

Never for him.

We wept for us, girls who vanished into darkness and were never looked for, as if we had never existed at all.

We buried him where he had always buried us, under the looming, all-seeing oaks who groan and mumble in the wind.

He had buried all of us there, and at first it broke our hearts to let him rest among us—but what is left of our hearts to matter?

So now he lies among us, and we dare you to find him.

Come looking for him, if you can bear it.

Come, uncover our crime, and see what we have done at the heart of the forest—but before you reach his bones, you will find ours in rows of teeth and narrow shoulders.

Before you find him, you will have to face us.

CHAPTER ONE

THEY WILL SAY, LATER, THAT IT WAS A FACTORY WORKER on his way home who found the body at the edge of the Patuxent. They will say that, because when I found the body first, I left it where it was.

I was headed back from the boxing gym, sweaty tank top clinging to my skin, legs sore from the workout. The river was as dark as night, little eddies carrying last year's leaves down, down, down. It was a break in the darkness: a flash of white.

It was his eyes. That was what I saw first. The eyes, wide open, the whites visible. It was one of the only things recognizable about a body that had been in the water as long as his had.

I knew him, anyway, because of the badge clutched in his hand that still read, in faint letters, his name. Charles Aisley.

I left the main road, walked through the long, half-dead marsh grasses, and peered over him. He was still half-submerged, and in the water pooled in this little inlet I could see my reflection next to his face in the water.

My own dark brown eyes, wide. My closely shaved head with nothing but pinpricks of black hair, in stark similarity to the bald head of the dead man.

The two of us, there in the water together, my face just a mirror. Nev and Charles. Charles and Nev.

And then, of course, I left. Not just because men like Charles deserve an ending like this one, though they do. But because a foster kid like me—an emancipated foster kid, no less—is going to have suspicion clinging to them as soon as the police get involved, even if I had nothing to do with it.

But that wasn't the only reason I left him there without telling anyone. Wasn't the only reason I went back to the little apartment I'd been living in and blew up the semblance of a life I'd built.

No, it was because the body in the Patuxent is what first gave me the idea. The way his bloated hand clutched his badge brought back a memory that had been buried, somewhere in my aching bones, in my chest cavity where I am mostly hollow. There was that, and the fact that my first lease would be up at the end of May, and despite what I had told Mandy-the-Way-Too-Perky-Social-Worker, I hadn't renewed it yet. Hadn't found a new one, either.

It was something she had warned me about: the frozen state of indecision, feeling as if nothing I did mattered. As if nothing I did could change the outcome. So I did not stay, and I did not sort out a lease, and I did not call any social workers.

No.

No, I was going to pack my bags, and I was going to disappear.

Just the way I was always meant to.

• • •

Build a routine.

That was the first rule on the crinkled flyer Mandy had left on the apartment's kitchen counter when I moved in.

Build a routine, as if brushing my teeth in the morning and working at the same time every day will keep me from becoming one of the kids she has to refer back into the system, ones who can't handle being emancipated at seventeen.

But I did build a routine, a bit, built something just to keep me from standing still for too long, so I had something to do every single day. So I never had enough time to—

Remember.

The first piece is this, more important than any of the other building blocks that make up the routine: At the end of my shitty little street, over potholes and past boarded-up storefronts and beside the cruel depths of the Patuxent, there is a little two-room gym and a sign with most of the letter lightbulbs burnt out. FABIO'S. And beneath it, in faded script, the words MARTIAL FIT.

I go almost every day. The days I do not, I practice at home. I visualize one person when I strike and kick, and only one.

So there is a routine, first.

And then there is a body.

And then there is a half-formed idea that maybe now, finally, I am ready to face it all. Or at least to try.

Find them.

Find *him*.

It doesn't solidify much more than that, even when I lie awake when I should be sleeping, staring at the cracks and stains in the ceiling.

The body is found the morning after I saw it there in the reeds, and the news is full of his face and his name and pictures of Avan Island, where he is from and so am I, in all the ways that matter.

I give myself one more night here in Johnstown before I let Avan Island pull me homeward. And on that last night, I follow my routine one more time, and find myself at Martial Fit.

The gym is at the edge of town, and just like every piece of the life I've built here, it is easy enough to disappear from when I need to.

Martial Fit stands at the end of a nearly empty street. The other buildings used to be shops or businesses, but they're boarded up. Fabio's gym is the only place on this road still open, and beyond it the ground slopes sharply down toward the river.

The rush of water whispers to me as I walk down the dark street, and I catch glimpses of it between sagging structures.

It is a sound that haunts me, though tonight I can't quite remember why.

I have sounds, smells that call up things I can't quite grasp—islands of memory, things I am sure of in my bones but cannot speak aloud. This sound—the river, calling to me—is one of them.

Late May here is usually warm, but tonight the last edge of spring is sharp, and I shiver in my sweatshirt. When I enter the gym, I welcome the warmth and the light.

"Nev." The instructor nods to me.

The mats are worn, the punching bag more ragged still, but the smell is familiar and the people don't talk too much.

It is a good place, this one. No bullshit, just self-defense.

Well, maybe a little bullshit.

Because here is the truth: I want to hit *hard*.

It is controlled here, though less than outside. We spar, and our fists strike pads and nothing more. We hold back, take care of our partners. We are polite, even here.

Sometimes, my foot hovers for a moment before I fire a kick, and I imagine how it would feel to kick the way I want to. I imagine how it would feel as they came apart. I play nice like I am supposed to, though. I *do*.

But I am so *fucking* tired.

If you are a foster kid, you are expected to be grateful, always. But if you are a *girl* in foster care, they want even more: kind and soft-spoken but strong enough to weather any storm, sweet but stoic.

They are hoping for nice girls, and they are looking for martyrs.

I am neither.

I refuse.

"Fabio." I nod back in the direction of my instructor before I make my way to him, slowly.

He stands well over six feet, at least a foot taller than I am, and he never says much, even when he's teaching.

"This is my last night." I scuff my foot against the pads beneath my feet, the ones Fabio keeps talking about replacing but never does.

He leans back against the wall and raises an eyebrow.

"I'm traveling," I say. "Going to visit some family."

It is the closest thing to truth I have about Avan Island. The rest—the rest is as scattered as the leaves in the forest around us.

Fabio scowls. "Bullshit," he says. He looks around at the others—three men lining up to spar on one side of the gym, a boy hitting the bag, and two women practicing locks near us. More will trickle in over the next ten minutes before class starts. Fabio leans closer, his voice lower. "You okay?"

I shrug. "Yeah. And I'm not lying about the travel."

He shakes his head, but says nothing, and as always it's his silence, his waiting, that makes me spill more than I planned to.

"I'm going back to Avan Island," I say, and regret it immediately, because even if he didn't follow the news, most people know what it means to be a girl like me from Avan. "My sisters are from there." That last truth spills before I want it to.

There is a look in his eyes that I never wanted to see, not here. "You okay?" he asks again, and this time it means something different.

"I'll be back," I say. "I don't know how long I'll be gone. A few weeks, maybe."

His dark eyes are heavy and sad, and he doesn't quite look like he believes me.

Girls like me, we don't usually come back.

And if I'm successful—if I find *him*, if I find my sisters—

I am not sure I intend to come back.

"I've got tuition, though." I hold out a fistful of cash. The department store doesn't pay much—but then again, I don't have to pay rent on the apartment next month. "For the whole summer. For when I come back."

Fabio hesitates, and then he takes the cash from my outstretched hand. "That's not what I'm worried about."

"You shouldn't be worried at all," I tell him.

He sighs, the sound soft, and then he shoves the cash into the drawer below his desk and folds his arms. Looks down at me, waiting for more.

"What are we doing tonight?" I change the topic with an incline of my head toward the others, now joined by a handful of teenagers

I vaguely recognize from school. They're not from the group home I'd been emancipated from, though, and I don't really know them.

"Sparring," Fabio answers, but his eyes are still focused on me. "Mariah is teaching the junior belts while the senior belts go in rounds."

I practice alone first, shadowboxing in the air, first with my fist curled shut and then with my elbow, a more powerful strike than a closed fist.

There is a poem from my days at the Avan Island group home, Sister's Place, one that I use to ground myself. It's an old children's rhyme, one with counting, and I use it now to count my strikes in the air.

One for sorrow—

A closed fist, shattering an invisible target.

Two for mirth—

An elbow, finishing what I began.

Three for a wedding—

"Partner off," Fabio calls, jarring me back to the present.

The mats are solid under my feet and sweat is beading on my brow. I look around at the other students.

The other senior belts pair up with one another quickly, too quickly for me. I'm the odd one out, and I'm partnered with another odd one by default.

He's my age, maybe a year older. He's lean and wiry, but he's taller than me, bigger than me. My body tenses when he moves closer.

When he smiles, fear squeezes my throat. Everything about this boy is thin: his paper smile, his spindly legs, his skinny torso. He is a spider, and his hands are reaching, and nothing about my brain is rational right now because I want to scream and I want to run and instead I just shove his hand away.

"Sparring," I manage. "*That's* what we're doing. And Fabio hasn't said *begin* yet." I repeat the rules like there's a chance in hell that he's forgotten, and the boy smiles again, his hand lingering.

"I think I know you from school," he says. "You're not usually here for the sparring classes."

I ignore the question in his statement.

"I'm Cole."

I don't care.

"You don't talk much."

You don't shut up much.

"You're one of the girls from that place, right? The group home, the new one they built in the middle of town?"

That place.

This time, I meet his eyes. It doesn't matter that I got *out* of the group home. Or the one before it, the one they've *all* heard about. I'm the girl from the group home.

"What're you in for?" Cole leans closer. "I mean, why'd they stick you there?"

I feel Fabio's eyes on me, but I don't look in his direction. I stare down the boy and let my lip curl. "I didn't die when I was supposed to," I say, and behind me Fabio lets out a sharp breath.

"Begin."

The word unleashes something in both of us.

In all of us.

For a moment, the rest of the world—dead bodies and lost sisters and small towns holding a death grip on their secrets—ceases to exist.

Cole throws the first punch, a straight-line toward the bridge of my nose, and I parry and strike low, my fist colliding with his ribs.

The ribs are protected beneath his hogu, but he winces nonetheless, and counters with a hook toward my head.

Adrenaline kicks in and then the rest moves slowly to me: his shoulder dropping, his hand firing, my elbow jamming into his bicep to block the punch.

He catches his breath, and I drive him backward with a side kick to center mass.

But it's a smile on his face now, and that can't be right. "I heard you were feisty," he says.

His breath is hot against my ear as he passes. Too warm. Too close.

He moves before he finishes his sentence, lunges for me—and my foot swings high, and then smashes down. Axe kick across the collarbone, to the gap in the hogu where no padding protects him.

No holding back.

And he comes apart.

CHAPTER TWO

I AM GONE THE NEXT MORNING.

My roommate, Clari, a quiet Puerto Rican girl with soft brown eyes and calloused hands, watches me from across our small kitchen as I swing my backpack onto my shoulder.

Where will you go? I think of asking her, but she won't give me an honest answer, just like I won't ever give her one.

I'm emancipated. There are records of me, such as they are—in foster care when I was young, in the group home on Avan Island for the in-between years, the Cutter's group home here in Johnstown, Maryland, and now, as an emancipated teenager on the edge of town.

Though of course, many of the records are sealed, at my request. And every time the other girls who survived Avan Island reached out, I made myself smaller, made myself disappear further. Not because I didn't want to see them. But because I couldn't, couldn't resurface, couldn't let *him* finish what he started.

Still, there are records I exist, if you know where to look.

But my roommate? I'm not even sure I know her real name.

"You're headed out, too?" I ask instead.

She shrugs. Her room was emptied overnight, her car packed only lightly. There's more in the dumpster. More she's just leaving behind, as if she's disappearing just like me. "Good luck out there, Nev," she says softly. "I hope you find what you're looking for."

I don't, not really.

The thing that's driving me back to Avan Island isn't *hope*. Isn't *want*. It's something else, something that's been building inside me for years and sometimes, in those moments when I lose control, explodes out of me like it did last night when I broke that boy's collarbone.

It's anger—and something more.

Clari is looking at me, waiting, even though she didn't ask a question.

"You be safe, too." I hesitate.

My memories of my last days on Avan Island are as scattered as the leaves that drifted down and covered our bodies. As empty as the hollow shed in the forest, the one I do not always remember.

But Roan. The oldest, after Zara was gone.

She gave me a switchblade to take with me.

I haven't spoken to Roan since. Haven't answered her calls. Haven't shown up when she's asked to meet. There were posters around town after she became a journalist—asking for anyone who'd lived at the Avan Island group home to come forward.

But I'm not a story, and anyone who wants to turn what happened to me there into a clickbait article—even if it's one of the people who survived it, too—isn't someone whose call I'll answer.

"You have what you need?" I ask Clari finally, turning the switchblade over and over in my pocket. "To defend yourself?"

Something clouds her gaze, and she nods, just once. "And you?"

I shudder, thinking of the boy last night, of the wail that ripped from his mouth when I broke him just for coming too close. Think of the look in Fabio's eyes when he looked at me and *saw*, for the first time.

"I'll be all right."

I leave first, backpack slung over my shoulder, duffel in hand.

"Vera." Her voice, soft and sure, stops me at the door.

I turn back to her, just once.

"That's my name," she says. "Vera."

For a moment, it hangs there between us. Then I reach out, push my switchblade into her hand, and curl her fingers over it.

I have others, of course. But this one matters to me, this one is from Roan, and it feels, somehow, as if it might keep Clari—*Vera*—a little safer as a result.

Something flickers in her eyes, a layer of emotion she hasn't shown me before.

She thanks me with a nod, her hand ghosting over mine, and then we both disappear, Clari—Vera—fading away behind me as I pull the apartment door shut behind me.

We could have been friends, Vera and I. Could have been more than a handful of words, an *are you safe*, an exchange of names.

But she is like me, and I am like her.

I linger at my car, considering the phone in my hand. There are so few numbers there—my social worker's number, which I haven't bothered to save, but exists in the text threads. Vera's, with a few messages about utility bills and apartment maintenance.

And Roan's, despite the fact I haven't answered her calls or texts.

How do you cross a chasm that wide? Roan knew a girl who no longer exists.

Still, before I go, I send off a text that just says—

Call me.

And then I have one last stop to make before I disappear.

• • •

The world is quiet this early, a frigid, hushed feeling hanging low over the mossy ground. The gravel of the parking lot crunches beneath my feet as I approach the morgue.

I have been here before.

Three times.

When they took me from Avan Island, I was twelve. Seven of the girls in my group home had gone missing. And sometimes, in those early days, when the police had found a girl—any girl—in the river nearby, they would call me, ask me if I recognized her. And each time, each time I had to come here to this morgue and tell a pale, sharp-eyed officer that *no, this is not my sister.*

If they asked the other surviving girls, like Roan, I never saw them there. And since I never answered calls or texts, I never asked them, either.

But the bodies they brought me in to identify were never mine.

They were just girls like us. We wash up on banks like this one all over the state, the country, the world. We are all different and we are all the same.

But no, I tell them every time, this one is not my sister. Nor this one. Nor this one.

They are not in the river.

That much I know.

Today I am here for a different cadaver.

The man at the front desk is white, middle-aged, unkempt, his eyes small and frigid. "Are you lost?" he asks sharply.

"I want to see him," I say.

The man cocks his head at me. "See who?"

"The body," I say. "The man they found on a weeknight at the end of May, half-submerged on the Johnstown side of the Patuxent where it empties into the Chesapeake." I say it like it's words that I have memorized, like it's a story I wrote, because if I don't step back, don't dissociate far enough from the man and the girls and the grave, I will be dragged right back in. "I knew him. And I want to . . . say goodbye."

The man's face softens, if only slightly. "He hasn't had any kinfolk come for him," he says. "He was identified by the forensic pathologist, actually, who knew him and contacted some of his friends from their hometown. They're moving him today. Taking him home. I'm sure they won't mind if you stop in to pay your respects before they do, though."

I do not look particularly vulnerable—shaved head, perpetually scraped knuckles, ripped black jeans and heavy-soled boots. But I do look young, and I do look femme, and for some—this receptionist included, apparently—that is enough.

"Thank you," I say, and I follow him down.

At the door to the morgue, we are met by the medical examiner, a man I have encountered more times than I have wanted to. Each time I have come to identify a body, each time I have wanted to look away from all the dead girls and not been allowed to—each time he has been here.

I asked him, only once, why they called me at all. Why he couldn't make a positive identification himself.

We had known the same girls.

They all looked the same to me, he told me.

So they called me for the next body and the next.

He was on Avan Island, of course, before he was here. A doctor on the board of directors at Sister's Place. A man who did not believe me. But those memories are less sure; those are slick mud beneath my feet and not solid ground.

"Nev," he says unpleasantly.

"Dr. Goodwin."

"Why are you here?" His gaze flicks from me to the receptionist. Lingers on me.

"To pay my respects," I answer. I watch him carefully, watch and wait for the widening of pupils or the quickening of breath.

Dr. Goodwin, who is so old he looks more at home downstairs with his cadavers than he does upstairs among the living, his eyes shifting from the receptionist back to me again. "Well then," he says finally. "Come in before they move him."

There is less air down here, and it's colder and quieter already. This far below ground, I can't even hear the river, the touchstone I am always listening for, something that both grounds me to my body and haunts the edges of my memories.

Dr. Goodwin enters first, and then turns back to me. He's standing beside the body, one hand resting idly on the steel table.

Charles Aisley looks much the same as he did when I found him at the edge of the river. Pale, bloated by the water. His eyes are shut now, though, no longer wide with fear.

"Do you remember him?" Dr. Goodwin asks me curiously. There's another question there, layered beneath it: *What* do *you remember?*

"No," I say. "Not really."

It's true, and it's not. I have missing memories, but I remember Charles, vaguely.

He was one of the cops, a detective, investigating our disappearances back on Avan Island. Detective Aisley spoke in a loud, booming voice about runaways, girls with behavior issues, girls with records. *They have to* want *help*, he'd say, shaking his head.

They have to *want* help.

Did he want help, before the end?

"How'd he die?" I ask.

Dr. Goodwin's pale eyebrows shoot up a little higher. "I thought you were here to pay your respects," he says.

"This is me. Paying respects. Very respectfully." I grit my teeth against the wall of emotions that crash through me at the slightest trigger. A memory rises from the silt, swirls in the river water around me, curling around me like it will pull me down with it.

Dr. Goodwin, standing shoulder to shoulder with the board of directors, saying, What a disrespectful little girl. Girls like these, they lie. Pathologically, sometimes.

"I'm glad you've decided on respect." Dr. Goodwin meets my eyes before they sweep up and down my body.

Not in the openly lecherous way that some do, their gazes raking up and down my body and lingering at my ass, my chest, whatever captures their attention. No, Dr. Goodwin's gaze is just as unsettling as it always has been, but coldly clinical, as if he sees me the way he sees the bodies laid out on his tables.

"I remember how upsetting that runaway epidemic was for you," Dr. Goodwin says.

The word *runaway* is a nettle burrowing into my chest every time someone says it.

This is what people do when they knew you as a foster kid: If you were messy, if you were wrong, if you were loud, if you were hard for the grown-ups around you, they never, ever, ever let you forget.

Girls like these, they lie.

They lie.

They lie.

I clench my fists. "You avoided my question," I say.

A pause. A small one.

"This one is looking like a sad accident, Nev." He leans forward, reaching one long-fingered hand out as if he is going to pat my shoulder sympathetically.

He can't touch me.

He won't.

But if I rip his fingers back, stretching the joints until they pop, the cops will never let me leave for Avan Island. So I step back, holding my breath as I make for the stairs again, leaving Dr. Goodwin and the dead behind me.

The morgue is belowground, only one way in—or out. When I emerge onto the main floor, the fresh air is a welcome relief. How they ventilate *any* air down to the morgue is beyond me, but what does make its way down is stale and thick with the stench of chemicals and death.

Though the dead don't mind, I suppose.

The police precinct is attached to its morgue on the other side, and I shove my way through the wrong door first. The building is small but buzzing with noise: men on phones, men laughing with one another at the watercooler, men leaning against the doorframes and chatting with a few passing beat cops. Men. Men, everywhere.

And then me.

I may be the only girl in the whole building, unless you count bodies in the morgue.

I shiver, turn on my heel before anyone with a badge and a uniform decides they have questions for me.

They might press charges, Fabio had told me last night when the boy's parents helped him into their car. *Watch your back*.

But whatever happens when I find *him*, charges will likely be the least of my worries.

CHAPTER THREE

WHEN I REACH THE PARKING LOT, THERE'S A PICKUP truck and a small Volkswagen with chipped red paint between my car and me, and two people outside of them: one a bulky man with tight dark curls and a beard and brown skin, laugh lines around his eyes. He's carrying a small video camera.

And beside him:

Roan.

My Roan.

She's speaking into her cell phone, and despite her makeup she looks older than I remember, the dark circles beneath her eyes pronounced even though she's still in her early twenties. Not quite twenty-three, if I remember correctly. She has the same dark brown hair, pulled back into a scrunchie behind her head.

And—and she's *alive.*

My heart catches in my throat.

Roan's eyes widen when she sees me.

The professionalism evaporates as her expression shifts to concern. "Nev?" She stares at me as if she cannot quite believe her eyes. "*Nev.*"

Then her phone drops to the concrete with a clatter and she walks toward me. She pauses, arms outstretched. "Can I—"

I step closer, wrap my arms around her, too. She smells of cloves and citrus, and it reminds me so much of being back in Sister's Place, that I almost want to cry.

I step back, hastily, because I cannot break, not here, not today, and certainly not when I go back to Avan Island.

"Holy shit," she says, staring around the parking lot, and then at the precinct and the morgue. "Are you okay? What the fuck are you doing here?"

"Came to visit an old friend," I say, drawing back far enough that I can catch the tears and force them back down. "Dear old Chuck is dead, Roan, didn't you hear?"

I don't ask her if she got my text. Don't ask her why she didn't call.

I didn't call her any of the times she asked. Did she wonder if I'd been lost to the forest, too? Did she wonder if eight girls had gone missing after all, in all those years in between?

Roan stares at me with a mixture of concern and—something else, something I can't read. She nods at the other reporter, a man wearing a *Johnstown Tribune* press badge, and he steps back, giving us some space. She picks her phone up again, brushing dust from the screen protector, before she hangs up with whoever she was talking to.

"Nev."

"I came to pay my respects," I add, when she doesn't say anything more than that. Just my name.

Roan releases a soft sigh, something weary, as if she is used to this from me, even after five years of not knowing the person I became. "Are you okay?"

"Great."

We stare at each other for a long moment.

"They're sending me to Avan Island," Roan says after a long beat. "I... I write stories like this one now. For a newspaper. I'm, uh, a journalist?"

This isn't news to me, of course. I watched her graduate college on Instagram and post the few-and-far-between pictures of herself, those haunting dark eyes staring back at me, never quite smiling, in every picture of her.

"Stories like this one," I repeat. "A dead man is worth a story?"

Roan shifts slightly. "My boss saw the news and assigned me this story. But I suggested there might be more to explore—a connection. Because Charles was the one who investigated—five years ago. Everything that happened."

She doesn't say *runaways*.

Even now, even after nobody listened to us five years ago, Roan doesn't call us runaways.

"Why?" I blurt. It's not that I don't think Roan's a good journalist; of course she is. But she has to be the most junior reporter, even in her small independent company, unless—

"Avan only speaks to its own," Roan says. "You know that. *Johnstown Tribune* is sending someone, but they don't have anyone on staff from Avan, so the reporter they're sending—Merrick, he's a friend of mine—asked if we can do some collaboration on this story."

I stiffen. "Is he going to dig into what happened five years ago, too?" I ask.

Roan shakes her head. "No, he's going because he—and his boss—thinks there's something to this. But, Nev, why now? Why are you really here?"

"I wanted to understand," I answer finally. I don't know how to explain more than that—how to say the words churning in my gut.

The names. The girls. The loss.

The boy who started all of it.

"I wanted to see Chuck."

"Nev, you don't need . . . you don't need to see the body. You can't be serious."

"Dead serious," I tell her. "Dead as good ol' Chuck."

"And did they let you go down there? To *see* him?" She shakes her head with disbelief. "They wouldn't even let *me*, and I'm a whole adult."

She's not that much of an adult, though, at only twenty-two, fresh-faced enough that she must still get carded anywhere she goes, even if *I* can see the weary look behind her eyes.

"You're press," I say. "I just told them I wanted to say goodbye to a friend."

Roan sighs. "Nev, I don't know what you're playing at, but you need to go back home, okay? You've seen enough. You're not part of this."

You're not part of this.

But I am. I am. I am.

I want to tear at my hair, but it is too short now, too short to be grabbed and dragged, too short for me to have something to tear at now.

I am a part of this.

So was the man on the table.

"Chuck," I say, just as Dr. Goodwin pushes open the front door and exits, still in his lab coat. "*Chuck* was part of this."

"Roan." Dr. Goodwin nods to her. "What are you doing hanging around this case? I would have thought you'd had your fill of Avan Island, after all those runaways."

How many times can he say *runaway* in a single morning?

I turn away from him. "Chuck," I repeat.

"Excuse me?" Roan says finally, weariness heavy in her voice.

"That was his name," I say. "Chuck."

"Charles," Dr. Goodwin corrects. "Charles Aisley."

No.

Charles Aisley was the only detective in town, served on the board of the Hunting and Fishing League *and* on the board of the group home. Charles Aisley was an elder in the church, too. *The* church, because it was the sort of small town that only had one.

The memories come and go without a shred of context. I have his face, or what it looked like before it was purpled and bloated by the river, his voice, a vivid flash of him sitting at the table with the other board members on Avan Island. The rest of the memories are disconnected from each other, floating in and out.

Charles Aisley was only one of many faces in the dark.

But now he is not Charles Aisley.

Now he is Chuck, a corpse on a table, a question mark, a body, an object, a nothing.

"Chuck," I repeat. "How did he die?"

"Nev," Dr. Goodwin says finally, as if I were ever talking to *him*. "I told you as much as you needed to—"

"They think it may have been an overdose of some kind," Roan answers. "There were a few injection sites." She shrugs when the doctor's sharp gaze settles on her. "Source at the precinct. Complain to them if you don't like it."

Dr. Goodwin draws himself up, his jaw set. "Get out of here," he tells me. "Whatever you thought you were doing here today, move along. Go back to your life, Nev, and stop disrespecting men who once tried to *help* you."

I have to dig my fingernails into my palm to keep my hands still.

A few men in blue uniforms are loading a large black van with something that is discreetly covered but is definitely a body.

I grin, lift my middle fingers in salute at all of them, Chuck included. "Have a terrible day," I tell them pleasantly, and then I shove my way past Roan.

Roan follows me across the parking lot. "Are you—are you okay?"

I shrug one shoulder. "Are you?"

"No," she says after a moment. "We— I tried to get in touch. Last I called your group home, some girl answered the phone. I don't think she was supposed to tell me, but she said you got emancipated. Living on your own?"

"Yeah."

Roan glances down at her phone before her gaze snaps up to mine. "Nev," she says softly. "You texted."

I don't meet her gaze. "I did," I say.

How can I explain why? Why now?

The truth of it is not something that I can share: that while Roan may have only been seventeen when I knew her, only as old as I am now, she was the closest thing to a safe grown-up any of us had. And when I saw Chuck's purple lips and bloated hand around his badge—

I didn't know what else to do.

"Is—is this what you wanted me to call about?" Roan asks carefully.

There's a mist hanging low over the precinct and the parking lot. It rolled off the river during the night, and the morning has not been able to shake it.

I take it in, listening for the river, imagining I could dive into the murky depths and resurface with more lost memories, before I answer.

"Was he killed?" I ask. "Is that why your friend thinks there's something to look into?"

"At first they were saying it was possible he drowned," she tells me, her eyes wandering toward the precinct doors, toward the van where Chuck now lies. "That he shot up, that he was high. The injection sites were in a strange place, between his toes, but the body had been in the water too long to know if he had anything in his system when he died."

But she doesn't sound all that sure even as she says it, and I know she is thinking of *him*, of the reason we all went missing before.

And it's not an answer to the question I asked, not really.

"Roan?" I ask. "Who's driving Chuck home?"

She tilts her head at me. "I think they're sending Dr. Goodwin," she says finally.

Roan's friend from the *Johnstown Tribune* has stowed his gear and walks over to us.

I've seen him on Roan's Instagram occasionally—Merrick, she called him. He seems friendly, and he's tall, broad-shouldered, probably about Roan's age. Easygoing even when Roan clearly never figured out how to be, which is a mark in his favor. And they're friends, even though they seem to chase the same stories.

Okay, so I may not have texted back or answered any of the calls.

I may have stayed invisible. But that doesn't mean I stopped following what Roan was up to. Even if I had to use a finsta to do it. When I could pull up her profile and see she'd posted a recent pic, it almost felt as if we were all a little less lost if Roan was still out there. Still okay.

"Morning," Merrick says to me. Nods at Roan.

She ignores him.

"Roan?" I say. "It's like a two-hour drive down there. Won't Chuck get a bit stinky on the way to Avan?"

It's not that Avan is far, exactly, not as the crow flies. But the road that winds its way inland to Avan Island comes with sheer drops into forested ravines on either side.

Avan Island is not a true island, or perhaps it has just forgotten it is an island. The river splits just north of it, flowing miles away from itself, Avan Island the gaping wound in the middle. Big enough to hold a town and a forest, small enough to have only one way in or out of town, a single bridge across the ravine.

Not exactly the easiest place to reach—or the easiest place to leave.

"Who's Chuck?" Merrick asks me, tilting his head as he looks down at me.

Roan flattens her lips to suppress a smirk.

"The dead guy," I tell him. "Chuck."

"Charles," Roan corrects. "Nev, we are not nicknaming any cadavers."

Merrick's eyes spark with mirth. "It's impolite," he says, and I can't help my grin.

"I don't think Chuck minds."

Merrick turns to Roan now. "What's she doing here? It's a bit much for a kid, don't you think?" He looks back at me. "You related to him?"

"*Is* it a bit much?" I ask, wrinkling my nose at him. Because really, what's one more body?

At least in Chuck's case, I'm not even a little bit sorry.

Merrick's eyes cloud. "Woulda freaked me out as a teenager," he says. "But as long as you're okay."

"Are you going with Roan?" I ask him.

Merrick shakes his head. "I'm heading down this weekend to talk to folks who knew him," he answers. "But my boss is waiting on some funding clearance, and he thinks they'll open up to a local more than me. So Roan is heading there without me. Did she tell you about the piece we're working on?"

"Yes, and she's heard enough about all this," Roan cuts him off. "And Nev is going home now."

"Yeah," I tell them. "Yeah. I'm going home."

Merrick says his goodbyes and gets into his truck, but Roan lingers.

She flips the keys in her hands and turns to me, but all the darkness in her eyes cannot mask the fear in her face, the tremble in her hands.

A flock of crows takes flight from the oak outside the precinct, and she flinches.

She opens the car door, and I peer up at the murky sky.

"A murder," I say, and point.

"The hell?" She stares back at me, jaw set fiercely, and I want to tell her:

Hands cannot shake if you close them over the steering wheel. Hands cannot shake if they are tight around the keys. Hands cannot shake if you have a weapon at your hip and you are about to drive far, far away from the Johnstown police station and from the people who want more than you have to give.

"A murder of crows," I clarify, and she shakes her head.

"Nev," Roan says softly. "Nev, what are you doing? Go home."

"I am," I tell her, and now understanding dawns across her face, sharp and sure and clear.

"No," she says. "No, Nev, you can't."

But the corpse and the boy last night and Dr. Goodwin's stark pale hands resting against the glinting table in the morgue—they shook something loose inside me, some longing sharpened by the years and what I lost to them. Roan might be going to do her job, to ask questions and spin a story, to explain something as unknowable as Avan Island to the world at large.

But I am going to Avan Island to face the things there I cannot forget, to find the things there I cannot remember.

And maybe I am going so that no one on Avan Island can forget what happened to us there—and so that *he* cannot forget that I know.

"Roan," I tell her. "I'm *ready* to go home."

She cannot stop me, but by the look in her haunted brown eyes, she would if she could. "Where are you staying?" she asks. "And are you—are you sure that's safe?"

"I'm fine," I tell her. "And I have a place to stay figured out."

I *am* fine, because I have been getting in fights for years. I have been training at Fabio's gym for years. The girl who left Avan Island with her long hair and hollow expression is gone, lost somewhere to the river and the winding road and the trees she once played beneath.

I am what remains—and I will not be broken by Avan Island this time around.

"Nev."

"I'm *fine.*"

"Why now?" she asks. She is staring at me, expression unreadable, her car keys in her hand. "You haven't gotten back to us in years. We've tried. We've *all* tried. And—and we *missed* you."

That familiar tightness constricts my throat again. In a different life, I might tell Roan that I'm sorry for that. That I missed her, too, missed all of them.

But in this one I stare back at her across the foggy parking lot, my hands curled into fists at my sides. "Because I'm ready," I tell her again.

It's as much truth as I can really tell her.

I can't tell her that I looked at Chuck's body in the water and did not falter. That I broke a boy for touching me.

That I am ready, at last, to find my sisters and face the person who took them from me.

Roan sighs softly. Then she reaches out and squeezes my shoulder briefly before she gets into her car, the Volkswagen with the chipped paint I saw earlier. I get into my sputtering little Honda Civic, lift my hand in a wave to Roan as I go.

And then we are off, winding our way back up a fog-shaded river toward a town both of us have been trying to leave behind. Two girls and a body going home.

CHAPTER FOUR

CHUCK WAS NOT THE FIRST BODY, OR THE LAST.

He was the first body they gave a shit about, because the rest were girls like me.

Five years ago, the world decided that seven missing girls were nothing but runaways. There was a police investigation, or at least they told us there was one. There was a touching tribute by the Avan Island mayor, Graham Portman, at a town hall. There was a single news article in the *Johnstown Tribune*.

And then they decided to fucking forget us.

I drive faster than both Roan and Dr. Goodwin—no surprise there—so soon enough I cannot see her car or the mini-morgue behind me. I don't even see her flash by when I stop for gas just under an hour out from Avan—the last real gas station until I reach Avan, if the town is as I remember it.

The road winds along the river, steep and curving and sharp as a blade or a needle, the kind that would fit between a man's toes and empty death into his bloodstream.

I wish I could remember more about Chuck.

I must have met him outside of the police station or those insufferable Sister's Place board visits, during which we had to dress up in uncomfortable church clothes that had been donated and pretend we were happy to be there. There must have been more to Chuck than judgment in his eyes when he looked at us girls, but if there ever was, it is all rotting in the back of Dr. Goodwin's van now.

I wish I could remember a lot of things.

The sun knifes through the cloud cover as I'm a few miles out of town, and I slow my car, dangle my hand out the window to feel the cool wind through my fingers.

As I drive across the bridge, the swollen river is so close it feels as if it is reaching for anyone who drives across it.

I run a hand over my scalp, over the hair I have buzzed short, my promise to myself.

I wonder when it will be time to say it, to make Avan Island face it: that if someone went looking, Chuck's body would not be the only one they would find.

Chuck retired a few years ago. That much I knew from the times I've been called to the Johnstown morgue, Dr. Goodwin keeping me abreast of the things that happened on Avan Island, no matter how disinterested I seemed.

I think again about both Roan and Merrick, drawn to Avan Island by Chuck's death. Roan looked for answers about five years ago, but Merrick—Merrick isn't from here. Maybe he noticed the same thing I have as I drive and think of all I have lost to this town:

If Chuck retired years ago, why was he found holding his badge?

• • •

Once I reach the border of Avan, the sun is obscured again, never breaching the fog this deep in the forest.

I don't go in too far.

Not close to the butcher or the farm store or the precinct—or the church. I am not ready for the church.

I think, again, of Chuck's naked, bloated body. I think, again, of a wall of powerful men standing before me and saying, *Runaways, they were just runaways. Girls like that, they lie.* I think, again, that I am glad, glad, *glad* he is dead.

There were few places to stay when I was here at the group home. No hotels, no Airbnbs, nothing beyond one shitty motel at the edge of the forest and three small apartment buildings, each only two stories high. Twenty-four units, total.

A short dirt road appears in the forest, a gap in the trees just as the road drops and the forest pulls away to reveal the town. I turn the car—the road is scarcely labeled, the lettering on the small green motel sign nearly worn away—and end up at a long, low building with eight or nine rooms. There is an office, if you can call it that. It is nothing but a little box the elderly property manager sits in.

I pull up in front of my new home just after one p.m., shrug my hood up, and avoid eye contact.

The manager is a dull man, pale and old and not distinct enough to remember after I've turned away and lost sight of him. Blurry at all the edges. He gives me a key, and I give him cash and a fake name he does not bother to question, because the money is in his hand, and there is enough of it.

"Most of these rooms is empty," he tells me with a shrug. "So if you don't like yer unit, pick another."

"Are there more keys?" I ask him.

"Just mine," he says.

I lift his spare from the desk the moment his back is turned.

The motel room is sparse—a twin bed, a lamp with a fine layer of dust that shifts when I pull the chain to turn it on, and a narrow minifridge whose rumble can be heard from the door. Aside from the lamp, there is a single light fixture on the ceiling, cobwebs dangling from it.

I borrow a broom and vacuum from the motel owner/property manager/resident contestant for World's Most Forgettable Man, run over the place once, and then toss my backpack and duffel beside each other in the corner.

It is home, as much as any place ever is. It is enough, for me, for now, while I do this. If there are answers, if there is anything that can fill all the missing gaps, I will find it here.

Or perhaps, if I close my eyes here, so close to home, so close to the place where I lost them, I will wake and they will be beside me again. My hair will be thick and unshorn, and Lily will be there next to me, her golden hair contrasting with mine. Jordan will be humming, eyes slipping past ours. Saem will be tuning her violin or fighting with her girlfriend.

They will be more than the curve of a rib cage or a splinter of bone in the forest.

I dig my fingers into the skin of my forearm, hard, harder, until I pull myself back. I am Nev. I am on Avan Island. I am newly seventeen.

I am here for answers. I am here because Charles Aisley washed up from the river. I am here because I want—not justice, no, it has been too late for that since I refused the grave that was dug for me and ran for my life. No justice. Not for me.

But answers, maybe. And, with them, revenge.

• • •

Settled is maybe the wrong word for what I have done by vacuuming the dusty motel room one time and tossing my bags down, but it'll have to do.

And next—

Home, properly.

The old group home is walking distance from the motel through a thick patch of woods that will spit me out onto another dirt road that curves away from town toward more forest and eventually the river. The walk feels short enough, especially during the day, but I drive anyway, because the path through the forest has never been safe. Not for me.

It's just a house, a small farmhouse, tucked under some willow trees at the end of a long gravel drive.

When I reach it, I park at the far end of the driveway, blinker on as I work up the nerve to follow that trail.

I am here. I am here. I am here.

Is *he* here, too? What has he done in the years between?

Will he find me, once he knows I returned?

As the sun starts to slip toward the edge of the forest, and I lose longer moments of time, I turn the car around.

I am Nev.

I am seventeen.

I am here on Avan Island.

And I cannot do this alone.

• • •

I find Roan and the dead before I do anything else.

The shadows have grown long, the sun sinking past the edge of the trees that have grown in, so close their branches brush the edges of the small brick mortuary.

Roan's car is parked outside, and she is standing, hands on her hip while she talks to a manager from the local funeral home while two attendants unload the body, still wrapped in its black body bag. Dr. Goodwin is nowhere to be seen—maybe inside already.

Roan catches sight of me, and I grin, lift a hand, and wave at her.

She stalks over to me, so, for good measure, I pull a cigarette from my pocket and shove it between my lips.

"Roan," I say around the cigarette.

She shakes her head. "For fuck's sake," she mutters, but she just looks at me expectantly, as if waiting for an explanation.

The Roan I knew—the teenage Roan, tough as nails, sharp at all the edges and direct every time she opened her mouth—that Roan would have told me off for showing up here.

But she is hesitant, as if just by her saying the wrong thing, I could disappear again, fade away into the forest that was once my playground and once my grave.

I shrug one shoulder. "It's a public space," I tell her.

"Nev," she says. "Coming back to Avan Island is one thing. Following the body around is another."

When I don't say anything else, Roan sighs. "Can I buy you dinner?" she asks. "We can . . . catch up. Okay? After I'm done with—" She waves her hand in the direction of the body.

I look, though I am not sure, suddenly, that I can handle seeing the body again, not when I'm so close to it all. Not when I am *on* Avan Island.

But as it turns out, I don't have to look at him. Roan makes sure of that. She is taller than I am by four inches at least, and she stands between the body and me just in case my morbid curiosity prevails.

"How was the drive?" one of the attendants asks Roan as they shut the van doors. She nods curtly, still facing me.

"Fine," she says. "Thanks for taking a minute to talk to me."

"Glad you made it here safe. That stretch of highway has been so slick with all the rain," the other comments. "I always worry someday someone's gonna lose the road and go right off the side of that bridge. Easy enough when it's foggy."

"Yes," Roan says. "Easy enough."

They exchange more pleasantries—Roan must have already gotten a statement from them for the piece she's working on—but I stare past her. In the black bag behind Roan and the funeral attendants, Chuck is very, very quiet.

Fury uncurls beneath my rib cage, because this is a memory I am sure of:

None of us ever got body bags, or funerals, or even a grave of our own. We got the forest and the river and the forgetting.

"You look pretty young to be a reporter," one of the funeral attendants says, glancing past Roan to me. He looks as if he is close to Dr. Goodwin's age, and his gaze is just as off-putting, just as hungry. A few years ago, the kind of smile twisting his face would have undone me, but today I smile right back.

"You look just the right age for a funeral home," I tell him cheerfully.

Roan steps between us, her face hard. "That will be all," she tells them, but her eyes are on me, dark as the river and just as violent.

I peer around her and grin at the men one last time. "Later, boys."

As soon as they are back inside the building, presumably storing the body in a freezer or some shit, Roan is all nerves again. For all her quiet calm in front of the others, like Dr. Goodwin and the men from the funeral home, Roan is a damn mess. "You need to keep your head down more." She shakes her head. "I should have called your social worker as soon as you mentioned coming back here."

For the first time today, I look at her eyes, really look. Deep and dark, brown as the oak trees looming over the road. "He started it," I say. "And you don't have her number."

Or I really *hope* Roan doesn't somehow have Mandy's number, because Mandy would be horrified to learn that I've returned to the place that, in her words, had a "deeply harmful impact" on my "development," or some shit. I never really listened when Mandy was talking.

A hiss escapes Roan. "They always start it," she says. "But that doesn't mean anything. You're from here. You know that."

The smile I give her is more bared teeth than mirth. "Then you know I know how to survive this town."

She flinches as if I have struck her. "I do," she says softly. "You do."

The pause hangs there between us, and then her face softens. "The diner is probably still shitty," Roan says finally. "But I'm buying."

The diner is, in fact, still shitty.

It is as I remember it, shockingly enough, one of the few memories without gaps in it a mile wide. It is not just the dingy curtains or checkered tiles, or the general smell of ketchup, grease, and existential dread—it is the particular sounds, the click of keys on the old-fashioned cash register, the clink of a cheap fork dropping to the ground, the scuff of slip-proof New Balances on greasy tiles.

"Well," I say. "Smells like home."

Roan's shoulders are hunched in on themselves. "Yeah," she says. "Sure does. The usual?"

My memories stutter and blur.

For a moment, I am eleven years old, tagging along because the older girls were going out and the alternative was staying home with one of the group home attendants.

We are at the diner, piling into a booth, and even though I am the youngest, and even though they do not want me here with them, not really, I pile in, and they make me scoot into the very center, the farthest I can be from the table of old men from church or the judgmental stare of that one nurse at the clinic who thinks, *Group home girls are trouble.*

Girls like that, they lie.

Just runaways.

Roan and Zara have me sit between them. Zara, the oldest, turning eighteen in just a few months. Roan, just behind her, newly seventeen. Me in the middle, only eleven.

Even now, even as the tagalong and the youngest, even now they are protecting me. Even now, Roan looks older than—than sixteen—or seventeen—or twenty-two—even now—even then—

I cannot keep it all straight.

"Nev."

She sets a hand over mine, so soft her fingers feel like a ghost's.

"Roan," I say. I force my tone to sound bright, cheery. I am here. I am Nev. I am sixteen—no, seventeen, now.

Roan is twenty-two. She drove home today. She is buying me dinner.

There is no group home, because it closed, and I am no longer anyone's little sister. I left them all behind a long time ago. I answered no calls, no texts. I held my breath and my tongue, and I did not speak the names aloud, and so he did not kill me.

I am sitting in the booth alone, opposite Roan.

She holds out one laminated menu, unchanged from the early days. "I asked if you wanted the usual?"

"Yeah," I say.

The food is as tasteless as always, but when it is finally on our table, I devour it quickly, realizing only then that I have not eaten all day.

"So." Roan sets down her cup, ice cubes clattering. "I'd like a straight answer. Why the fuck are you here?"

And there she is, the girl I knew.

I cough, a dry bite of hamburger and bun going down the wrong way at her bluntness. "I want to know," I say, and then stop. "Why did Chuck die?"

"You're not here because of Chuck."

"No," I answer her. "No, I'm here to get some closure. Is that so bad?"

I am here to find them. I am here so that nobody can pretend this didn't happen.

Chuck didn't have to face it before he died—but I'll be damned if the rest of them have that option.

"Why *now*?" she demands. Her knuckles are pale where her hand has closed over the edge of the table in a death grip. "Why—what were you doing before?"

"Waiting," I say before I realize the truth of it.

The word settles, heavy and uncomfortable between us.

"For what?" For the barest of moments, she looks like she might cry.

"I don't know," I say. "I— It wasn't much of a life. I couldn't go anywhere until I aged all the way out. That was one of the terms of being emancipated. The apartment and the job and I had to go to *school* or they would send me back to Cutter's—the other group home, the one in Johnstown. And I could . . . I could have left. But I didn't want to be a—a runaway."

It is the easiest thing to say when a girl like me goes missing and no one is all that interested in looking for her.

"And then Chuck—Charles," Roan corrects herself, hiding a shadow of a smile. "He washed up. And that reminded you of . . . all this?"

"Pretty much." I tip back my glass, drink because I can't think of anything to say.

It isn't that I want to find out the details of what happened. *Those* memories? Those memories are so vivid they cut me open every time I close my eyes.

No, there's something else, blurry and murky at the edge of it all. The one thing that haunted me after all of this: Why was *I* one of the ones who survived?

"How long will you be here?" Roan asks me, when I don't offer more.

I don't tell her about the motel, though she's likely staying there, too, so she'll know sooner or later. I don't tell her about the job I was thinking of asking about either. I don't tell her about the little notebook I brought or the map I've been drawing of the forest I'm afraid to reenter. I don't tell her that I'll probably end up at the abandoned group home most days, walking beside my sisters. I don't tell her that I already stopped there, hands trembling on my steering wheel while I parked down the road.

Instead, I shrug a shoulder at her again. "Not long," I say. "Not long at all. You?"

"Not long," she repeats my own answer, her eyes hard. "Nev, I have a story to write—my boss has asked me to dig into what happened five years ago, to put together an investigative piece on our—our sisters. And when I do that, every single person who brushed it under the rug is going to start coming out of the woodwork, because it's probably going to make them look bad. I don't want you caught in the cross fire."

She means *him*, of course. More than any of the rest of them.

Still, I breathe in sharply. *"Probably?"* I snap. "It will *probably* make them look bad?"

Roan meets my eyes. No pretending now. "Do you *want* to talk about everything that happened? Do you . . . do you *remember*?"

Can she see it in my eyes, that the memories flicker and fade and sometimes stay just out of reach?

"I remember enough," I tell her.

For a moment, Roan doesn't look at me at all.

"Then hopefully you remember how badly this town wanted to pretend nothing bad happened," Roan says slowly, as if weighing her words carefully. "Nev, we didn't even know—we weren't even sure you were alive all these years. Please don't get involved in the shitstorm that is coming for this town."

"But what if I'm not done?" I ask her. I set the glass down on the table harder than I need to. I could smash it into pieces on the ground. I could crack it down the middle and hold the sharp part out, away from me, toward whatever threat reaches for me out of shadowed forest and night-dark river.

And what if I'm right—what if Chuck isn't the last body?

What if I don't want it to be?

Roan folds her arms across her chest. "What do you need?" she asks.

"I just—I want to go see the girls," I say, and then my chest tightens around the rest of the words. "Just. The house. I mean the house."

Because Kess and Jordan and Saem and the rest, they're not there anymore. They're not gone, no. But they're not waiting for me back at home.

"Okay," Roan says gently. "Okay, Nev. How about I drive you tomorrow morning? We can go together. Where are you staying tonight?"

"At a friend's place."

Her eyes narrow. "All right," she says finally. "I'm out at the motel at the edge of town. You have my number if you need anything."

Of course I have it. She was the first to call, after that night.

They drove me away at first light. I know this because my social worker told me, but not because I remember it.

Traumatic, Mandy called it. *To be taken from your home so suddenly, to leave behind girls you cared about.*

Roan called, begged me to call back.

And then Jeza, and then Priya, and then Maraam.

So yes.

Yes, of course I have her phone number.

I nod.

"Okay." She stands, looks down at me with eyes that are as haunted as the forest closing in around us. "Nev? Please be safe."

I don't need to be protected, though. I can break a boy for touching me. I cannot be dragged back into the forest.

More than that, though, there is nothing left that this place can take from me. There is nothing it has not already stolen.

"You too," I tell her.

"Can I walk you to your car?" she asks as we make our way to the door. "Just—for my own peace of mind?"

Roan has known what I have known, what it is like to see your sister one moment, to turn around and realize she is gone, to know in a place deep within you that you will never see her again. So I let her walk with me down the narrow streets of Avan Island beneath streetlights that flicker and sputter, desperate defenses against the gathering dark.

She shivers in her thin sweatshirt but shakes her head when I offer her mine.

Our cars are the only ones in the parking lot outside the morgue, the funeral attendants long gone.

For a long moment, Roan looks at me. "Meet me for breakfast in the morning? And I meant what I said. Call if you need anything at all."

I nod. "Stay safe."

"You too."

She's still in her car, dark eyes on me as I drive away.

CHAPTER FIVE

I WAKE EARLY THE NEXT MORNING, DAWN JUST CREEPing over the edge of the forest and through my curtainless window. I plant my hand on the chipped wood of the bedside table and listen for the river. Outside, its low, steady murmur pulls me back into my body even as it reminds me why I am back on Avan Island.

Vaguely, I remember slipping between the blankets in a room that once was mine.

No, that isn't right.

The motel. The bed in the motel. Not the group home. That's where I am.

I am here. I am here. I am *here.*

When I meet Roan outside of the diner later, she looks as exhausted as I feel.

"I was thinking," she says as she settles in across from me. "I could go back to Johnstown with you, when you go? Make sure you're safely home. I've been making connections, and I have a few interviews scheduled for today, but I can reschedule them."

"Making *connections*," I say through a snort. "You know them, and they know you. You just have to see who'll talk to you and who's gonna treat you like you're still group home trash."

Roan flinches, sitting back sharply against the faded red vinyl of the booth. "Something like that," she says. "But you avoided my question. And my suggestion."

"What's it to you?" I ask. "Where I go and what I do?"

Her eyes flash. "Nev," she says firmly. "This town is a *pit*. Last time—"

"Don't," I snarl, lunging forward, only impeded by the booth between us. "Stop fucking talking about *last time*."

Roan catches my wrists in her hands before I can shove her or grab her or whatever else I was going to do. Her grip is tight, unflinching. "You know what was all over town this morning?" she hisses. "'That girl, that little girl is back on Avan Island, and shit is happening.' *You* are bigger news than the dead fucking body they brought back here yesterday. Do you know how dangerous that is? To have everyone in this town noticing you? To have *anyone* in this town noticing you?"

Girls like that,

they lie.

"Good," I say, yanking my hands back from hers.

The waitress comes by, takes our order—Roan's is the same as it ever was, and so is mine, and we order it without pausing to think about it—and then Roan turns back to me.

She looks as if she is in physical pain. "If it's really closure you want," she says softly, "then come with me, okay? We could call you my intern. I could have some help, you could have some closure. My boss thinks it's an interesting angle—someone connected to the group home, a board member and former investigator, dying under mysterious circumstances. So she wants me to talk to each of the remaining board members. The police captain, Ramsey, is still there, so I'll talk to him, the mayor too. Anyone on the board, if they'll talk to me."

"Anyone?" I ask. "What about the interns—Brett and Jake and—and—"

Him.

His name sticks in my throat though, trapped there by hands that wrapped around my neck, crushed my voice until it was nearly gone forever.

"Yeah," Roan says softly. "Anyone. So I'll make you a deal, Nev. I let you come with me as I ask questions. I take you to the group home so you can pay your respects. And..."

"And?" I pause mid-sip and look at her over the top of my water, which is in a Coca-Cola branded glass that would be called vintage anywhere else, but on Avan Island is just average. The world moved on long ago, but this town has stayed frozen in time.

Just like I have.

"And," Roan continues. "I... A few of the girls are still here."

My head snaps up. I know, of course I do.

In the woods, in the ground. We never left.

Roan's eyes are so impossibly sad that I know she understood exactly what I took her words to mean. "Priya," she says. "She... You remember her?"

Priya.

Long black hair, braided down her back. Sharp brown eyes, long lashes. *Fast.* She ran with Zara and Eva and Roan. She climbed trees so fast you'd lose her in the foliage if you didn't keep your eyes on her.

Priya, here. *Here.*

"I remember her," I manage.

"She's a photographer now who contracts with the police department when they need a crime scene photographer," Roan tells me. "I talked to her last night. She'd love to see you, if you're up for it?"

I swallow hard. "I'd like that."

"Okay." Roan breathes out, the *whoosh* of breath sharp. "Then my terms."

I arch an eyebrow at her. "I don't know about *terms*."

"I'll drive you around town, I'll let you ask questions, I'll let you be closer to this than I probably should," Roan says in a rush, as if she's desperate to get it all out before I cut her off with sarcasm or dismissal, something she must expect from me now, though she never would have from the little girl she remembers. "*My* terms are: You don't take unnecessary risks. You don't poke your nose into dangerous shit. And the second I am done interviewing locals and putting together a picture of what's happening here, we go back to Johnstown and I make sure the place you're staying is—well, safe."

"Oh, is that all?" I glare at her. "I'm not a little kid, Roan."

"No, that's not all." She levels me with her gaze. "Talk to anybody you want. But not the Portmans."

For a moment—just a moment—I freeze.

Mayor Portman was the head of the board. And his son—his *son*—

I take a breath in. Out.

"I rented a room at the motel for a month," I tell Roan, because I can't talk about the Portmans.

"You— A *month*? The motel?" Roan pinches the bridge of her nose. "Are you out of your mind?"

"Quite possibly."

"What are you doing," she asks slowly, "that you need to be here for a month?"

I shrug again.

This time, Roan folds her hands and looks at me. "Fine," she says. "I still want you to leave Avan Island as soon as we've gone to the group home together, and you've had some time to say goodbye. But when we get back to Johnstown, I get to talk to your social worker. So do we have a deal?"

I tilt my head and stare up at her. "What's it to you? If I do dangerous shit?"

"What's it to me?" Now she just looks pissed. Furious, even. "What's it to me if you die in this godforsaken town like the rest of us?"

The breath rushes out of my body so fast I stagger, nearly tumble out of the booth onto the floor. Priya and Zara and Roan and I. Jordan and Lily and—

Roan's hand closes over my forearm. "I'm sorry," she says. "Jesus. Nev, I'm sorry."

"Fine," I rasp. "Yeah. Okay. I get access to all the assholes you talk to, and afterward I'll be a very good little girl and go home just like you want."

Roan pinches a finger over the bridge of her nose. "Okay," she says. "Yes. Thank you."

"How do we explain this to your friend when he gets here?" I ask as the waitress sets our orders in front of us.

There's an extra order of hash browns, because Roan always orders extra so that nobody goes hungry.

She slides it across to me, shrugging one shoulder. "He's chill," she says. "And he works for a different paper than I do, so even if he has something to say about how I do my job, he can save it."

Like me, Roan explains as little as she has to, and I don't expect more than that.

After breakfast, I leave my car parked in front of the diner and climb into Roan's passenger seat. The car is neat, nothing out of place, unlike mine, which has fast-food bags and empty Mountain Dew cans littering the back seat.

Roan is right, even if she doesn't know how right she is. I shouldn't be here. I never had any right to survive this town at all, let alone return to it.

Still, it feels right as I sit beside Roan. And as the door clicks shut behind me, the forest and the girls and the ghosts and I breathe out as one. As if, finally, we are all about to get exactly what we've been waiting for.

CHAPTER SIX

"WHAT ARE YOU GOING TO ASK THEM?" I ASK ROAN AS we pull up in front of the police station.

"Well, Charles Aisley was the only detective on the force five years ago," Roan answers, as if she is still unsure what I remember of them and what I don't. "And Captain Ramsey, he helped with the investigation. I want to interview Ramsey today, ask him what he remembers about the girls." She doesn't say *disappearances*. Or worse, *runaways*. She says *the girls*, and despite myself, it makes my shoulders relax a little. Because Roan, she won't let them forget. She won't.

She's like me that way.

I open my mouth to ask her how she stays calm when they act like this is all some easily explained case of girls running away, but when I look at the fierce set of her jaw I think I have the answer to my question: She doesn't.

She just masks her anger better than I do.

"And it's part of our deal?" I say. "That I get to help you ask the questions."

"Yes, if they let you stay in the room with us," Roan says. "But I'd like to know what kind of questions you're going to ask. For closure."

If that was really why I was here, where would I even begin? How are you supposed to move on, when half your heart goes missing in the forest and nobody fucking cares?

"I want to ask to see the file," I say. "What they investigated, where they looked. How they decided not to keep looking."

Roan nods. "And you remember him? Ramsey?"

Ramsey is loud at the town hall, his voice filling the space after I open my mouth and say, *I think someone might have hurt them.* I am twelve, shrinking smaller and smaller until I'm nothing at all. Just a hollow space, an empty chair. There's only space for him, announcing that there isn't anything more to be done.

For girls with rampant behavior issues, we've still done everything we can. I've done everything I can.

Everything.

But we were still missing.

"Nev?"

"I remember him."

"And you want to go in?"

I don't answer that question. "Is Priya here?"

Roan shakes her head.

I follow Roan inside. It's smaller than the Johnstown precinct, a few rooms and a few cells tucked in a wing of the building that houses the precinct, the morgue, and the town hall. Basically everything except the church—though knowing Avan Island, I wouldn't be surprised if they started holding services in one of the conference rooms here.

When we enter, the front lobby is chaos—uniformed men running, a loud, familiar voice bellowing orders.

"Get me Johnstown on the phone!" Ramsey is standing behind the front desk, pointing one long finger at a uniformed officer, who looks pale as hell.

Ramsey's eyes lock on us. "Shit," he says. "No."

That's exactly the look I like to see on a man's face when I walk in: abject horror.

But I don't make pig noises at him, because that might be a bit much to allow, even for Roan.

"No," Ramsey says. He takes a full step back. "You're not supposed to be here."

Roan sidesteps slightly, her shoulder a barrier between Captain Ramsey and me. "Hi, Captain, I'm not sure if you remember me, but I'm a journalist from Johnstown, and I grew up here. We spoke on the phone?"

He jabs the finger my direction. "*She* is not supposed to be here."

I'm not supposed to be alive either, but here I am. Here I fucking am.

"Lovely to see you, too," I tell him.

I am not twelve. I am not small. My hair is not long, and nobody can drag me by it.

"You and I are going to need to reschedule," Ramsey says. His voice shakes, a strong reaction for someone seeing a girl he didn't expect. "And come back without her."

"I'm the intern." I wave and offer up an approximation of a cheerful smile, though it doesn't soothe the worry on his face.

"We've had a . . . complication," Ramsey says, then his eyes flicker to Roan's again. "Nothing we can comment on. You need to leave."

"This is a public building," Roan begins. "And if you need to reschedule, I'm happy to do that, but—"

"Sir, Johnstown can't send anybody," the uniformed officer interrupts. "They can send us the new ME, though, to process the bodies—"

He stops talking as Ramsey's face flushes hotly. "Get the fuck out of here," he tells Roan and me again.

"The bodies?" I ask.

The bodies, *plural.*

Not just one. Not anymore.

"Who's dead?" I ask bluntly.

"The medical examiner," the cop at the desk blurts.

Ramsey looks ready to strangle him, but it's elation surging through my chest, and it shouldn't be, it shouldn't, if I were a better person it wouldn't be. But I'm not, so it is.

"Dr. Goodwin is dead?" I ask.

Roan steps farther in front of me, blocking me from Ramsey's gaze.

"He . . . he died downstairs sometime during the night," Ramsey says with a noise of defeat. "Don't you dare print this shit, Roan. You of all people should know how hysteria and panic can almost ruin people's careers."

Hysteria.

I would lunge forward, if Roan wasn't in my way. Which is probably exactly why she is.

"I'd love to get any statement you're able to give," Roan says, her voice impossibly even.

But I see her, I see the gaps in her mask where her hands shake, where her shoulders and neck are so tight they look as if she can hardly move them. It's anger, there, too, barely contained.

"You know what? Fine," Ramsey says, throwing his hands up in frustration. "If it gets the fucking press out of my goddamn precinct, then yes. Edwards, get started on processing what you can of the scene downstairs."

The only person not in uniform—presumably the detective—turns and rushes back out of a door, disappearing down a set of stairs.

Ramsey points to the officer with the phone in his hand again and directs him to call Johnstown again and make sure the new ME can get here within twenty-four hours. Then he invites Roan back into his office but glares at me. "She stays here."

Roan mouths *I'm sorry* at me, but I give her a thumbs-up. I have questions, yes. I have so many questions for a man who reduced seven missing girls to hysteria and dismissed us like so much trash.

But this serves me right now, because with Ramsey busy, and his little uniformed men running around, I can make myself at home.

If you walk somewhere confidently, people tend to believe you belong there, so when I walk past the desk and into the records room, the uniformed officer—who is once again on the phone with the Johnstown police department—doesn't even look up.

They still keep physical copies of records, as if it's the 19-fucking-90s back here, so it's not hard to find. Like many small towns, the records are abysmally kept and not locked up, or at least not locked up well.

Nothing a penknife and some determination can't open, at least.

That year is thin on files: A few drunken and disorderly. One haphazard file on a burglary at the edge of town.

And—

There.

Sister's Place, written in thick black marker. And over the top of it, in brutal red Sharpie, CLOSED.

It's a viciously thin manila folder, only a few papers shoved inside.

The whole world tightens, the trees outside squeezing in around this place.

They forget, they tell me. *They forget.*

Don't let them.

And I won't, Zara. I won't. Not you, and not Cezanne, or Lily, or Saem, or Jordan, or Eva, or—

"What the fuck are you doing back here?" It's Ramsey again, his voice filling the entire room until there's no air left to breathe at all.

Behavioral issues . . . All those runaways . . . Girls like that, they—

I shove the folder up the front of my shirt, tucking my flannel tighter around me to hide its presence before I turn. "Just waiting outside like you said," I tell Ramsey.

He looks paler than before, which means whatever questions Roan asked him scared him or angered him or both.

But that doesn't mean I can't ask him my own.

Don't let them forget.

"Do you think he's dead because of them?" I ask Captain Ramsey. "Chuck? Or Dr. Goodwin? Or both?"

He startles and takes a step back out of the doorway of the records room.

"I think you need to get the fuck out of here," Ramsey repeats. "Before I decide to stick you in one of the cells for a night for trespassing. And a girl like you, a girl your age? Bad idea."

He said that to me once before. He did, a memory that ripples back into my consciousness as he says it now.

I am twelve, and I am loud, just once. I ask him, *Why, why, why won't you look for us?*

And then I'm interfering with official business and I'm loud and I'm bad and it's all hysteria anyway and I'm unruly and am I threatening a police officer, and do I want to spend a night in a jail cell, and a girl like me, a girl my age?

Bad idea.

"See you around, Ramsey," I tell him as I step back. I don't have to walk so close. I don't have to take up so much space.

But I do, on purpose, jostling his shoulder with my own as I go past him.

I shouldn't, shouldn't throw my cards down on the table and show that I'm angry, that I'm here for answers, but what else is there? What else is left to lose?

Roan is waiting for me just past him, eyebrows raised.

"Be safe," Ramsey tells us as Roan shoves the precinct door open.

It doesn't sound at all like it does when Roan says it to me. Because he doesn't mean *I hope you get home safe*, he doesn't mean *I hope this isn't the last time I see you*, he doesn't mean *I hope you're more dangerous than the danger that finds you.*

He means *Watch your fucking back*. He means *Stay out of my way, if you know what's good for you.*

I don't, though.

"Let's go," Roan tells me softly. Her hand is so gentle on my arm, guiding me toward her car, that I can barely feel her at all. "Let's go, and let's find somewhere to stretch our legs, take a break from this for a bit. I'll tell you what I learned on the way."

Out here, in the open air, I can breathe again. I can hear the river. I can hear the trees and the wind and all of it.

Don't let them forget.

And as I get into Roan's car, the forest lets out its breath in a gust of wind.

Roan looks at me as soon as the car doors are safely shut. "Dr. Goodwin killed Charles Aisley."

I suck in a sharp breath.

His bloated hand, clutching his badge. His wide terrified eyes, staring up from the Patuxent at me.

I had known, I had known then, that there was a reason they were calling me home.

CHAPTER SEVEN

THE FILE STAYS TUCKED BENEATH MY SHIRT, THE EDGE of the manila folder pressing against my hip.

"Roan?" I ask her. "What do you mean he killed Chuck? He said it was... accidental."

There's an answer somewhere out beyond the edge of this car, this town, this body. There's an answer somewhere caged in memories I don't quite have, and girls whom I will never forget.

But Roan is here, solid and real and strong, and committed to being the reason this story doesn't get buried the way ours did. "I'm not sure how much I should—" She stops, shaking her head.

"You're not a rule follower," I say, aghast. "Roan. You can't be serious. I can handle it. Whatever it is."

What's one more body, and one more after that? What's one more horror?

"Dr. Goodwin did the autopsy on Charles and wrote up a report declaring it accidental," Roan says. "Fentanyl overdose."

"I knew that much." I shift the folder beneath my flannel. "What the fuck changed?"

"At some point—whether he did it in Johnstown or did it once he got out here—Dr. Goodwin carved a word into the body," Roan continues after a beat. "It's a little gruesome. The note he left detailed his plans to die by suicide, and now they need a new ME to reexamine the bodies and determine the official cause of death for *both* now that Dr. Goodwin's autopsy report can't be trusted."

"Are they sending more cops, too?" I ask her, running my thumb along the edge of the folder.

Roan pulls over on Main Street in front of a battered brick building and looks over at me. "Ramsey always wants more cops, and more money for his precinct. But no, I think they're just sending an ME and getting Priya for crime scene photography, and—they have a forensics tech, someone I was going to interview. Nev? I know you keep saying you're fine—"

"I'm not."

The car idles while we stare at each other.

"Nev."

"I'm not fine," I tell her. "None of us are. You aren't, or you wouldn't be here."

Hurt flashes in her dark eyes, her gaze slipping from mine toward the long, empty street.

Main Street is wide, dotted with a few historic storefronts and other buildings, spaced apart like they can't bear to stand too close. The diner. A one-room library on some historical register or other, but it hasn't been open in years. A dilapidated house, tilting sadly to one side. A bank, solid brick, the only new thing on this route.

Trees grow in thick, hanging over the buildings here, casting long shadows.

"I'm headed back to the motel to write up what I've learned and send it to my boss," Roan says finally. "They'll rush Merrick here now, with this new twist. Maybe it's easier to get funding when bodies start stacking up. *My* boss is laser focused on five years ago, though, and convinced they'll have the next great investigative journalism piece on small-town America. Maybe even a Pulitzer."

"A Pulitzer? For— It's not even the *Johnstown Tribune*, is it?" I snort. "Who do you work for again?"

"I know." A slight smile plays across Roan's face. "And it's a small independent journal. Covering . . . disappearances like these."

I freeze.

I had judged Roan, when I first saw her posters around town and on social media, asking survivors to come forward. I had thought that she, like so many others with their true crime podcasts and tell-all TikToks, was capitalizing on what I only experienced as pain.

But maybe she's just been looking for answers, looking for *us* in all this.

"But that's not why you're here, Roan," I say softly.

"No," she says. "No, and it's why I need you to be careful, Nev. I . . . You know that the truth about what happened to all of us at that group home never came out. Avan Island loves its secrets and closed doors. But I can make a difference, with this story. I can. You have to trust me to tell it, though. And you have to keep your head down, don't be so . . ."

"Aggressive?"

She shakes her head no at that, smiling a little. "I like that you're aggressive," she says. "Hold on to that fire. But if people know you're hunting down answers, if they know you're knocking on doors they want kept shut... I'm worried, Nev."

But I won't be the next body.

That's something I've known for so long. I've already been the girl in the woods. I've already been the tragedy spread out across the pages of someone else's story. I won't do it again, not for anyone.

Not even if *he* is still in this town.

"So I shouldn't steal files from the records room anymore?" I ask, tugging the file folder out of my shirt and flipping it open.

Roan startles, then reaches to grab it, but I lean away, holding it out of her reach.

I knew the folder was light, knew it from the feel, but staring down at it is a different matter.

There is a list of us—seven girls. No, eight, one name crossed out.

Because I came back.

The report itself is just as short—less than a page, single-spaced, about evidence of girls planning to run away together, about eyewitness testimony stating that girls were seen headed out of town or hitchhiking. About no evidence of foul play, no blood, no DNA, no injured girls.

It's not true. None of it is.

But it's in the official file all the same.

And at the back there is a photocopied page of a book, containing the rhyme I've carried with me for years, chanted in my head as I learned to throw a proper punch and break a board with the force of an elbow strike.

One for sorrow,
Two for mirth,
Three for a—

I slam the folder shut.

"Give that to me," Roan says softly. "Come on. Nev. Let me drop you off back at your car, and tomorrow we'll see Priya and do some more interviews. It'll be all right."

She's using a coaxing sort of tone, as if she is speaking to an injured child, but I do not need softness. Not from her, not from anyone.

I hand her the file anyway. It is trembling like a leaf in a storm, my hands not my own.

One for sorrow, one for sorrow, one for sorrow.

It was in a book I'd read as a child. I know that much. Some memories aren't fully gone. Some are just strangely shaped and hard to take off the shelf, hard to hold in your hands, and this is one of them.

I am young and terribly small and I am struggling in school. I have a tutor, a beautiful boy with blond curling hair and blue eyes.

But how did the rhyme make it *here*?

I close my eyes as Roan drives me back to my car, and I block out the rest.

• • •

Being on Avan Island is like swimming to the bottom of the river and sifting through the silt. And when I resurface, I do so with more pieces of me returning home.

I am ten years old in a home for girls between the ages of ten and eighteen, and I am so desperately, dangerously young. Any younger, and they would have had to find a foster home. It's a different, quieter sort of aging out—you turn ten, and nobody wants you anymore. I am the youngest in a house full of the desperately, dangerously young in a town that feeds on us.

They take us to the local county fair on a rainy gray day at the end of August, the chilliest day of the summer.

They call it an outing, one of the few we get as group home girls. The board of directors, who manages the group home, waits for us to be grateful for the charity tickets the fair donated to Sister's Place and the money the church donated for us to ride one of the traveling carnival rides. The fair is sprawled across the only wide-open space in this whole community, a vast field at the edge of the looming, waiting forest.

The forest calls to me, even at ten.

Even before *he* drags me beneath the trees by my hair and steals every last bit of me away.

At the fair, one of the group home attendants leads us to the rides last, after we have suffered through barns full of animals that do not want to be here anymore than we do.

The rides are here just for the week, set up at the farthest edge of the open field, close enough that I can see the weathered trunks of the oak trees that are calling, calling, calling me home.

"Pick a ride and be back here in thirty minutes," the group home attendant tells us, and the older girls wander off in pairs.

"You should come with us," one of the oldest girls tells me, worry in her dark eyes. Perhaps it is Roan. Perhaps it is Saem. Perhaps it is Lily. It is all of them in my memory, and none of them. "Guys? Wait up. The kid's coming with us."

The others look at me with that indifference born of living in a group home, living as girls no one cares about. Nobody here has the energy to care about one more, not when there is so little left of ourselves.

I look around at them, my eyes stopping on one of the oldest girls. Her dark hair is loose, a cloud around her shoulders, and her eyes are worn and soft. She says nothing. They all say nothing.

"No," I say. "I'm okay."

I walk away before I can see the pity in their tired eyes. Before a group home attendant can make me stay with her the whole time.

It is enough that I am the youngest. I will not be the weakest, too.

The first ride I visit is not running. It is raining harder now, but I look up, up, up anyway. The ride is teacups that turn in circles along a narrow, rusty track. The teacups are faded, paint chips bleeding off the side.

"It don't ride for just one." The man who runs the ride is closer, so much closer, than I had realized, and I shrink back farther.

He spits, a long stream of tobacco juice that arcs through the air and lands between my feet. He is a wanderer, the saddest kind, the men who move with carnivals and fairs. The kind that just might want to take a girl like me with them when they leave this place.

I shudder.

"I could make a special exception." He smiles, and that is worse.

I run.

I run, through mud and animal bedding mixed with shit that farmers' boots have carried here, through ugly laughter and watchful eyes toward the forest.

Beyond it, the river thunders in my ears, and the trees lean closer, waiting.

The house of mirrors is at the very edge of the field, haphazardly set up for the few patrons who have made it this far.

"It costs two tickets." The girl at the entrance is sixteen, maybe seventeen. Another wanderer. She has a large bruise on her throat and rings of purple climbing her forearm, and I meet her tired, tired eyes. She holds out her hand for the tickets. "You sure you want to go in there, kid?"

I nod, placing the tickets in her outstretched palm.

She shrugs once and steps aside to let me pass.

It is dark inside, and my eyes are everywhere.

Wide, so wide, staring back at me with hope and wonder and fear. I shiver. This is too much of me, too much, too much. And then, and then—

There is another pair of eyes in the dark, and I stifle a scream.

I move to brace my hand on a mirror but find a man instead. No, not a man. A teenage boy, maybe seventeen or eighteen, though his eyes look older.

They will remember this: I reached for him first.

He is taller than me but short for a teenager, stunted and narrow, and his eyes are as cold as the silt at the bottom of the river, but I'm here, I have to keep going, dive deeper until I can make sense of this memory amidst all the others.

I am ten. He is eighteen. His smile is a hungry thing in the dark house of mirrors. I notice these details long before I recognize him, the danger clearer than the boy.

He is my tutor. A good boy. A nice boy. A boy I am supposed to trust, so I do, don't I? I tell my body I don't believe it, I tell my pounding heart be still, I tell my legs not to run, because that would be rude, because he's good, because I trust him, because he's good, because I trust him, because—

"Sorry," I whisper. "I didn't see you there."

"No problem," he says, and he steps closer to me. "You need help finding your way out of here?"

I shake my head no. "I'm okay."

"You sure?"

"Yes."

Please go. Please go please go please go please leave me alone.

But he doesn't.

But they never do.

Not the group home girls.

Not even the ten-year-olds.

He reaches for me and I don't trust him, he's not good, I don't trust him, I scream.

I scream and I scream and I scream and I scratch his face, my nails digging so deep he bleeds, three long marks stretching from his eye to his chin, and then I put both my hands on the mirror closest to me and push.

And the entire house of mirrors comes down around us.

UNSOLVED DISAPPEARANCES, TWO DEAD IN AVAN ISLAND, MARYLAND

by Roan Ellison

A body found in a river. A community rocked by an unexpected accidental death. This could be any small town in America.

But Avan Island, Maryland, is a little different. And so is Charles Aisley, whose body was recently found in nearby Johnstown after failing to return from a fishing trip.

Five years ago, Charles Aisley worked on an investigation involving seven girls who disappeared one by one from a local group home called Sister's Place.

Now Charles Aisley is dead, and another man connected to the group home, former board member Dr. Abel Goodwin, claimed credit for Aisley's murder. Dr. Goodwin's body was found beside Aisley's in the Avan Island morgue.

Questions linger in Avan Island, and law enforcement remains reticent about any possible connections between these recent deaths and the disappearances of girls from Sister's Place.

An agent in the local VCAC (Violent Crimes Against Children) Unit, speaking off the record, said that they have not been contacted by local law enforcement for support on the unfolding case. This is an ongoing story.

CHAPTER EIGHT

THE NEXT MORNING, ROAN KNOCKS ON THE DOOR OF my motel room and then drives us to the other side of town, near the wide-open field where the church boys play games of kickball on Saturday afternoons and where, once, they hosted a county fair.

There's not much in this part of town other than the church—that, and the Norrycs' farm store, which has been here for decades. The church has been here longer, and it's painted white, chipped a little since I've seen it last. Its steeple reaches one lone, gnarled finger up toward God, silhouetted by the green all around us.

Roan kept the file yesterday—or brought it back to the police; she didn't actually tell me what her plan was, but the last I saw of it, the folder was sticking out of the top of her bag.

"Are we talking to the pastor?" I ask her. "Who else are you interviewing for this article?"

"The pastor, the mayor, and one of the boys who interned at Sister's Place. Jake Norryc."

"Just the young Norryc? Or is the old one still around?" I shrug on my jacket, hunching my shoulders against the chill of the morning air. The young one was a teenager when I lived here, often hanging around the group home because he dated one of the girls, Jeza.

"The old one's dead," Roan tells me abruptly. "Jake Norryc owns his dad's farm shop now," she adds, watching me carefully, as if wondering again how much I remember, but this—him—him, I remember.

• • •

I am ten, and I am no one's child. It has been so long since I was a child at all.

Jeza is third oldest—first Zara, then Roan, then Jeza.

Jeza is fierce, taller than the rest of us, and strong, too, muscles rippling in her shoulders.

She seems unbreakable to me, even then.

She has the boyfriend who promised he was the safe out, the escape from the house that raised her, until he wasn't.

It is late on the night I arrive to the Avan Island group home when I first meet him.

"Your boyfriend is here," one of the girls tells her.

Jeza has been holding my hand, her grip firm and solid, but at the mention of her boyfriend, her hand goes slack in mine. All I cannot remember, but this I have with so much clarity: Jeza's hand as limp in mine as if it belonged to the dead.

I see him at the door of the group home, a tall, broad-shouldered boy with fear and violence in his eyes.

I see Jeza's bruises.

And I remember.

• • •

The farm store is a long, one-story building with a single window at the front and a security camera pointing toward the door.

When Roan and I hunt him down, Jake Norryc is at the back counter of the feed shop, in front of the wall of rifles and handguns available to purchase. He stands the way he always has: stance wide, arms crossed. That old, ugly fear is still there, flickering in his eyes like a dull, dying flame that gives light to nothing.

"How can I help you girls?" he asks, and at the word *girls* a muscle in Roan's jaw clenches. He's only a few years older than Roan, and he's as tall as I remember.

A force to be reckoned with, they used to say about him. He was smart, too, good at math when he was in school, and when people talked about him, they talked about *potential*. He's still here, though, working the back desk of his dad's farm store.

Roan shows him her press credentials and tells him about her assignment, and then recognition and fear fills his expression as his eyes flick back and forth between us.

"We just have a few questions for you," I tell him, loudly enough that the other two employees behind the counter glance over at us. "I'm sure you boys don't mind if we take a minute?"

"Perhaps somewhere private?" Roan suggests.

He nods once, jerks his head toward a door to our right. It's a small supply closet with a chair and a table, a calculator, and a handwritten ledger.

Jake Norryc shuts the door behind us and then moves to stand between us and the exit, arms still folded across his chest. "Roan, you know I'm happy to talk to an old friend, but what kind of paper do you work for these days?"

It is a power game, and that was a power move. And while Roan may be playing diplomatic, I am playing to fucking win.

"Does it scare you?" I ask him. "That two men from the Sister's Place board are dead and we don't really know why?"

"Nev?" Recognition hits him only when he sees my anger.

"Yes," I say.

Roan is not so different now than she was: same dark hair, same slight build, even nearly the same sense of style—sweaters and thick combat boots.

But I was a long-haired, wide-eyed child who wore fear like a cloak. And now I walk through the world having made fear my companion and friend. I am taller, my head shaved, more wiry muscle than before from years spent in a martial arts gym learning to *fight*. It haunted me for so many years and it haunts me still: Why he chose the ones he chose. Why he took me.

But regardless of why, I spent the years between making sure I would be someone he'd think twice about choosing.

"I—I didn't know you were back in town," he says. He is at least three shades paler now.

Roan smiles, her expression lethally gentle. "You don't look well, Mr. Norryc," she says. "Why don't you sit down?"

He does.

It is all backward, that he can't scare us, that we caught him off guard with our questions, with my presence, that Roan gave him an order.

That he followed it.

"We're so sorry to hear about the loss of two members of your community, of course," Roan says softly. "And to answer your earlier question, I work with a paper that covers unsolved disappearances."

She may be new at this, may not have as much confidence as a seasoned reporter, but none of that shows on her face now. She is cold, and sure, and determined.

"Jake," I say. "What did you tell the police five years ago when they questioned you?"

Roan clears her throat and looks at me, but Jake's face goes from white to red to a version of purple I've never seen on a human face before. "What— What the hell do you mean? I wasn't— I wasn't interviewed by the police. I just— I told them what I knew about the girls. But they didn't think *I* was involved." He is staring at me, not at Roan.

They didn't, of course. But when Jeza broke up with him, Jake Norryc went to the police and said, *All those girls are talking about running away.* Just because Jeza had confided in him about aging out, about the fear and the freedom.

"We can return to the disappearances later. Can you tell me a little about Charles Aisley?" Roan prompts, ignoring his question. She shoots me a look, one that maybe means *chill.*

I won't, of course.

But it's a nice thought.

"He was my father's friend," Jake says finally. His eyes slide between us, narrowing as he looks at me. "I . . . It's not like I knew him well."

Roan scribbles something on a yellow notepad.

Jake leans forward to see, but she lifts it just out of sight.

"But he was well known in the community, wasn't he?" I ask. That's what they told *me*, when I was so little, when I demanded to know why nobody questioned Charles Aisley's version of things. "So you must have known him, at least from that?"

He's a pillar of the community.

He's a detective.

He's well-known, been here for years. We trust him.

"Well," Jake says, shifting a little in his seat. "It's just so hard, of course. He was such a good man. The whole community loved and respected him. To hear that he was dead . . . well, of course we're all just devastated."

It's a touching story, if you're the kind of girl who believes a man like Jake Norryc.

The knuckles on his right hand are scraped slightly.

"What happened?" I point to his knuckles.

Jake startles before shoving his hand into the pocket of his jeans. "I like to work out," he says. "Kickboxing."

"Mmm," Roan says. She scribbles something else down on the yellow notepad, her handwriting just as lopsided as it was years ago.

If I didn't know better—if I didn't know how much this job and this story mean to her—I would almost think she was scribbling more just to make him squirm.

"How aware are you of the circumstances around Charles's disappearance and eventual death?" Roan asks, pen paused above her paper.

"He . . . he left on a fishing trip," Jake answers finally. "That's all I know. I think it was a solo trip?"

His eyes flick back and forth between Roan and I as he says it.

"Does he take those often?" I ask.

Jake's look stutters to a halt on me. "I— Yes, I suppose."

"Usually alone?"

He clears his throat, and then shakes his head. "That doesn't seem terribly relevant. Anyway, it's horribly tragic. I lost my own father a few years back, and it's—it's always so unexpected."

"Is it?" I lean forward. "Maybe you can tell us more about the town, then. Is this a safe community? Has any crime like this been committed here before?" I want him to see it in my eyes, that I remember, that I know the years of bruises he left on Jeza, that I know he *knew* about the rest and said nothing. I want him to know that he should be afraid.

"No," Jake says. Now it is just pure confusion on his face. "No crimes. I trust the law enforcement around here. They're not like those city cops. And I'm proud that this community—" He looks like he is trying to summon his bluster and his bullshit, but I have confused him, startled him, tilted the power in this room just a little too much. "Wait. Are you saying Charles was murdered? When Captain Ramsey told us about it, he said it was probably—"

"Murder," Roan tells him. "Of course, it's such shocking news. Can you tell me more about Avan Island? Most folks around here say you know everything that goes on in this town."

"Yeah," I add. "The kind of local who's been here forever and is a fixture of the community. Just like poor Chuck."

Jake was always bragging that he was smart enough to get out of this town and go places, always talking about the fancy Ivy League schools he'd get into and the football scholarships that would get him there.

Now he looks belligerent, as if he has recovered his wits at long last. "This is a beautiful town," he says. "Good people. But I'd hardly say I'm a *fixture* of—"

"There's no one in this town that you can imagine having a

propensity for violence?" I lean even farther forward, our faces close to each other, and he jerks back as if the proximity makes it hard for him to breathe.

I know the feeling.

"We're not implying anything," Roan says quickly, nudging me with her elbow. She has already been lenient, I know she has, risking her own job by letting me tag along with her, and asking questions when she is supposed to be gathering material for her next article in the series. But I find I cannot quite pull back now, like the momentum carrying me forward is as sure and relentless as the current of the river.

"No," Jake says. "Of course not. And I have to get back to work." He stands, but he has it all wrong.

Because Roan and I, we are the ones between him and the door now, Roan with questions that floor him and me with the axe kick that can take a man apart.

"Oh, I just have a few more questions," Roan says politely. "Maybe you could sit down with us a little longer? I'd so appreciate it."

And Jake Norryc does.

Roan says it so politely, but there is a current in the air, charged and dangerous, as if there is only one option Jake can safely take.

He did this, often enough, with Jeza. He didn't say she couldn't leave—he said, *You're really going to leave while I'm feeling like this?* And he said, *Come on, come on, I was just joking*, when anyone called him on it.

Anger flickers in Jake's eyes as he looks at me. "A few more questions," he agrees. "But if this is some kind of witch hunt, I don't consent to have my interview printed."

"No witch hunt," Roan says easily.

"It can't be a witch hunt if the people accused are actually guilty," I share politely, just for accuracy's sake. "Have you seen—"

For the first time, my own words falter. I haven't said *his* name. The blue-eyed boy. The tutor. The one I trusted. Didn't I?

I take a breath, force the air back into my lungs.

All these men in this fucking town, and there is only really one I am here to see.

"Have you seen Cal recently?" I ask. It is supposed to sound casual, but all three of us pause. For a moment, I'm so far away I am watching my own body, standing opposite Jake, spine ramrod straight and eyes fixed on his.

Even Roan is frozen, just for a brief flash.

"I'm not sure what Cal has to do with anything," Jake answers icily. "He still lives with his father a few miles out of town."

"Thank you," Roan says smoothly. "My intern is—eager. I'd like to ask you what you remember about the disappearances that occurred five years back? My team has actually asked me to focus my piece on that."

I watch Jake as he formulates an answer, and as I do, I wonder who it was that taught him to wrap rage and violence around fear so tightly it was almost invisible, if he had someone who once treated him like he had always treated Jeza.

But it is too late for Jake Norryc, really, too late because he stands and says the words that damn him—

"An article? Just about all those girls? They were nothing but runaways."

CHAPTER NINE

WHEN WE ARE OUT OF THE FARM STORE, ROAN TURNS to me. "You asked a lot of questions for someone who was supposed to just be my intern," she says finally. "Did you get—did you get what you needed?"

"A chance to verbally bully an asshole from the past?" I dust off my hands. I'm not sure I'll ever see Jeza again, but at least—at least one of the people who hurt her had to suffer through an uncomfortable hour. "Yeah, Roan, I did. Thanks for that, by the way. Where to next?"

She hesitates. "Nev," she says finally. "I know they're scumbags, all right? I want to see them get a taste of their own medicine as much as you do, but—"

"No," I say.

I want them dead.

That is what I nearly say, but around me the forest shifts and the wind whispers, *Not yet, not yet, not yet.*

"What I'm trying to say," Roan continues finally, "is please, *please* be more careful. And get some rest after this, okay?"

She is looking down at me as if I am something small and tender, something to be cared for and treasured, not as if I am something to hate or fear or discard or fight. Not as if I am a weapon sharp with rage and slick with blood.

She looks at me the way she did when I was twelve, as if I am something precious, and I can scarcely bear it.

But because I am not brave enough to push her away, even after all this, I let her rest a hand on my shoulder, gentle on a body that was never made for gentleness.

• • •

Roan drops me off back at the motel, waiting until I'm in my room before she pulls out of the lot.

I do the thing Roan asks me to: I rest, at least for a little while. I nap, fitfully, and wake closer to evening.

And then I do the thing that would make Roan worry more than she already seems to: I walk through the woods beneath the shadows that grow longer, and I may not have kept this path or this map in my head, but my body has kept it. My god, my god, my body has kept it all.

So I find my way through the forest without thinking and without knowing. I walk a path that only deer and lost girls walk.

And I find home.

Sister's Place.

It is a two-story white farmhouse with faded trim that has seen better days and shutters that hang precariously from rusted bolts, age and disuse marring them.

I scrape my hand over my scalp and suppress the urge in me to cry.

Green and grief have crept up over this house, the only memorial my sisters truly have.

The windows are dark, curtained by cobwebs. No lights flicker there, and the door is locked. Behind the house, the little woodshed. It was my job, at ten and eleven and twelve, to fetch wood for the fireplace. It was the longest I had ever lived in one place—floating between foster homes until I landed there—and it felt almost like a tenuous routine, a tenuous place to belong.

One night, one night, I was late doing that chore. One night, one night, Kess volunteered to go with me, because it was dark, and I was afraid of the dark.

One night, one night, we went into the dark together and only I came back.

Now I look up. I run my hand over my scalp again, and the only real thing is the way the hair prickles against my hand. The rest of my body is not real. The rest of my body is not here.

Zara is at the door, a smile on her face, and behind her, the coat of paint is fresh and the windows are warm with light and there is nothing out there beyond the woodshed, waiting for me. Maybe Roan is just inside, too. Maybe Priya is listening while Saem plays the violin.

Everything will be okay.

Because Zara is at the door, welcoming me home.

• • •

When you grow up in foster care, you fight for each scrap you get. You hate the ones who are the prettiest, and you hate the ones who are the ugliest, and you hate the ones who are the loudest, and you hate the ones who are the quietest.

They are the reminder, always, of the price of not falling in the middle. The price of not fitting in the box they give you, parameters as narrow as a coffin.

I was one day away from turning twelve when she went missing.

Her name was Zara, and she was breathtaking.

She was the most beautiful of all of us, and I loved her anyway.

I could not help it. None of us could. She was laughter and sunset and warm summer evenings, her curls dark and her brown eyes bright, no matter what happened.

On my first morning in Sister's Place, after a group home attendant had scolded me for wetting the bed the night before, Zara took my hand in hers—her perfect, flawless, golden hand—and led me to the laundry.

She washed the sheets and the clothes and let me wear her sweatpants and her favorite shirt, the one with the embroidered daisies that an older girl had given her as a hand-me-down when she aged out.

Zara sang everywhere she went, and she fought, and she kissed another girl—Saem, a girl from Baltimore who talked about cellos and Zara and getting out of here to see the ocean—in front of the pastor himself.

We feared for Zara.

There were twelve girls in Sister's Place, and I think we always knew she would be the first of us to die.

Because who among the boys and men of Avan Island could see someone so free, so beautiful, so untamed, and not try to destroy her?

She was almost eighteen, too. The closest to being *free*.

I like to think that she was one of the ones who made it. That maybe, just maybe, Zara and Saem were the ones who got away across the wide expanse of river.

That they have a little house at the edge of the sea, where Saem plays her violin and the cello she always wanted and Zara dances for her in a dress embroidered all with daisies.

But I know the truth.

I saw the grave where he buried them.

Where he would have buried me.

And I knew her, even her bones, still wearing that little shirt with the daisies.

• • •

When I come back to my body, everything aches the way it did when I found Zara. The scar on my shin aches furiously, *One for sorrow, one for* sorrow.

I am huddled in the overgrown grass outside of Sister's Place. The shadows are longer, evening quickly approaching.

I am scarcely breathing when I call Roan.

"Nev?" she asks softly.

I have barely a bar of service, but I cling to the sound of her voice, scratchy with the poor connection, anxious and harried and tired.

"Please come," I whisper.

"Nev," she says. "Where are you?"

"Home," I say.

The line disconnects, and I stay there, huddled in the grass, waiting for Zara and Roan to arrive. They will be with me. They kept me between them, one on each side of me, because I was theirs. I was theirs, when it mattered.

Roan's headlights cut the growing dark, and then she is out of her car, hands outstretched toward me. She says nothing, just pulls me to my feet and then close to her.

I'm sorry, I try to say, but my voice is lost, wandering in the dark, looking for daisies.

CHAPTER TEN

IT MUST HAVE BEEN LATER THAN I REALIZED WHEN Roan picked me up, more time lost to the grassy yard behind the group home than I knew, because after she brings me back to the motel and nods her head at the other bed in her room, I only get a few short hours of sleep before the sun is streaming through the windows. Roan is already up, gathering her notebooks and a small microphone set for her next interview.

"Merrick will be coming up tonight," Roan says. "I told him that you've stuck around and I offered you an internship. He had some questions—they're pretty strict about what interns can and can't do at the *Tribune*—but my boss doesn't have the same hang-ups his does. And if he wants my help, which he does, he'll be cool with you tagging along. Also, I heard a rumor that the other precincts finally figured out who to send, so the new medical examiner will be coming up tonight, too."

I nod my head sleepily at her, bracing my palm against my forehead as if I can push away the pounding headache that has chased me since visiting Sister's Place last night.

"Who are you interviewing today?" I haven't forgotten that Roan promised me the mayor.

"The pastor," Roan tells me. "Maybe the mayor, too. I want to fit in as many board members as I can before they start clamming up on me."

"Or dying like good ol' Chucky boy," I say, reaching for a sweatshirt.

"Maybe we don't share that nickname with Pastor Williams? Or that sentiment either?"

"Whatever you say." I follow Roan out the door and into the grassy lot in front of the motel. "It's lonely out here, just you and me."

Roan nods. "It is," she says. "You can keep staying in my extra queen if the quiet out here gets to be too much."

"I'm peachy keen," I tell her flatly, because I can't tell her it isn't as silent for me as it is for her. My sisters whisper when I wake, all of them but Kess. Sometimes I hear their laughter beneath the trees where we used to roam and play, the forest our only oasis—until it wasn't.

Roan is staring at me as if I've missed a question, or even missed time, so I right myself, force a smile to my face.

"Roan? Stop worrying so much, and let's go get our pastor."

Her nose wrinkles in disgust, but she doesn't argue with me. Doesn't say much, really—just drives us into town, stopping at the coffee shop across from the church for croissants and chai before parking in the church parking lot.

Pastor Williams must have agreed to this interview—I'm still fairly certain Jake Norryc was mostly ambushed by Roan and me yesterday—because he is waiting in the front entrance.

Pastor Williams's beard is grayer than it was when he made me apologize to the boy in the ruins of the house of mirrors. I have few memories of him other than that—glaring down at me, arms folded over his chest, telling the group home attendants, *Get your house in order.* Few memories of him at all beyond that and the occasional flashes of sitting through various sermons, all of us lined up in a row on a narrow wooden pew. I must have more, hidden, buried in the forest waiting for the right breath of wind to shake them loose.

"Roan, dear," he says. "I'm glad you are here, despite the circumstances. We have all missed you."

I force myself not to shudder, but Roan stands firm. "Thank you for having me. Can we come in?"

"Of course," he says smoothly. "And who is this lovely young lady who seems so preoccupied with her phone?"

I raise a single eyebrow at him as I look up from my phone. "I'm glad you think I'm lovely," I say, and then I bat my eyelashes in an exaggerated way that makes Roan stifle a snort.

Pastor Williams reddens, and for a moment joy sings through my chest.

I have always had a talent for turning the language of men back upon them. *Isn't it strange?* I ask them. *Isn't it strange to call a teenager lovely, when you're a grown man?* But it only seems unsettling to them when I'm the one using their words.

"This is my intern," Roan answers, swallowing the smile that had played across her face.

"Come on in," Pastor Williams says, recovering himself.

I stare at him evenly.

"I'll be taking notes as we work, but please let me know if there's something you would prefer would remain off the record," Roan tells him. "And please feel free to stop me if you have any questions."

Williams waves his hands. "Oh, of course, Roan. You do what you need to do. How wonderful that you've made something of yourself—I always knew you were one of the bright ones. And now you've got yourself a little gig covering local stories, is that what I hear?"

"Do you want us both, Pastor?" I ask as I follow him down the hall. "Where do you want us?"

He falters.

Again, again, I rip power back out of his hands.

"Both," he manages. "Both of you are welcome."

He leads us down a hallway under bright fluorescent lights. This was carpet, once. Red carpet, faded with years.

Now it's a laminate masquerading as a light brown hardwood. Same trim, though. New coat of paint.

I remember this hallway. All of us crammed in here, one by one, waiting for private counseling. Anger issues, for some of us. Compulsive lying. Stealing. Struggles in school. There was a label for each one of us, and Pastor Williams was here to save us, one by one.

It's why they could say *behavioral issues* later. It's why they could say *Girls like that, they lie*. It's why they could say *runaways*.

Because Pastor Williams had already handed them that story, neatly packaged.

We enter his office and sit down across from him. Roan pulls out her notebook and pen, and I pull out my phone.

"As you know, we are here to ask about your friend Mr. Aisley," Roan says. "You worked with him on the board of directors at Sister's Place, correct?"

Pastor Williams waves his hand. “Enough of the formalities, Roan,” he says. “We’re all friends here. Yes, Charles was an elder for years at the church and helped establish the group home. In fact, I remember when you were a teenager in this town—”

“When was the last time you saw Mr. Aisley?” Roan cuts him off, tapping her pen against the notepad.

Watching Roan manage Pastor Williams in the same office where he once was so hard on us might be a new favorite pastime of mine.

Pastor Williams swallows. “Two weeks ago,” he answers. “He was going on a fishing trip closer to the coast, and then he was going to make a stop in Johnstown to pick up some groceries and supplies we don’t get all the way up here. You know, I just saw someone you’ll probably remember. Priya? She and Maraam volunteered at the church just this morning. I’m sure they can—”

My whole body jerks at the name.

Not just Priya here, but Maraam too.

Of course, of *course* Maraam is still here. She never would have left Priya in this town alone.

“He told you this before he left?” I manage to ask. “Chuck. He told you he was going fishing and then to Johnstown?”

“Yes.” Pastor Williams shifts in his leather chair, surprised at my question. “Our church leadership team met on Monday morning as they always did, and then I saw him again at a council meeting. We’re both still on the board for community development, if you remember? Then afterward he told us where he planned to go. The boys you grew up with, too—Jake Norryc, Brett Fairchild, and the mayor’s son, too. I’m sure you remember Cal?”

I dig my fingernails into my palm sharply. I will not lean over the table and grab the pastor's shirt, haul him forward and demand to know where Cal is right now, where I can find him. I will not.

Roan dutifully writes down the timing on her notepad as he talks.

I dutifully look for ways to make Pastor Williams feel increasingly uncomfortable. "Sounds like nothing has changed in five years."

Pastor Williams's eyes narrow. "Do I know you?" he asks. "Were you . . . here?"

I smile at him. Again, I am not as easy to recognize as Roan.

"I knew him." Roan's voice is as cold as the river, and I feel it as viscerally as if I've been submerged.

I knew him, too.

And oh I remember, I *remember* him.

My self-restraint evaporates like mist beneath the sun.

"Where is he?" I blurt.

Both Roan and the pastor stop, Roan's pen stilling above her paper.

"Cal?" Pastor Williams asks. "Isn't your article about Charles?"

"My article is actually focused on the disappearances from the group home," Roan answers smoothly. "But I'd love to hear more about the timeline if you feel that's relevant."

"I— Of course it's not relevant." Pastor Williams looks at me again.

"You don't think Charles was relevant?" I ask. "He was on the board of directors. He investigated the case. And now he's been killed."

Pastor Williams sits up straighter. "It was an accident. They *told* me it was an accident. Do you . . . do you really think he was killed?" He is asking me. Asking Roan.

"Yes," Roan answers. "I'm sorry to break the bad news to you."

Her tone is professional, her expression neutral, her body language nonconfrontational. But there is a hard note in her eyes that tells me she is not sorry.

She is not sorry at all.

It felt as if Chuck was waiting for me, eyes wide in the river. Waiting for me to find him. Inviting me home with one river-bloated, outstretched hand.

"You don't think it's connected?" I ask. "You don't think it's strange that two former board members are dead, and one claimed to have killed the other?"

I wish I had access to the note Roan mentioned, to pore over the details of this case so I could understand what exactly Dr. Goodwin had planned.

A memory untangles from the rest:

Dr. Goodwin in this very office, talking to Pastor Williams and to *him*. A casual conversation after a board meeting. All of them so friendly with one another.

Girls like that,

they run away.

"No," Pastor Williams answers me, glaring at Roan as if she will offer him any help. "Of course they aren't connected. Roan, I really feel that these questions from your intern are inappropriate. Perhaps this is something we should only be discussing with the police? Do they know you're poking around all this?"

"Of course," Roan says smoothly. "As a journalist, I operate regardless of the comfort level of the police, though they are aware I am writing a piece on Avan Island's many disappearances. But if you need a break from questions, I'm sure we can find another time. This is certainly an upsetting topic."

Pastor Williams nods gratefully, clearly unsettled in a way he did not expect to be.

I stare back at him, unabashed.

"I'm happy to talk to an old friend," Pastor Williams manages finally. "But maybe your intern is not ready for this type of work?"

He is trying to put pieces together, but who could recognize me? Who could recognize me, when they were looking for a weak, helpless child?

"You don't think someone could have murdered him because he had covered something up?" I ask, folding my hands and leaning my forearms on his desk. I take up space. I take up so much space he leans back even farther. "Something like seven missing girls?"

"Jesus Christ," he whispers.

"Language," I reprove him. "We're in God's house."

Roan sits back, a troubled expression on her face. "I'm very sorry about my intern. She's still learning. There's nothing else?" she asks.

"No." Williams's voice is very quiet, as if we have taken something from him he cannot get back. When he opens his mouth to say more, I cut him off again.

"Theodore," I say, because this is the deal I made with Roan. More or less. This is why *I* came back to Avan Island. "Theodore, what do you think Chuck Aisley knew about all those missing girls?"

But the ashen man in front of me never gets to answer my question, because doors slam somewhere in the church, and the sound of running footsteps and then a fist pounding the office door interrupt us. The sound makes my stomach drop like a stone in the river.

"There's a body," a voice is screaming. *"There's another body."*

CHAPTER ELEVEN

I KNOW THE YOUNG MAN AT THE DOOR, WEEPING FOR this body as he never once wept for all the other souls who died in this godforsaken town.

"Brett," the pastor is saying. "Brett, calm down. What's happening?"

I stare at Pastor Williams as he learns another body has been found. He is gaunt and sallow, and it is not quite surprise that shows in his face.

He looks as if he is already dead.

"It's Jake Norryc," Brett at the door is saying, and he's sobbing onto Pastor Williams's shoulder like his heart has broken. "Jake Norryc is dead."

Jake Norryc, who answered our questions with fury and fear.

Jake Norryc, who left bruises on Jeza's wrists.

Roan is standing very close to both of the men, and I stand, too.

"Brett," she says. Despite the situation, her face and posture are calm, composed. "Can you tell us more? Where is Jake? Has anyone called the police?"

"He's out on the road near the motel," he manages, making my body stutter to a stop for a moment. "I called the station. They were sending a few cars, and—I just, I just needed *you*. Please come," he says to Pastor Williams. "*Please* come." He startles, taking Roan in. "Roan?"

She nods.

"What are you— Are you all right?" he asks.

She reaches out, squeezes his shoulder, the gesture comforting.

I have no comfort left to offer, so I step back and let her.

When Pastor Williams walks Brett back out, arm over the younger man's shoulders, Roan turns to me.

"I can take you to the motel," she says. "I—I think I should go. They probably won't let me close, but reporting live from the scene would...would probably be something my boss would want. She said to send updates for our social media account."

Roan's face is drawn and grim.

"Can I come with?" I ask. "I won't bug you. I won't ask anybody any questions. I just—"

If I say I'm afraid to be alone, she'll relent, but that's not fair to her. Roan, it would seem, is the one person I'm not quite capable of lying to. How do I lie to the older sister who, despite five years of my silence, is trying to take care of me at every turn?

"I want to stay with you," I say.

Roan nods. "Okay," she says finally. "But please don't go near the actual scene. Just stay by the car, and I'll bring you back over to the motel after."

We take the winding road, the only one that goes in and out of town. We pass the turnoff to the motel. Roan is quiet as we drive.

But my body calls me toward the forest, toward the shortcut I know, the footpath I ran on that night long ago, running from the hands reaching out in the dark and the grave at the heart of the forest that is waiting for me.

I did not die when I was supposed to.

Pastor Williams is in the car behind us, and Brett Fairchild is with him, still weeping in panic.

I remember him, but this memory is not so sour as the others.

• • •

I turn twelve the day after the first girl, Zara, goes missing.

Girls like her, they run away all the time, the mayor says, and tells the police to stand down. Of the whole town, here are the people who help look for her:

Jeza and Roan and Saem, walking the forest and the river together and finding nothing. And Brett Fairchild, who spoke up and said they should be allowed to go looking.

• • •

Roan pulls the car over behind a silver truck on the side of the road. The truck is parked at an odd angle, skid marks behind it like it spun out of control, and both the front tires are flat. There are only two police cars on all of Avan Island, and one is parked beside it already, red-and-blue lights flickering. Captain Ramsey is standing there, hands on his hips. One of his uniformed officers is next to him, staring as if he is in shock.

There is a dark lump in the grass a few feet away from the truck and the squad car, and when Roan puts the car in park, she turns to me with a glare.

"You will stay here," she says. There is not an inch of room for negotiation in the sharpness of her voice.

Pastor Williams's car pulls up behind us, and he gets out, followed by Brett.

I can't hear what they're saying, but by Ramsey's body language, he's furious that Roan heard, that she's here at all. She holds up her press badge and shrugs her shoulders, and he keeps gesturing, leaning over her. She stays far enough back from the dark lump in the grass, but she does stay.

I get out of her car and lean against it until Brett Fairchild walks over to me. His face is red and puffy, eyes haunted.

"I'm so sorry," he says. "So sorry you heard all that. Are you okay?"

He is the first man in this town who has ever apologized to me.

"I can take you away from the scene if you want?" Brett continues. "I'll—I'll drive. A kid shouldn't be here."

I ease back, my shoulders curling in on themselves despite myself, because the thought of being trapped in a car with a man, any man, in this town makes my skin fucking crawl.

Brett seems to read that in the look on my face, because he stops and steps back. "I'm sorry," he says again, more quietly. "I can—I can leave you alone if I've made you uncomfortable."

"Men can't make me uncomfortable," I tell him, and I know by the look on his face that he believes me. They almost always do, now.

"Okay," he says. "I know you, don't I? You were . . . You lived at Sister's Place, didn't you? You were . . . the youngest one?"

Pastor Williams couldn't place me, but Brett Fairchild, I suppose, was always more observant.

"Yeah."

"Why are you back on Avan Island?" he asks quietly.

I glare at him, I brace for the accusations that I'm a liar, a behavior kid, not to be believed. "I'm working as Roan's intern," I say.

I really need to prod Roan for more details, because I don't know that I've actually even gotten the name of the press from her.

"This must be—hard. Being back here. I'm sorry," Brett says, and this, this second apology makes rage boil up in me so fast and so hot that I am volcanic, ash and disaster, the earth and the mountains split apart.

I don't stop to think about my promise to Roan. Instead, I stalk toward her and the heap in the ditch that we interviewed just yesterday, the heap that said *nothing but runaways*.

He's wrong, he's wrong, my sisters, they're more than that. But Jake Norryc?

Jake Norryc is nothing but a corpse in the ditch.

Roan's eyes flash with danger. *"Nev,"* she snarls. "What the hell did I say? Go back to the car and stay there."

"No," I say. *"No."*

Something like understanding enters her eyes, and I hate her for it.

"You don't have to be in the car," she says. "But sit your ass down next to it, or so help me, Nev—"

She is standing between the body and me, but I see him.

He is face down in the grass, but his head is all wrong. The wrong shape.

Flattened.

There are bits of his head smeared across the grass, and darkness rolls through me like a wave, because Jake Norryc died just yards from the motel. Just miles from town. Just hours after we spoke to him.

"Who's the kid?" the uniformed cop asks. "She needs to stay back. You both do."

"She's my intern," Roan says.

"Oh *hell* no." Ramsey approaches, obscuring my view of Jake's body. "Both of you are going to get out of here. Press credentials doesn't mean you get to fuck up my crime scene."

Pastor Williams lingers at the edge of our small gathering.

"Does *he* have to leave?" I ask. "Or is there a special reason he's allowed to be here?"

"Comforting the bereaved," Pastor Williams answers before Ramsey can.

I lean slightly, looking past Ramsey again.

And then I stand there, frozen to the spot. There is a fragment of bone, sharp as a knife, lying on the ground only a few feet from where we stand. It reminds me of something I cannot name. It makes my body ache at a faint half-moon scar just below my knee.

Roan puts her hands on my shoulders and turns me forcibly around. "By. The. Car." She says the words through her teeth, but I am grateful for her hands because they are the only thing holding me to the earth.

This was not just some car accident.

Not when his windshield is intact but his head looks like *that*.

"Roan," I say. "Roan, someone bludgeoned Jake Norryc to death."

Her face remains expressionless. "Yes, Nev," she says. "They did. And I do not want you to see." When we leave the scene, Ramsey's angry gaze following us even as the car pulls away, I close my eyes, one hand curled around my phone, and rub my free hand over my scalp. The familiar, scratchy feel of my buzzed-short black hair is enough, enough.

Enough.

They killed Jake Norryc.

"Roan?" I ask. My voice sounds small, too childlike. I need to be harder than this, unbothered by gray matter smeared across ditches. I don't want to sound like the littlest sister. I don't want to sound like I'm begging Roan to let me stay with her. "You said—" I clear my throat, try to make my voice sound bigger. "You said I'd stay with you?"

Because I'm not scared. I'm *not*.

"You can be at my side as long as you want to," Roan tells me. "And we'll go back to Johnstown the second you say the word."

"Roan," I say after several long minutes of silence. "Why do you think this is happening? After all this time, why *now*?"

I don't have to ask why *them*. We don't have to know all the details of how, of why Dr. Goodwin killed Charles, or who killed Jake, to understand in our very fucking *bones* why this is happening.

"Nev..." Her voice trails off, buried beneath moss and the dark, rich soil of this forest that has fed on so many bodies before. "Nev, I don't know what we're up against."

But she should, and so should Brett, and Ramsey and Pastor Williams and everyone else.

We all should.

Silence can only last so long.

The dead of this forest have not rested, not since they were dragged to their grave screaming and begging. And now the dead have come for those who were silent when they should have spoken, for those who stood still when they should have gone looking.

I know it as surely as Roan knows it, deep down.

As surely as Jake Norryc knew it, far too late to save himself.

Nothing but runaways.

It looks like he was one, in the end. Fleeing town, dead before he could cross the river and leave it behind. Nothing but a runaway.

Above me, the oak trees whisper to one another, their branches clicking and scraping over and over and over.

The forest breathes—a gust in, the sharp exhale out—and I shiver at the sudden cold. If I listen closely, I can hear all the other girls lost in this wood.

I run my hand over my head, and I breathe deep, because Brett and Pastor Williams and Roan and Captain Ramsey, they're all scared, but not scared enough.

The dead are coming for us all.

CHAPTER TWELVE

I DID NOT DESERVE GENTLENESS. I WAS NEVER GENTLE, not once. I pushed down the house of mirrors. I clawed at the man who touched me. I broke a boy, a day ago or a lifetime ago, because he touched me.

But Roan has been gentle, and I am weak enough to want that, especially now. Especially tonight.

Lily was gentle, too.

I gag, my stomach heaving, and Roan slows the car.

I throw up the entirety of my breakfast on the side of the road, and Roan stays beside me, silent, her hand on my back before she helps me back into the car, as if she has not just borne witness to me falling apart.

. . .

I stare out the car window away from it all, toward the oaks and maples outside that lean close to us to whisper. *We remember*, they tell me, their branches brushing the windows. *Do you?*

When we were all children in this town, Maraam and Kess and I would race in the pasture behind Sister's Place, running back and forth barefoot through the grass, unheeding, uncaring. Free. Zara would stand at one end, cheering us on, and no matter whether Maraam won or lost she always hugged Kess and I close to her when the race finished.

Roan looks down at me, her eyes haunted.

"Can we see her?" I ask Roan as she turns the corner back into town. "Can we stay and see Priya before we go back to Johnstown?"

My hands tremble, and I run one over my shaved head, back and forth, feeling for something that isn't there.

Roan puts a hand on my shoulder, her touch featherlight. I've known ghosts with heavier hands than hers, but I welcome the touch all the same. "We'll go see Priya tomorrow."

I lean into her hand, just slightly, but I do not let myself believe her, not really. Priya is not the only sister I thought I would see again.

"I'm okay," I tell Roan. "It's all okay."

Roan nods, but not quite as if she believes me, and when she parks outside the diner, she tells me to stay put while she picks up her order.

Zara is beside Roan when she returns, her eyes soft. There are daisies in her outstretched hands.

"I will keep you safe," someone says.

And perhaps it is Roan handing me takeout and telling me I will be safe. And perhaps it is Kess. And perhaps it is Eva.

The trees lean close, one branch brushing my window like a long, gentle finger.

I will keep you safe.

• • •

We are driving again, and I am dreaming.

Not asleep, because sleep—and facing what I see when I do—takes a strength I am not sure I have today.

I do not question Roan when she tells me, again, that I am staying with her instead of alone in mine that night. I just grab my backpack from my room—which is on the far end of the motel from Roan's—and then hesitate and grab my duffel, too.

Night has fallen when I make my way to Roan's room, and the trees seem closer, calling, calling, calling to me.

The shortcut, they whisper. *The way you knew.*

The way the others did not.

There are eyes in the dark, and I must not let them see.

My ankle twists in the lot outside the motel—there is no parking lot here, just indents in the long grass beneath the oaks—and I let out a sound before I can stop myself.

Roan slows her pace and reaches out her hand. "You okay?" She takes mine, and despite myself I hang on, because mess or not, she's strong.

And I need strong.

"Yeah," I whisper. *The trees, they want me to fall*, I want to tell her. *All the way down, down, down, in the grave made just for me.*

The flickering overhead light in our motel room is the most welcome sight I have ever laid eyes on, and I shut the door hard behind us.

I run my hand over my hair but it's *long*, it's growing out just a little bit and it doesn't feel as close-cropped and spiky as before even though that's impossible, so I curl up on the bed and I. Don't. Move.

Roan turns on the TV, flips through channels, most of them empty blue screens because service is limited here, until she settles on one where there's an old black-and-white movie playing. Something with birds, and the crackle of sound recorded long ago, background noise to what's playing out right in front of us. I'm grateful for the noise, and I think Roan knows it. "You okay?" She's looking at the TV, not at me.

I nod, curled into myself.

There are three bodies in this town's morgue now, and a new ME on their way, but for now it's just Roan and me in a town full of death.

And even though I chose this, *I chose this*, I don't know if I'm strong enough.

I close my eyes, but the tears leak down my face all the same.

"Do you want to know more about what's going to happen next?" Roan asks gently. The other bed creaks as she stretches out across from me. "Or would you prefer quiet?"

"Tell me," I whisper. *About the girls.*

Because Chuck be damned, that's why I'm here. It's why we're here. Because they deserve truth, and I have all its pieces, if I could only fit them all back together long enough to see it.

"It sounds like they couldn't get a medical examiner," Roan answers. "So they're sending an assistant ME. Because all the precincts argued about whose job it was to help out here."

"Because Dr. Goodwin killed somebody." I shiver, hug my arms around myself a little as I press my body back against the bed.

"Because Goodwin is dead." Roan shows so little emotion in response to the death of these men, and I wish I could emulate that—wish I could shrug it off and keep moving.

"Did I tell you?" Roan asks, her tone suddenly more cautious. "Who they have working in the lab?"

I flip my phone in my hand, pushing my thumb under the edge of the shatterproof case idly and then letting it snap back. "In the lab? Is it someone I know?"

"Pastor Williams brought her up today. It's Maraam."

Maraam, who raced me across the sunny pasture, legs pumping, laughing no matter who won.

Maraam, who is still here, with Priya. Maraam, who is working this case.

Fear snakes down my spine and winds around me a moment later, settling in the pit of my stomach like a dull weight. Because if they're still here—and *he's* still here—and they're asking questions—

I stop the thought.

"Are we interviewing—*him*?"

For a moment, the silence that falls is absolute.

"After we talk to everyone else," Roan says finally, staring into the dark, her face cast in shadow.

I hear the part that's unspoken: Roan doesn't want me there when she does.

So I let my head thump back on my pillow. "Do you know the ME assistant they're sending?" I ask. I don't know why I ask. How the fuck should I know some random assistant medical examiner from the small towns in this part of the world?

But something tugs at me. Something old, a memory buried under too many layers to look at properly.

Roan hesitates.

"Jeza," she answers finally. "The precincts know that's how Avan Island works. So they're sending her."

I close my eyes again, both hands pressed against my shaved scalp. "Avan always calls us home," I tell her. "Always."

But it hangs at the back of my mind even if I can't bring myself to ask Roan—

All of us, back home on Avan Island, just like last time.

And what if *he* decides, just like last time, to do something about it?

• • •

Cezanne was the second girl to go missing. She was our dancer.

She was tall and long-limbed and she moved like sunlight through branches and the river in the early days of spring.

She had waist-length dark hair and freckles, so many fucking freckles.

And I say that girls in foster care have to hate each other because we're told to, because only a few of us survive and we each want that survivor to be ourselves so we have to push each other away—but I think I am lying, because all I am ever able to feel for Cezanne and Zara and Saem is love, is love, is love.

I was ten when she caught me as I fell.

I was clumsy and timid and wide-eyed, and one day I broke a communion glass in church, knocked it over and smashed it, breaking both the glass and the quiet of the sanctuary.

Pastor Williams was angry and everyone was angry and all the adults were looking at me and looking and looking until I wanted to die.

But it was Cezanne, who looked like she was dancing even when she walked, who came to clean the pieces up and take my hand. "It's okay," she whispered, and I wanted to believe her. "I'm here with you, and if we're together, no one can hurt us. Sisters, right? And we're sisters."

We're sisters.

Oh, Cezanne.

Oh, Zara. Oh, Saem.

Oh, sisters.

I remember her near the river that final summer, her eyes closed like she was praying and her face heavenward, listening to the music in her headphones as if she was hearing god. Roan tugging my hand, saying we would be late for dinner. Jordan touching Cezanne's arm, so softly. Jeza, posture rigid, eyes fierce with pride and affection as she watched Cezanne dance.

We could not hear the song Cezanne danced to, and she could not hear the world around her. She stayed until we all went home.

She stayed until it got dark.

And we never saw her again.

Maybe that was it. Maybe the only reason he took her is that it was easy, that she was there, that she was alone.

You didn't talk to her when she was like that—eyes closed, music pouring into her—but I wish we had.

I always thought that must have been how she died, eyes closed, headphones on when he found her. All those pieces in the middle—the order of things—the holes and gaps I cannot fill—but my sisters I remember as vividly as if they are still here beside me.

I hope Cezanne never saw him, never heard him.

Never felt him.

I hope she died dancing.

DEATH TOLL RISES, QUESTIONS REMAIN UNANSWERED

By Roan Ellison

A third death has rocked the town of Avan Island: Just outside the city limits, an influential young man was found brutally murdered. Jakob Norryc, who owned a small local business, was found at the edge of town.

The baffling questions remain: Jakob Norryc reportedly worked as an administrative intern at Sister's Place, the same group home both Charles Aisley and Dr. Abel Goodwin were connected to. Local law enforcement refused to comment on any possible connections between these deaths, or between the deaths and the missing girls from Sister's Place.

While official investigators maintain that all seven of the girls were runaways, none of them have ever been found.

FBI agent Maria Martinez of the VCAC (Violent Crimes Against Children) Unit announced that their team would be coordinating with local law enforcement and providing additional support if requested. The mayor's office could not be reached for comment.

CHAPTER THIRTEEN

I WAKE TO THE SOUND OF A SCREAM.

No.

No, not a scream.

It is just the phone—the motel phone ringing violently. When my eyes jolt open, Roan is lying in the other queen bed, her eyes wide as if she had not been sleeping at all, the blankness of her expression unsettling in the near-pitch darkness.

"Answer it," I tell her softly when she doesn't move.

Roan holds the phone close, cupped against her ear so that I cannot hear.

"What's going on?" she asks quietly.

The person on the other end says something, too muffled to hear, and Roan sits up slowly.

"Is it Merrick?" I ask. "Is he here?"

She shakes her head. "There's been an accident," Roan tells me. In the darkness, her eyes are as wide as mine must be.

I sit up, wide awake now. *"What?"*

Roan listens for a minute longer and then sets the phone back on the receiver with a little click.

"Roan?"

"Captain Ramsey was leaving town," she says. "Someone shot out his tires and he went over the side of the bridge. He's dead, Nev."

I scramble out of bed, tugging on my sweatshirt. "Who called you?" I ask. *"Roan."*

I meant to talk to Ramsey. To demand time, to demand answers. To sit him down and ask why he didn't listen to me or my sisters when we told him someone was targeting us, hurting us. I wanted to ask him if he knew the whole time. Or if he only cares, now, when other board members are dying.

"Jeza found him on her way to Avan," Roan tells me. "I'm going out there so she's not alone in the woods."

Because—because *he* is out there, hunting again.

"You stay here," Roan says. She reaches into her boot and pulls out a knife that's nearly as long as my forearm. "Keep this. You know how to use it, yeah? Don't open that door for anyone who isn't me. Stay here, with the lights off and the door bolted, and you'll be safe."

She's gone, without waiting for me to promise that I'll stay put.

And I can't. I can't stay here, not with my sisters out there. Roan and— I know now it was Jeza's voice at the other end of the phone.

I pull on my black jeans and tuck the knife into the waistband, and then I go—

It is raining outside, and between this and the wind in the trees, all other sounds are blanketed. It terrifies me. You would never hear footsteps approaching behind you, hands reaching for you in the dark—

I don't turn on my phone's flashlight, not here. I let my eyes adjust, waiting. If I am caught out here, if *he* finds me tonight like he found so many of us, I will not go without a fight.

I take a shortcut through the forest to the main road. It is not long, not long at all, and I go, I go because I cannot lose her to this forest and this ancient, aching, malevolent town.

I will not.

When I arrive, it is to a truck half-submerged in the river. Roan's car is parked behind a pickup truck and another small car, two police cars with red-and-blue lights flashing behind them.

Ramsey's crime scene is just yards from Jake's, so close it feels like, somehow, the malevolence Jake left behind him could have caused it all on its own.

I go to the river, cloaked in night. I hold the knife in my hand, and I stare and stare until my eyes adjust again.

Captain Ramsey was a tall man once. He looks small and fragile in death. He is half-submerged, seat belt still buckled, his body nearly cut in half by the windshield that had folded in. I look away, still the trembling in my hands by force.

One for sorrow, two for mirth, three for a wedding, four for—

The poem, the one in our police report, rushes into me like water rushing into a submerged vehicle. I shake my head, as if that will be enough to clear it of the cobwebs.

Captain Ramsey's eyes are open, his head turned toward the window as if he was watching his own death approach.

His back tires are still on the end of the bridge, only half of the truck over the edge. Both tires are brutally flat, torn sharply.

I shudder.

Whoever wanted him in the river, glass and metal folded around him like a shroud, wanted it to be thorough.

Voices jar me, bright beams cutting the forest near the river, so I run, skirt the edge of the woods as cops make their way down the bank toward the body.

And because it is all too much now, horror washing over me like a drowning wave, I emerge from the trees and find Roan.

She startles, her hand reaching for something on her hip—a weapon, maybe, a Taser—before she realizes it's me.

"Oh *fuck* no," she says. "Jesus, Nev. What did I say? And how did you *get* here? These woods aren't safe."

They were safe, once. Or at least they felt that way, when I was too small and naive to know better.

Now, though, Roan is right. The forest is not safe.

I am not safe, though. It's hardly a consideration before I act, though I don't know how to tell her that.

A man approaches us from the throng gathered by the squad cars, and Roan shakes her head at me before I can say anything—not that I could justify going through the forest alone even if I did.

"We'll talk about this later," Roan promises.

The man approaching is tall, broad-shouldered like Jake Norryc, and I almost flinch before I recognize him:

Merrick.

Thank *god*.

My breath catches in a glad little sob, despite myself. In front of me Merrick opens his arms wide and Roan walks into them.

"Are you okay? Roan?" He's tall—she's tall, too, but she still disappears in his arms.

She draws back. "I'm okay. It's good to see a familiar face."

He turns to me. "Nev? What are you doing here?" He turns to Roan. "Roan, what the hell? Why is she . . . *here*?"

In this town, in this forest, at this crime scene? And how can I answer that? How can I tell them, that I came because I miss Zara and Saem and all the rest?

I nod at him. "I'm fine. I was—in town."

"Why the fuck are you out here in the middle of the night?" Merrick asks bluntly.

How do I explain the rest? That I needed Roan and she came? That I could not be alone so Roan let me stay with her?

"Roan? This is no place for a kid—"

"I'm her intern," I blurt out.

Roan sighs.

"Yeah, I've heard that whole story," Merrick says, unmoved. "And *your* boss might be okay with a teenage intern, but she definitely wouldn't be okay with her coming to a fucking crime scene. *Roan*."

"I know," Roan says. "I *know*, all right? I'm not any happier about this than you are."

Merrick lets out a breath, folds his arms. "You look cold," he says finally. He shrugs off his jacket and reaches out toward me.

When I step back involuntarily, he nods, holds it out to me more slowly.

Even more slowly, I take it.

A woman in a brown leather jacket, black leggings, and black boots walks towards us. "Jeza," she says to Merrick. "I'm the ME. Well, I'm his assistant. I'm the only one they could spare. You're Roan's colleague, right? The reporter with the *Tribune*?"

Jeza.

Jeza.

She's taller than me, dark-skinned and dark-eyed, and the look she gives me is familiar. I have a sudden flash of memory, disjointed from everything else. Jeza, five years ago, on Avan. She's on the soccer field across from me, and Cezanne and Eva are beside her. Zara is beside me. They're team captains, Zara and Jeza. The sun is bright, the fog hasn't settled yet, my sisters are still here.

Jeza's home.

She called, too, in the early days after I was taken away from Avan Island and Sister's Place was closed. She called and texted and said she just wanted to know I was *safe*.

And because I could not bear to look at it, because I had to bury so many memories, many of my memories of Jeza were buried too, stirring now as I look at her.

Roan is introducing Jeza and Merrick—Jeza, a friend from before, Merrick, a friend from now, she's so sorry they're meeting this way, and so glad they're safe, and tomorrow, of course, not right now, it's all so awful, Jeza would be so happy to talk to them both.

Neither of them look old enough to be here—not Roan, on her first real assignment. Not Jeza, still an assistant, not even finished with school.

In fact, framed in the red-and-blue lights in the middle of this dark, endless forest, they hardly look old enough to distinguish from the rest of my sisters, the girls who are with me no matter where I go.

Jeza and Zara could still be playing soccer together. Roan could still be braiding my hair and adding extensions to Jordan's. We could all still be the girls we were.

"It's been a while," Jeza is saying, shaking Roan's hand, her grip firm, and I'm back here in the forest in the middle of the night, surrounded by bodies. "I'm sorry to meet again this way. Thank you for coming."

"Of course." Roan nods. "How many people do you have with you? What can you tell me about tonight?"

"I was in the first car," Jeza answers. "I saw Ramsey's vehicle off to the side of the road, and when I got out—he was gone. I blocked the road off with my car and my hazards on, left flares in both directions to mark the incident. We'll need to look for casings in the morning."

"Who?" I ask. "Who shot his tires out?"

Merrick looks at me, confusion on his face—that I'm here, that I'm asking questions, that anyone at all is allowing me to.

Jeza's eyes fall on mine. Like Roan, she shows little of her emotions at first glance, but her eyes flame when she glances my way. She takes a breath and then looks away again, as if she cannot quite bear to look at me. "We don't know that yet," she says.

Bullets ripping through his tires. Ramsey, half-submerged. Like Charles, eyes wide in death.

The road and bridge are steep here, the ditch steeper.

"I'm sorry you arrived to all of this," Roan says finally. "I'm here for whatever you need."

Roan and Jeza exchange a look, a long, unreadable one.

Merrick shifts, looking down at me. "Can I get you anything?" he asks. "I got Gatorade in my truck. Snacks, too. You... God, kid, you shouldn't be here."

I bristle. "Not a kid."

He waits, ignoring my tone, for an answer about the Gatorade.

Finally, embarrassed, I shake my head.

Merrick stays beside Roan and I, close and silent, and I am grateful.

Half of fear is the part where you're alone, and he makes us both feel less so.

And in this town, that matters more than I can say.

• • •

Dead girls whisper to me while Roan talks to Merrick and Jeza about the uniformed officers who are down at the scene because there is nobody left in charge. I turn away from them, because there, beneath the low-hanging trees, is Eva, with the cold breeze lifting her hair, reaching out to take my hand.

Come, she says. *We are sisters, survivors, and wind—*

And we know the way.

I take a step toward memory, toward sisters, and then there's a hand on my shoulder.

"Nev?" It's Jeza, and her voice calls me back out of my memory, and then Eva is gone, *gone*, and so is the memory she was about to unlock in my mind.

"Nev," she says again.

I stare over her shoulder toward where Zara had stood, beckoning me closer. "What?" I ask. Whatever flash of memory I had was gone, disappearing into the forest with Eva. *This way*, Eva was telling me. For the briefest moment, I hate Jeza for interrupting me, for knocking that memory out of my consciousness.

We know the way.

Jeza opens her mouth like she's about to say more, or maybe like she has just found a lost memory of her own.

"Don't go off in the woods on your own," she says. "Seems like a bad idea, all right?"

I see daisies and black dirt and flattened skulls. I see a cut just below a knee and a crow taking flight. I am huddled in front of Sister's Place, arms wrapped around my knees. I am staring into the dark forest and seeing a way home. I suck in a lungful of cool spring air. It tastes like damp, packed leaves and moss clinging to exposed roots.

Jeza's eyes flick to me. "It's not safe out here," she continues. "I need to help these cops with the body and make sure the forensics team is safe, but you—" She looks at Roan and then at me.

"I'm fine," Roan says. "I can stay out here with you, if you want. I'll stay off your scene, I promise. I just . . . I don't want you to be alone." Roan's gaze falls on me next. "*You* need rest, though."

"I could go back to the motel. I don't mind walking." *Eva* was there just now—and what could possibly happen to me if I was with one of my sisters? If I went into the forest, I would see them again, the sisters, the survivors, the wind. *We know the way.*

"No," Roan says flatly, and Jeza nods her head.

"You're not walking anywhere," she says, and she doesn't meet Roan's eyes, doesn't acknowledge all the shared history standing in our midst, but she does back Roan up. She always has.

"Can I drive you back to the motel?" Merrick asks finally, his gaze flickering between me and Roan. "You're not staying in any official capacity anyway, right?" he asks Roan. "You're just here to drive your friend back at the end of this?"

Roan looks at me, waiting.

She will believe me, if I tell her no, I can't get into the car with him. She won't ask questions. She won't be upset on behalf of Merrick, even though he's her friend. She'll just nod her head and let me get into her car and wait.

But I trust my gut more than I trust anything else, and when I see Merrick I do not need to run my hand over my shaved head to make sure I am still here. When I see him I do not reach for the knife Roan gave me or think of an axe kick.

So I nod. "I'll go with you," I say, and the forest around us lets out its breath.

I follow Merrick to his truck. He doesn't say anything, and I tip my head so I can lean against the cold glass of his car window, my breath foggy against the pane.

The fog distorts the flashing blue-and-red lights, but I stare past them, toward tire tracks and Captain Ramsey's black police truck as I imagine the moment he came apart.

CHAPTER FOURTEEN

MERRICK GETS A ROOM AT THE MOTEL, SMALLER THAN Roan's with only one queen. It's beside Roan's, a few doors down from mine. After he gets his key, though, he lingers outside. He looks down at me for a moment, and then, unexpectedly, his lips quirk upward. "Have you nicknamed the other cadavers yet?"

My laugh is so loud in the stillness that I startle a crow from a nearby tree, and if Roan was here, she would be glaring at me.

"Not yet," I tell him. "I'll keep you posted."

He grins, but his eyes move past me, sweeping the area—forest, lot, everything—and I see the tension in his shoulders. "Kid, I—I don't know the whole story here," he says finally.

I take a step back, shoulders back, chin high. "That's correct," I tell him.

He nods, slowly. "I know Roan looks out for you," he says. "I trust her to do that job right. But if you want to go home—and it might not be worth much, but I think you *should*—I'll take you home, okay? I'll drive you back to Johnstown if you need a ride."

"I *am* home," I tell him. "I'm from here. Didn't you know?"

My question is a jab, because sometimes it feels like everyone I meet in Johnstown knows who I am and where I'm from. I'm the girl left alive. I'm the girl they call into the station to identify the other lost girls, only none of them are ever mine, and somehow that's worse.

But it's also a lie, because I can't go home.

Something was taken from me here. Something was taken, and I can't go home, won't ever *be* home until I get it back.

"Okay," Merrick says quietly, holding up his hands. "Okay. Let me know if that changes."

He waits until I have shut and locked my door, and then I see him through the windows, broad shoulders curved with exhaustion, as he steps inside his own room and shuts the door behind him.

• • •

I wake later, though it's still dark, to Roan's headlights in the grassy lot outside the motel. I am up, knife in hand, waiting at the door.

Merrick must have heard her, too, because I hear the rumble of his voice.

I throw open the door, jamming the knife back into my boot at the last moment.

Roan nods to me, but Merrick raises an eyebrow.

"Did we wake you?" he asks.

"Did you go back out there?" I ask him.

"No," he says, and offers no explanation.

I almost say something sharp and vicious about not needing him to stay here and look out for me, but Roan cuts me a look that probably translates to something along the lines of *don't show him the fucking knife in your boot* or *don't say any weird murder shit*, so I just shut my own mouth tightly.

Merrick glances at Roan. "Roan?" His voice is hesitant. "We have a contract photographer, a brand-new lab tech, an assistant ME who hasn't even finished school yet, and you have a high school intern. This town doesn't have a cop in charge, let alone enough law enforcement to guarantee *our* safety. Do you think we should talk to your boss *and* mine about getting security? Or just . . . going home until they get reinforcements out here? I mean, the goddamn police captain is dead."

They came for him, I want to tell them, because this truth at least is solid in my whirlwind of memories. They should know, they should know, but when I open my mouth, the trees tell me *Not yet.*

Or maybe it is *him*, here to finish what he began.

I clench my hand, nails digging into my palm. "You should probably get out while you can," I mutter, but neither of them hear me.

"Your boss will want you to stay until you at least *try* to talk to the mayor," Roan says. "And my boss said it's up to me if I stay or not."

"So if you don't have to stay—" Merrick begins.

"I have to stay," Roan cuts him off, and looks at me.

I don't realize my hands are shaking until Roan's hand finds my shoulder again, gentle and insistent.

"So after we speak with the mayor?" Merrick asks, but he's looking at me with interest.

Have you seen Cal? I am asking Jake Norryc. Where is he now, now when his friends are the ones going missing? "If you still want to at that point, I'm down to get the fuck out of here," Roan promises Merrick.

Are we interviewing—him? I am asking Roan. Roan and I know what Merrick does not: that neither of us can leave until we face Cal Portman.

• • •

I sleep again after Roan returns, though fitfully, and when I wake the sun filters through the trees beside the motel as if the fog and rain of yesterday were nothing but a dream. While Roan talks to Jeza near the cluster of vehicles, I stand in the long grass and stare up at the oaks.

Cezanne loved this—the light, the warmth of the sun, the feel of grass on bare feet.

I pull my phone from my pocket. I don't have service, but miraculously the shitty motel Wi-Fi lets me connect to Spotify. I pull up my most repeated playlist, a strange mishmash of everything from blues to pop music to Ludovico Einaudi. Ludovico plays first—"Le onde"—and I freeze, chilled even beneath the warmth of the sun.

This was it.

Cezanne's song.

And then she's there beside me, swaying beneath the trees, and I'm ten and barefoot, and I want to take her hand and dance with her and Priya and Zara until the last bit of light is gone.

"Ludovico Einaudi?" Merrick's voice pulls me back to *now*, to seventeen, to the forest of the dead.

"Yeah." I raise an eyebrow at him. "You don't seem like the type to know that."

Merrick's mouth twitches. "My little sister," he explains. "Lucy. She likes to compose music. She's good, too, at composing—but she also always makes me dance with her. And she is *not* a good dancer." His eyes are twinkling.

Impulsively, I stretch out my hand to him, and he grins.

"'Le onde'?" he asks, and when he spins me, my laugh fills the clearing. He spins me again, and the filtered sunlight and wild green spin, too, and Cezanne is here, laughing with me.

I stomp on Merrick's toes at least twice, but he's laughing and I'm laughing and I hardly realize we've lasted the whole song when he stops, breathless.

Jeza has gone back inside her motel room, but Roan is staring at us with something strange in her face. She looks around the clearing, her hand on her hip as if reaching for a weapon. "Come inside so we can get ready to go," she says.

Merrick nods in Roan's direction, but he still smiles at me. "You and Lucy would get along," he says.

"Yeah?"

"Yeah. She's also a big fan of stomping on my feet while she dances."

He dodges the punch I aim at his shoulder as we head for our respective rooms. But I—I give one last look over my shoulder, because my sisters are all here now, and they are all dancing.

For them, "Le onde" plays on, endless—Saem and Zara pressed together, moving as one, Cezanne twirling and reaching for Eva's hand. Lily has her face turned toward the sun, her feet barely touching the grass. Jordan is swaying in a slow circle, wreaths of irises in her hand. And Kess—Kess reaches for my hand. When I see my sisters, the others speak sometimes, but not Kess. Never Kess. My best friend in the world, and she cannot speak to me.

But now—now she does. *Keep dancing*, she whispers, and it's a smile on her face. *Keep dancing.*

CHAPTER FIFTEEN

WHEN ROAN AND I ARE BACK IN HER ROOM, ROAN SETS down some takeout that someone—maybe Jeza—brought for us while I was still sleeping and sits down on the bed.

"We'll have to be a little more careful today," Roan says. "With Merrick around, I may not be able to bring you to every interview, unless you can promise not to ask the kind of questions you were asking Pastor Williams."

"When are we talking to the Portmans?" I ask.

"Nev."

"Yeah," I mutter. "Your rule."

Five years ago, when my remaining sisters and I stood before the board and begged them to help us, I pointed across the room at Cal Portman, Kess clinging to my arm as I did.

Of course, of course Roan doesn't want me to see him now.

I pull out my phone, hunch over it so I can ignore Roan's attempt to plan the day with me. "It's fine," I say. "I'm good on my own. I'll stay out of your way."

"That's not what I said," Roan says. "Nev, I'm just letting you know it's gotta be a little different. I still want you to stay here, if you want."

"I'm good." I stand, reaching for my duffel, when a knock interrupts us.

I open the door, duffel in my hand, and it's Merrick, followed by—

Priya and Maraam. From here. Of course, of course, of *course* it's them.

Priya, who I have been waiting to see. She is tall—taller than she was at sixteen, when I knew her—with long dark hair that is pinned in a bun. Her camera hangs around her neck, stray wisps of black hair framing her face.

Beside her is Maraam, wearing a blue hijab and a matching navy-blue pantsuit.

They're mine and they're here and they're safe and *he* didn't take them from me.

Eva, I want to tell her. *Eva, look, they're here. We missed them, we missed them, and they're* here.

But Eva's dark hair falls past her face and she steps back to make space for Priya and Maraam, and I cannot let anyone hear me talking to them, so I hold out my hands to them now.

The memories are so tangled, but the feeling is clear, that warmth of remembrance I felt when I saw Jeza last night.

It all takes a moment to sort out, to get the memories into the correct order, to make some semblance of sense, but in this place, in this forest, there is enough of me to manage it.

"Priya," the tall one says, tucking a strand of hair behind her ear and shaking hands with Merrick and nodding to Roan and then turning to me. Before she was a photographer of the brutal, she was ours and we were hers.

"Maraam," the woman in the hijab introduces herself next. Maraam shared a room with Priya in Sister's Place. I can remember them arguing over conditioner. I can remember Maraam learning how to pin a hijab with no one to help her, of Roan trying her best and Jeza googling and Eva's deft hands holding pins out to her.

And we are here now, reunited because somewhere along the way this town decided it could only be served by its children.

I loved them once. I knew them once, and they knew me. We belonged to ourselves, and each other, and seeing Priya and Maraam here in this dark motel room makes my body ache with longing for that old world.

Now, I reach out toward them, and I wonder how much of them is left, and how much they left behind when our sisters were stolen from us.

I take their hands.

Jeza arrives soon after Priya and Maraam, and then Roan pulls me aside, her tone insistent when she calls my name.

Merrick is looking between the other women and me in this room with confusion, and I understand the feeling of seeing all the stray pieces and trying to puzzle out how they fit together.

My sisters, I could tell him, and I wonder if he would understand.

"I think we should talk about you heading back to Johnstown early," she says carefully. "Not now, not today, and I know you don't want to hear this, but... Nev, it's gotten pretty dark, and I just want you safe."

"I'm staying," I tell her. "Until this is *done*. Something is *happening*, Roan."

Her glance cuts to Merrick again, and then she jerks her head to the door. "All of you out," she snaps. "I need to talk to Nev."

Jeza's eyes meet Roan's the way they always have, the way they have since they arrived on Avan Island on the same day, when they argued over whose bedroom would be whose until it turned into an almost-fight and the adults decided to make them share a room as punishment.

Jeza is the last to leave the motel room now, her gaze lingering on Roan.

"Listen to me," Roan says. "I know you want to know. I *know*. But what if this gets worse?"

It did, last time. It will again. I have been sure of that for days now.

But there is something waiting for me here, and I will not, *cannot* leave until I face it.

"I meant what I said about wanting you with me," she continues when I say nothing. "So we'll stay a few days and you can berate any old asshole from the board you want to, or dump a laxative in Williams's coffee at the diner, or whatever the fuck you were planning to do, all right?"

"That's an idea," I tell her cheerfully.

She sighs. "Just a few more days," she tells me. "And then you and I head back to Johnstown, make sure you get there safely. Even if things aren't wrapped up here."

I will need longer than that. I want to tell her, to tell her I can do it, I can find the shed in the forest. I can walk the path and find my way, and I can find my sisters. I can find the girls, the girls who are not runaways, I can find the upturned earth and the dampened leaves and the daisies. I can do it.

I can face *him* even. Ice-blue eyes and a wave of blond hair and hands that reach in the dark. I can do it.

I just need—

Time.

"Let's go," Roan says.

She leads me past my sisters—Maraam and Priya, standing near their car. Jeza near Merrick's truck.

They do not feel quite real to me, any more than Eva felt real when she stretched out her hands to me in the forest last night or a lifetime ago.

Are they as trapped as I am? Are they hollow shells who keep coming back to this place, back and back and back? Or is it different for them, because they were not the girls *he* chose?

And will I ever be able to look at them and wonder why he chose us, chose *me*, and not them?

"Don't actually put laxatives in anyone's coffee," Roan says as we reach our cars. "That's a crime."

"But not a very *big* crime," I remind her. "Besides, there aren't many cops left in this town, and they've probably got bigger problems today, don't they?"

"Nev," she says. "I mean it. Merrick and I are going to try to get an interview with the mayor, or even a town hall. If you stick with us, you'll have to—"

"Behave myself?"

"Something like that," Roan says. "Are you going to join us, then?"

"Well." I pause to think about it. "Actually, I might go to the church and ruin the pastor's day. And when I'm done with that, I might set off a few firecrackers inside the mayor's office."

"I can change my mind about spending a few more days here," Roan tells me. "I could drive you back to Johnstown right the fuck now, and we could figure out your car later. I'll just take you straight home. What did you say your social worker's name was?"

I wince. Mandy has called me six times since I left Johnstown, partly because I am supposed to check in with her once a month and missed it, and partly, I'm guessing, because I broke a boy's collarbone. Sent me a text, too, even though she swore when we met that texting was only for emergencies.

"I didn't," I tell her flatly. "I don't think I'll tag along with you and Merrick today. Thanks, though. And I'll—I'll wait for you before I go back to Sister's Place."

Even in the warm light of day, I cannot say the name of my old home without shivering.

She nods. "I'll come get you at lunch. We can go then."

"Roan," I say. "Thank you."

She nods again, and then she is gone, her shoulders stooped with the weight of all she has been carrying.

And I am sorry, I am, for what I am about to do. And for the paper I slipped from Roan's bag before we left—the last page in our police report, the rhyme that has haunted me for years now.

Not for the reasons I should be sorry, no, and not sorry enough to stop, but I am sorry that I will cause Roan to worry.

• • •

Theodore Williams has been the pastor of the church on Avan Island since long before I was born. He is a fixture in the town. He is power. He keeps the peace. He prays and preaches and cares for his congregation, and once he saw my sisters disappear from us and all he could say was *amen*.

I bring him a coffee from the diner, paid for in cash, and I do not add a laxative, no matter how badly I want to now that Roan brought it up.

The church secretary is not at her desk, so I push open the doors to his office and walk in. He looks up, and then nearly jumps out of his skin.

"Lord have mercy," he says, placing a wrinkled hand over his chest.

"He won't," I say, kicking the door shut behind me and then setting the coffee on Williams's desk. "Hi. I'm here because I know what you did." I slam the poem down on his desk.

Not that I think he understands that piece of it any better than I do, really. But because I want him to *flinch* when I do it.

His already pale face goes another shade whiter. "I don't— Who do you think— Who gave you the right— I'll be calling for—"

"Spare me," I tell him. My hands do not shake when they push the coffee toward him. My hands do not shake when I fold them and rest them on the table, my eyes never wavering from his. "Pastor Williams," I continue. "You're going to tell me everything."

"This is preposterous," he says. "You're that *intern*."

"Oh," I say. "Yeah. That. I'm not really an intern, so you can't blame the press for this. I just know what you're covering up, and I want answers."

I told him, I told him, I told them all.

And he chose not to listen to me.

He shifts. "I'll be calling Roan back in immediately." He reaches for his phone, but he's bluffing. "Or maybe I should skip straight to calling the police. This is unbelievable."

I lean forward and grab his wrist, *hard*.

Did you know?

That's all I want from him. Did he know we were telling the truth about what was being done to us? Or did he just prefer not to?

His wrist is cold to the touch. Cold as a cadaver.

"Or," I say, "I can send what I know straight to the FBI. But I'm sure you want to be helpful. I'm sure you want to help me uncover the truth behind what's been happening in your community these last few days."

"Of course," he says, his voice wobbling just a little. "Though I'm sure I don't understand what you mean about *knowing* anything. But I'll do anything to help find the person who committed these horrendous crimes."

"Good," I say. I have been waiting, *waiting* to say this for five years. "Then maybe you can start where we left off the last time. By telling me about all the missing girls."

• • •

Here is a memory I am sure of:

When I was a child, Theodore Williams made me apologize to a monster in a wide-open green space on the east side of town.

There was glass at my feet, shattered mirrors around me.

And by the time my sisters found me there, he had forced me to apologize to Cal, beautiful Cal with the golden hair and tan skin and straight-toothed smile. Cal, the eyes in the dark.

I am sorry, they made me say.

It brings me the greatest pleasure to hear him gasp like this in his own office.

"I-I'm not sure what you mean," he says.

"The girls," I say, and for a moment I am thinking of daisies and bones in the dark heart of the forest and I cannot say anything else.

"There was a group home here a few years back," he says finally, recovering himself. "Several girls unfortunately ran away, and we as a community realized that it was best for the remaining girls if they were moved to other homes. It seems that running away became a trend—maybe even a dare—among them. The girls had a multitude of behavior issues, but we did our best by them."

They didn't run away, I want to tell him. *They're in the forest.*

They're here with me now.

"And you were involved?" I ask. I am not recording. This is not testimony or evidence. But I need to know, and I need him to say it to me. "You helped run the home."

"I did." He shuffles his papers nervously in front of me, turning a document labeled SERMON NOTES, EXODUS, over and over in his hands. "I was on the board, among many other people. I was certainly not the *only* person involved in all of that."

"And—"

"Many of us served on the board of directors," Williams interrupts me. "I was a spiritual adviser, because many of the girls were . . . troubled. They met with me regularly, and Dr. Goodwin, too. But the day-to-day management, that was Charles Aisley, Captain Ramsey, and the mayor. Jake Norryc and Brett Fairchild were administrative interns and Cal Portman helped out as a tutor—all volunteer projects for school."

All of them, always.

In every room where power met, it was these men.

All of them, against all of us, and we never had a chance.

"What is it with these girls, anyway?" he snaps, and that facade of goodness and patience that had started to wear thin now slips off entirely. "Is this some kind of vendetta?"

Williams stands, all traces of nervousness gone, the shift in expression so quick I am almost disoriented.

Almost, but not quite, because I know how power works and I

know how games are played and I will not let him take back any of the power I have stolen from him today.

I lean across the table and place a hand over his like he always did when he *counseled* me or my sisters, a gesture that could be comforting but always instead was used to smother us. "Yes," I whisper.

He snatches his hand back as if my touch burns him.

"Yes?" he asks, horrified. "It *is* a vendetta?"

"You were told something was happening to the girls of Sister's Place," I say. "And did you know? Did you know it was true?"

"They were just difficult girls who ran away," he says faintly. "There was nothing more to it than that."

The words burn at the core of me as he says them.

"Why didn't you try to find them?" I ask.

Williams stares at me, at a loss. "They *wanted* to go," he repeats. "Of course no one went looking for them."

"That's not true," I tell him. "*I* did."

And that's when Theodore Williams finally recognizes me.

CHAPTER SIXTEEN

AS SOON AS PASTOR WILLIAMS RECOGNIZES ME, HE tells me to get the fuck out, so I do.

He tells me to never come back, so I decide I won't. There is nothing else for me here, no answers Pastor Williams will ever give me, no admittance of guilt or complicity, because as soon as he realized who I was he shut down completely.

I imagine the mayor telling all of them, *They were telling rumors about my son*, and everyone laughing it off. I imagine them saying *Girls like that, they lie* so many times until the truth was left only in our bodies and nowhere else.

But I won't know. I won't know if it was worse, if instead the mayor said, *Don't tell, but—*

And Pastor Williams and the rest just didn't care.

I bite back a sob, because there is no place for that here.

There is just me and this church where they met and led and created futures for us that we did not ask for.

We all met here, they would tell us later. *To decide to bring you all home to us.*

They would beam at us as they said it, as if we should be grateful.

It is not the first time I have picked a lock in this building, no. There was the summer I was ten, the first summer here, and Eva was twelve and Saem was fifteen and they showed me how to pick a lock, because Roan, who was fifteen, had shown them. That was the summer Eva and Saem and I broke in to get the communion wine. And the summer I was twelve, when I jimmied a window open and climbed through and listened to the men talk about what to do about all those missing girls.

The lock for the basement is easy to pick, an uncomplicated knob lock, and I am inside before I can stop to think about Roan's horror if she knew I was here instead of safe.

The basement hall stands empty. It once had church suppers and small group meetings—and meetings of that board of directors.

It is not the way it is in Sister's Place, the echoes of love and laughter and dancing everywhere I turn. Here it is just empty and a bit cold.

The last room before the sanctuary is a much smaller office. It was shared by the elders. It was where girls were sent to talk to Pastor Williams when they were in poor standing at home. When their grades dropped or they mouthed off or they did not do their chores or they were not grateful enough.

Jordan, Jordan, she was always sent there when school got too hard to keep up with, and school was never easy for her. She did not speak to us.

So they sent her here, to this tiny cubicle where men took up space and we learned to be smaller.

I dig my fingernails into my hand to keep myself here, but it is not quite enough. It is never quite enough.

• • •

I am almost eleven, and I am clutching *Blaisely's Treasury of Rhymes*. I have fared poorly in school, my reading abysmal, the letters slipping and sliding in front of me and rearranging themselves into nonsense.

But poetry I can understand. The white space helps, the font in this book, it helps the words arrange themselves in an order that makes sense.

Still, they tell me, one of the older students has volunteered to help me learn. A good student, bright and wise and so helpful, so kind to offer this to me.

When I tell the other girls, Jordan is afraid.

She sits at the top of the stairs, her own copy of the book of rhymes in her hand, whispering the words to her rhymes again and again. Again and again.

She has it with her when she goes missing. This I know: She is holding it in her hands. She is facing the forest, looking back over her shoulder at me with a small smile. I never see her again, not after that.

But first: Jordan on the stairs, whispering her rhymes. Jordan on the stairs, fear in her eyes.

When I sit alone in the little office with Cal Portman, the book of rhymes open in front of me and his broad hand pressed firmly on my knee, I understand why.

SISTERS

NEV DOES NOT WANT TO BE HERE.

We can tell she does not.

The door stands open, a yawning mouth of darkness, and she is there, head tipped back toward the cobwebbed ceiling, eyes closed, fists clenched at her sides. The copy of the rhyme is in her hand.

And she is so brave, our Nev.

She is so brave, because she pushes open the door and she flicks on the light and she bites down the scream, but it is all right, because we are all screaming. We are all carrying it for her and with her. Her pain is our pain, as ours is hers.

We feel the hand on her knee, firm and possessive, in those days before she learned how to strike with that same knee.

She is strong now, so strong we almost believe this version of her could have saved us.

She is older now than most of us ever were.

She steps inside, and she does not scream or cry. Instead, she whispers.

One for sorrow as she opens and shuts drawers.

Two for mirth as she lifts the rug and looks beneath.

Three for a wedding as she opens the coat cabinet and shudders.

Four for a birth as her fingers trail across the doorknob again, as she remembers all the times she longed to make a run for it.

Five for silver as she upends the cup of fountain pens just because she can.

Six for gold as she sorts through the bookshelf, scrubbing a hand across her face to wipe away the tears she would not want anyone to see.

Seven for—

And then she finds the book.

CHAPTER SEVENTEEN

IF YOU TELL, THEY WILL COME FOR YOU.

I do not come back to my body until I have walked halfway across town. Roan has said she will be at the funeral home, doing an interview with Jeza for her next article, and my body has remembered this, somehow. I am walking toward my sisters. I am always looking for my sisters.

They have Jordan's book.

It aches in my chest. Someone had her book. Someone saw her, after we did for the last time.

If you tell, they will come for you.

It does not matter who you are or how much good you have done, if you were one of the girls with the loud voices and the scarred bodies, they will crush the voice right out of you.

I am twelve when I learn this.

After Zara vanishes one day like smoke in the wind, Pastor Williams says, *If she's gone, it's because she wanted to be gone.*

Someone at church starts a rumor that she was pregnant, that she was talking to some boy from upstate online and ran away with him.

We know better.

Saem, the only love Zara ever wanted in her bed, knows better, and she is loud in her loss.

She stands up in church and she says, *My love would not have left without me.*

Saem was so many things in our house—the organized one to Zara's chaos, the musician, the poet leaving messages on little sticky notes all around Sister's Place. She was loud, her laugh bright and sharp like birdsong. She was *good.*

And then that day in church she stands there, alone, a reed in the wind.

I wish we could say that the girls around her with their crushed voices and scarred bodies found enough rage that day to stand, one by one, until we were all standing beside her in that godforsaken church, but here is one more ugly truth:

There is not enough rage in the world to survive some things.

Because that day in the church, with two girls gone in a span of a few weeks, Saem says a name.

A name.

The girls who say a name are the ones they come for first.

That is all the answer I will ever get to *why.*

Cal Portman, she says.

The boy in the house of mirrors just over a year ago, when I screamed and scratched and smashed everything around me, bleeding just to be free.

That night, Saem disappears.

I know she will, know it in my aching, twelve-year-old bones. Because Saem and Jeza and Roan, they went together in the forest in the morning, walked the woods all day looking for Zara. And then, and then, and then—we all go home.

I see Saem leave again that night, and I know then, when she goes again to look in the last place she saw Zara and then the last place we all saw Cezanne. I know, because in her eyes there is no more fear and there is only, only, only rage.

I hope when he came for her, she hurt him.

I hope she clawed across his face and smashed her elbow into his stomach and scraped a long line across his chest.

I hope she went for his throat.

It is the only hope left in my body, after everything.

I hope she made him bleed.

• • •

Roan is still busy doing an interview when I arrive, so I find a place at the end of the lobby to wait.

I am slumped on a faded leather sofa in the reception room of the funeral home, staring at the stark blue light of my phone and trying not to feel any of the sensations in my body when Jeza finds me midafternoon. The windows are narrow, the shadows growing long outside.

They are reflected in her face, her too familiar face, and I look away so I do not have to make eye contact with too many of my memories.

"Roan is making some calls," she says. She hesitates, her dark eyes careful as she looks down at me. Abruptly, she sits down beside me on the couch, at the opposite end. "Nev. Can we talk?"

I shrug, let my feet thump to the floor to make room for her on the couch. The echo of my boots is loud in the hollow space inside the funeral home.

The tables around us, usually full of food and drink for funeral attendees, are empty and bare, stark plastic usually covered by tablecloths and trays of cookies made by the women from church.

We never got the cookie trays and the tablecloths, though. We got the forest and the forgetting.

"What do you want?" I ask Jeza.

What can she possibly want with a girl who left everyone behind?

"What do I want?" Jeza repeats softly.

She called, too. Not as often as Roan, but often. They called and called for me, and I could not answer. I tried to tell myself it was about keeping myself alive, about keeping myself safe from being dragged into the woods a second time, or even about keeping them safe, as if *he* wouldn't come for them if they were not with *me*.

But all this time, maybe I was just afraid of what they would see when they looked at me.

"Yeah," I whisper. "Why are you all— Why do you care? That I'm here?"

Behind her, all around her, the rest of my sisters stand.

Kess is at the window, sun in her red hair. Saem and Zara are holding hands, fingers threaded together, nudging each other out of the way for the last peanut butter chocolate chip cookie. Jordan fidgets with the ring she always wears, the solid black band around her thumb.

They missed Jeza, too.

"Nev?" Jeza snaps me back to the empty funeral home, where everything aches. "You are—you are *ours*. Are you okay?"

This is usually Roan's job to ask. She is the oldest now, and I am the youngest, the burden my sisters could not shake. But now it is Jeza asking me in Roan's absence, her eyes sharp and waiting.

"Not really," I say. "But not because the assholes are finally dying."

Something flickers across her face. Something close to a smirk, though it evaporates like fog over the river. "Me neither," she says. "Nev. I'm not Roan. Not . . . gentle like her."

Roan *is* gentle. That's the cruelty of it all, that girls like Roan and Zara and Jordan were so gentle to begin with, and the world paid them back in brutality.

I clench my fist until my knuckles turn white around my phone. "Me neither," I tell her.

Jeza does smile, this time, though it's tinged with something sad. "I just wanted to ask," she continues. "What you remember."

My body jerks upright so fast my head spins, the chipped plastic foldout tables and dingy curtains and narrow windows folding in around me. "What do you mean?" I ask her.

Jeza shakes her head slowly. "Do you . . . do you remember *me*?" she asks finally. "That's all I was asking, Nev. If you remembered us. How *much* you remembered us."

I grind the heel of my palm against my forehead, fingers curling until my fingertips touch short-clipped hair and skull beneath. "I remember," I tell her. "I remember all of you."

You are what I see when I sleep. You are what I see when I wake. I remember all of you, and I remember none of you, and you do not let me sleep.

Some days, I do not remember which of you are safe, and which of you were lost to me.

I remember everything.

I remember *everything.*

"Oh," she says, her voice sounding suddenly frantic. "Oh shit, Nev, I didn't mean— I'm sorry. I thought— You didn't look like you recognized me last night."

I shake my head, rubbing at my eyes with one hand. "No," I say. "No, I remembered you."

The memories may be disjointed—Jeza and Roan arguing in the bathroom, toothbrushes in hand, while Lily tried to talk them down. Jeza teaching the rest of us how to play soccer. Jeza showing us how to throw a punch, though Kess never took the lessons seriously.

"Jeza?" Roan's at the door, silhouetted by the harsh lights of the hallway. "Nev? You're in here, too?" She looks back and forth between us. "Everything okay?"

I nod, run my hands over my thighs to wipe any trace of sweat or tears from them, and stand. "Yeah," I say. "Everything's just peachy."

"Glad to hear it," Roan tells me. "Priya and Maraam are doing an interview with Merrick, and I was out writing up my next article. Nev? What is that?"

I look down at my lap. The book of rhymes is still sitting there, worn at the binding. I snap it shut and shove it in the seat beside me. "Can I come say hi to them?" I ask. "I won't get in the way."

Roan cocks her head to one side. Her face is cast in shadow, the light of the hallway behind her, but I can imagine the worry creasing her brow. "Okay," she answers finally. "But no questions about the case. They can't give you details, all right?"

I nod. "Sure."

No questions.

Roan doesn't need to know that I barged into Pastor Williams's office and demanded answers he could never, ever give me. Or that I broke into the basement and found a book that will only really have significance to me.

Well, to me and to *him*.

"Okay," Roan repeats, offering her hand to Jeza.

Jeza takes her hand, their fingers lingering in each other's for just a moment.

And then Jeza is off, pushing past Roan, head turned away so I cannot see her eyes.

Priya and Maraam are in the funeral director's office, Priya sitting in the swivel chair and Maraam leaning back against the wall behind her, both hunched over a pile of folders.

They both look up when I enter, Maraam smiling and waving me in.

I have to take a breath, sort through the memories, both recent and far away, to remember when I last saw them. Did I see them in the forest? Are they gone forever? Or are they sitting in just the next room, waiting for me?

"Nev," Priya says, using a pin to secure some of the hair slipping from her bun. She used to wear it loose, flowing down to her waist. "I'm glad you came by."

Just like earlier, Maraam pulls me into a brief hug, warm and welcoming and sure as always.

I am suddenly twelve again, watching Priya pin Maraam's hijab with gentle ease, because they had finally learned just how, and then later watching Maraam's nimble fingers play with Priya's long hair, watching them linger together, always together.

"Where's Merrick?" I stare around at all of them, all of us, pulled right back into this world, as if someone is pulling these strings. As if someone *wants* us here. As if someone is waiting, waiting, waiting to finish what they started all those years ago.

"He said he was going to write up his report after he finished our interviews," Jeza answers, folding her long fingers and settling them on the desk in front of her.

Roan gestures to a chair. "Nev, take a seat. If anyone asks why you're sticking so close to us, this is . . . part of your internship."

Jeza snorts. "That's what you're going with?" She shakes her head.

"I think it's a great idea, personally." I lean back in the chair and manage a smile. I reach for the small knife tucked into the pocket of my jeans, my body stilling a little as I feel the familiar weight of it, hear the familiar *flick* as I open and shut it. "I make an excellent intern."

Roan rolls her eyes. "She's done being anywhere near the investigative side of my work," she tells the other girls.

"Priya? How did you and Maraam decide this was what you wanted?" I interrupt, flicking the knife open again.

"It was as good a path as any other," Priya answers softly.

All of their chosen careers make a sad sort of sense, though. That Roan would go looking so hard for answers she'd end up diving down rabbit holes like this one, writing stories about the towns and girls and ghosts everyone else forgot. That Jeza would need to unravel the secrets of the dead so badly she'd end up working in a morgue. That Priya would take the pictures, make sure the evidence was inescapably captured, after the board of directors didn't listen to her—or any of us—years ago. That Maraam would need to process more crime scenes just to come to terms with the fact that nobody ever found ours.

Maraam gives me a smile and lets Priya's answer stand. She slips something from her pocket into my hand. "These are my favorite," she says. "Priya always gets them for me."

When we were young, Maraam always had pockets full of fidgets. Sometimes, as the sun began to slip down over the edge of the forest and the river at the end of the day, its last rays reaching languidly toward our home, Maraam and Jordan and I would sit on the back step, Maraam handing us fidgets.

It's a small fidget, the thing she hands me now, a soft little animal so formless it's not really identifiable, but it's a gentle thing, the sort of thing you'd offer to an overwhelmed child. I take it all the same.

"Maybe use this instead of the knife?" Maraam suggests softly. "At least once Merrick gets back?"

"Oh." I hadn't realized I'd still been toying with it. I shove it back into my jeans.

"Anyway," Jeza says. "The cops are trying to trace the weapon used to take out Ramsey's tires, but they only found one casing. They're also trying to decide if he was fleeing town."

Roan shoots her a look, and Jeza pauses, then sighs when she looks at me.

"Are you supposed to be telling us this?" I ask.

"Do you care if I break the rules?" she shoots back, arching an eyebrow at me.

That's the Jeza I know, bright and fierce as a flame.

We're interrupted from any further argument over what I can or cannot be allowed to hear as Merrick pushes open the door, laptop in hand.

He looks back and forth between us, eyebrows raised. "Nev," he says finally. "You're here." He looks hard at Roan but doesn't bring up their argument again.

I almost reach for the knife again but stop myself, instead squeezing the fidget Maraam gave me. "Sure am."

Merrick nods slowly. "Hey, I saw there was some dancing at the community center in the middle of town," he says after a beat. "I saw a poster for it today when Roan was off on her solo interview. Maybe we could all go, dance a little like we did earlier?"

It's a kind offer, meant to take our minds off the horror we're nearly buried under, but I shake my head.

"They won't be playing Ludovico," I tell him. "Probably some awful shit like polka music or something."

He grins at me. "You're telling me you don't polka?" he asks.

Roan cuts in. "Can we talk?" she asks, all business.

They step outside, where the conversation shifts from polka back to me—I can hear my name through the door, pieces of an argument about when I should go home, and what I should or shouldn't be allowed near.

Maraam leans forward, her dark brown eyes bright as she cups my face with one hand. "You okay?" she asks.

I shake my head, whether I'm saying yes or no anyone's guess.

"*I* think polka would be funny," Priya says, tucking a loose strand of hair back into her bun. She laughs, and it's almost a giggle, and for a moment she sounds just like the teenager I knew. "Imagine Jeza relaxing enough to try some type of dance she's never done."

I snort. "I think we deserve to see it, personally," I say.

Jeza rolls her eyes at us but doesn't dignify this idea with a response, just pulls out her phone and scrolls, purposely ignoring the bait.

Maraam smiles, too, and it is so easy, with them, to slip back into the camaraderie of our childhood. "Polka night, then," she says. "After this is all done?"

"I'm not ninety-six," I tell her. "And neither are you. If we're going dancing, let's at least make it fun. Latin dancing?"

Roan storms back in, interrupting the conversation, Merrick at her heels. He looks around at all of us, eyes narrow as if he is trying to piece together too many fragmented truths that don't add up, finally landing on me as if I am the most glaring of all the things wrong with this picture.

But he doesn't say anything else. Just nods at Roan, once, and then at me.

"Thank you all for giving us statements today," he says. "I do appreciate it. And if you think of anything, you have our numbers."

Merrick is here, playing his part, despite his protests. And I can't help but wonder if he understands the true scope of everything that's happened here. Or maybe he is just a good man, and he can't bear to leave Roan and me behind.

I shiver as I look around at all of them. My girls.

Outside the funeral home, the forest leans closer.

Almost, they tell me.

Almost.

CHAPTER EIGHTEEN

I STAY CLOSE TO ROAN THE REST OF THE EVENING, AND Merrick accepts it without further question, though his eyes stray to me between interviews and meetings, worry and something more in his eyes.

When the sun is gone, leaving cold and fog in its place, the people of Avan Island begin to gather down the street near the government building. The police are speaking, a town hall of sorts, though Avan Island has never been as formal as all of that.

When Merrick and Roan sit down together in the little office Roan has commandeered, he looks closely at her. "Roan. You still doing all right?"

She nods.

He gives me a pointed look, which both Roan and I ignore.

"Anything else for us?" She drums her fingers against the desk. "Is Jeza still downstairs with the bodies?"

I startle.

Of course, of course Jeza is downstairs with the bodies—and one of those bodies belongs to her abusive ex-boyfriend. I shudder.

"How old were you?" I ask Merrick. "When you saw your first body?"

"Seventeen," he answers. To my surprise, his gaze meets mine and does not waver. Finally, he turns back to Roan. "Should we head to the town hall? Nev, you want a ride back to the motel first?"

"I'm good here."

Merrick hesitates, looking to Roan for guidance. "Let's talk about a safer—"

"I don't need your protection, *Merrick*," I snap, but I want him to hear the rest of it: *You cannot protect me.*

And also, equally: *This cannot scare me.*

"Let's go." Roan cuts us both off, and jerks her head to Merrick. "Nev? I'll give you a ride home after this town hall."

When they leave, I wait to be sure they won't return for something, and then I head to the front desk to make small talk with the receptionist for just long enough to palm a key card. Finally, I make my way to the floor below, the book of poems still clutched in my hand.

It smells worse than Dr. Goodwin's morgue back in Johnstown, if that is possible. Rotten and sweet.

When I enter, Jeza is at the table, her back to me, her tight curls firmly tucked beneath the surgical cap. She stands where Dr. Goodwin stood, beside the table, body straight, demeanor calm. Except now Dr. Goodwin is a body on a table, and it is only Jeza left standing.

Captain Ramsey, who we spoke with so recently, who said *They were just runaways*, is quiet and cold. He is naked, white rolls of flesh frozen in place when he died. His fingers are outstretched toward me in supplication that I do not answer.

Next is Jake. Jeza's boyfriend, once. Does it break her, being down here with him? Or does she feel nothing but relief, anger, all the rest?

I tiptoe forward.

On another table beside him is Charles Aisley. Chuck.

Just runaways, Saem hisses in my ear.

Girls like that, they lie, Eva whispers in rage.

My fingers curl shut as I look at them.

Their final pain is bare and intimate before me, but I do not shudder for these men.

I will not.

But there is a mark on Chuck's thigh not like the rest. A *word*, carved in familiar handwriting. A word, carved into a fucking corpse.

Sorrow.

I gag, bile catching in my throat, and the living and the dead turn to me.

• • •

I see it. Him. I see him.

"What is that?" I ask, because I see it, I do, but I cannot process what I see. "What did they carve into his body?"

Jeza turns to me, startling before her eyes cloud. "Oh, Nev," she says softly. "How did you get down here?"

"What did they *do*?" I ask.

Jeza hesitates, and then she answers me. She was always willing to be honest with me. She was always one who treated me as if I could handle the dark, because she knew I could, because I had always had to. "The word *sorrow*," she says. "Each . . . each of them has a word carved into them. I'm sorry, Nev. I didn't want you to see this. None of us did."

Sorrow.

The script is familiar, handwriting I knew once. The curl of the *s*, the sharp edge to the *w*.

I gasp, taking a lungful of the kind of air that makes me think suffocation would be better. It is the sweet smell of the room, rich with blood, and for a moment I think I'm going to pass out.

I straighten, my fingers curling around Chuck's table.

Jeza is looking at me carefully. "Not easy to look at," she says. "You okay?"

"Yes," I say. "I'm fine."

I step closer, but my eyes fix on Jeza, daring her to stop me.

"No," she says halfheartedly, but my eyes are already on the body.

"Why?" I ask, and the forest and the body and the ghosts do not answer me. "Why is this happening to them?"

"I have no idea," Jeza says. "Maraam is still analyzing DNA, and the cops haven't found a murder weapon yet. But it doesn't matter, Nev. What's happening to them . . . Well, you should let it go, as best as you can. Come on. Get out of here, go find Roan. Or I'm calling her."

"Roan's at the town hall," I say. "Don't bother her. I just—I wanted to know."

"Do you know how much trouble you could be in with the police?" Jeza continues lecturing. "If they find out you were down here? They're trying to figure out what—what all this means, and they'll latch on to the nearest thing they can find. Do *not* let it be you."

"*You* could be in trouble with the police," I shoot back.

"You're not wrong," Jeza says. "But I'm more worried about you, Nev."

As Jeza guides me out of the morgue, more of these memories shatter and shift inside me.

"You don't need to," I tell her. "You don't need to protect me."

Something jars loose. When I saw Chuck, his bloated fist wrapped around his badge. When I saw Dr. Goodwin, smiling down at me as he dismisses what I told him about Cal and the girls. When I saw the trees flash by me on the narrow road back to Avan Island. When the birds screamed in the trees above my old group home. When I woke to the ring of a phone and Roan's eyes, already wide open in the dark.

"I know the words," I say, and I cannot explain how I know that the words on the bodies are the words in my poem. Only that I am right, that the dead told me this, that I knew this because of the birds that circled above the open grave in the forest. I know, I know, I know. "One for sorrow, two for mirth—"

My voice cracks.

I shudder, look beyond Jeza. There are carvings on the bodies, not just on Chuck's. Not just on Jake's.

Chuck, *sorrow.*

Dr. Goodwin, *mirth.*

Jake Norryc, *wedding.*

Captain Ramsey, *birth.* Someone has left us a message, in handwriting as familiar to me as my own name.

And beside Jeza, I begin to tremble.

I don't want to see it.

I don't want to open my eyes.

I want to lean on Jeza and never stop.

"I didn't want you to see this," she says again, her voice cracking a little as she says it.

It's okay, I want to tell her. *I'm used to it.*

"Okay," Jeza says softly. "All right, that's enough. Let's get you out of here."

She is blocking me now, her body between mine and the naked, carved-up men at the back of the morgue.

"I'm okay," I tell her. I am as okay as I have ever been.

And I know another piece now. I remember another piece about the book, the book with a rhyme, and a man with the book, and a forest with a—

I take in another breath.

Tonight. Tonight I will go and find the piece that I need.

Jeza continues ushering me out, her hand on my shoulder. Usually, it would be a touch that keeps me here, keeps me grounded.

But I know, I know—

The crows are taking flight. The girls in the forest are not resting quietly. I know, I know what I have to do.

No matter what it takes.

CHAPTER NINETEEN

WHEN I TURN TEN YEARS OLD, THE STATE DECIDES TO throw me away. There are no more foster parents who want older children, especially a girl who glares instead of smiles.

My last foster mother is a tall, thin white woman who smiles often in a way that never reaches her eyes. I am the only child in her house. She does not like children. These are the only things I remember of her—the rest, her name, her face, the sound of her voice, all of it is gone.

And when she no longer wants me in her home, I am told by a social worker I barely remember that I am going to Avan Island. It sounds like a nice town to grow up in, the social worker tells me. It sounds like a haven. It sounds like a second chance.

But most of all, it does not sound like a place where girls like me go to die.

A van arrives to Johnstown and takes me away.

The men who run Sister's Place will someday tell me about how they decided *to bring you home to us*, but for now, I am a little girl in a van, clutching a black trash bag that contains my clothes, another pair of shoes, and one last stuffed animal.

I am ten, skinny and sharp at the edges, long-haired, fury barely contained by a small rib cage. And I do not know, not then, that I will never leave Avan Island. Not really.

• • •

Jeza does call Roan, no matter what I claim about being fine.

Roan comes back, Merrick with her, with the news that the mayor has been delayed, the town hall pushed back another two hours.

Then they argue again, just outside, about what to do with me.

They think that I cannot hear them when they drop their voices into hushed tones, but I have always been good at listening where I am not wanted.

"She shouldn't have *been* there, Roan," Merrick is saying.

"You think I don't know that?" Roan hisses back.

I stand farther down the hall, leaning against the chipped drywall and glaring at them both.

Merrick has never looked so weary. He raises his palms. "Roan, I think we're in over our heads here." He takes a step back. "Can I pick up some dinner for you before we head back over to the town hall?"

"I'll come with," Roan says. "I could use the walk." She looks down the hallway at me. "You in?"

• • •

Night has crept up over Avan Island, but we sit outside in the little park at the center of town, takeout containers from the small taco joint in hand.

I shiver when the wind bites, and both Roan and Merrick hold out their jackets to me before exchanging an unreadable look—and then a sigh when I refuse both of them.

Merrick knocks his knee against Roan's. "Who knew we'd be getting first-class dining with this assignment?"

She manages the slightest smile but says nothing in response.

"Wait until you try the diner," I tell him. "It'll blow your mind."

He laughs, leaning back against the bench. He takes up so much space, but I forget, at times, because he has not yet used it to make me smaller. "So, Nev, you're in high school, right? You'll be a senior this fall?"

"Yeah." It's technically true, I guess. Though my attendance has been as intermittent as I could get away with without triggering a visit from my social worker.

"Are you going to work in journalism, too?" he asks. "Is that why you're doing this . . . internship?" He says the word *internship* with a healthy dose of skepticism, and on the other side of me, I know Roan is smothering both a grin and a grimace.

"Hell no," I tell Merrick, nearly choking on my taco. "Your job *sucks*."

He tilts his head back and laughs. "So what then? What's the big dream?"

I pause, feeling the weight of Roan's gaze settle on me as she, too, waits for the answer to a question I've never really considered. "I don't know," I reply finally, honesty where I had not expected to share it. "I'm— I'd like a room of my own, I think." I glare at him, at Roan, at the whole town, daring anyone to laugh at a dream this pathetic. When they don't, I find that I open my mouth and continue speaking. "I'd like a few plants in the window, too."

Roan's expression drops.

I look away from her before I can hate her for any pity I see there, but Merrick just looks thoughtful.

"I recommend basil," he says. "It grows well in a window. Lavender, too."

Roan smiles—actually smiles this time, something that's a little crooked but realer than the one she offers the people she interviews. "I'm imagining you with an herb garden in your house," she tells Merrick. "I like it."

Jordan loves lavender, I try to say, but it doesn't make it past my lips, not quite.

Merrick launches into an explanation of the best way to grow herbs in your front window, but I'm still thinking about that. About the big dream.

A room of my own, and a window, and some plants.

After all this is done, that's what I want.

Some green and some space and some quiet.

SISTERS

WE GATHER THE TOWN TOGETHER, WATCH OVER THEM as Roan and Nev enter.

Ours, we want to tell this town. *Our sisters. Our home.*

Nev, she was ours and we were hers and we miss her. We *miss* her.

Roan straightens, her fingers landing gently on the hilt of her Taser. She was so good to us, all those years ago. She braided our hair and she made flashcards before our quizzes and she did our chores for us so that the adults in charge of us wouldn't be angry. And now her touch is so very, very gentle with Nev.

They are having a meeting for all the dead men.

They did not do this for us. There were no meetings. There was no worry.

We were gone. We were gone. We were gone.

Nev sits in the front row to Roan's left, her arms folded, a small smile playing across her lips, and we know the town is watching her. They called us liars.

They stood shoulder to shoulder and stared down at us and said we lied.

Nev is taller now, and the long hair of her childhood is gone, and they do not all recognize her, not yet.

Though they know that they should.

But who could recognize what that little girl became? And we are sorry, Nev. We are so, so sorry.

We are a rustle of wind in the trees outside. We are bones and grief, and we do not acknowledge his rules, his town, his people. We do not obey.

They are talking about dead men, about bodies and investigations and things we never had.

"And the missing girls," Nev interrupts them loudly, and there is a sharp, collective intake of breath.

We're here, we call. *We're still here.*

Nev is still smiling, her body calm and relaxed as if she is having a friendly conversation about the weather. Uncertainty has no place on her face.

We see her pain beneath it, because it is our pain. Our chests, cracked open. Our blood in the damp moss. Nev is carrying it all.

But they do not see this, this town whom she has transfixed. They see her *power.*

"All the girls who disappeared five years ago," Nev interrupts, pulling every eye to her. "Thank you for reopening the investigation. We know that's what Captain Ramsey would have wanted."

We sigh. The oaks brush against the windowpanes.

The fear is in all their faces now, pale and somber as if they know the kind of reckoning coming for this place.

She is their nightmare, this girl who lived to tell about what happened. This girl who refused to be silent. We look at all of them, their horrified faces staring back at Nev, and beside her Roan, beneath the flickering lights of this town hall. Roan's fingers brush a pink scar on her forearm.

"Zara," Nev says. "Cezanne. Saem."

Avan Island flinches at each name.

"Eva. Jordan. Lily," Nev continues, and we see grief bleeding through her calm for just a breath of time before she regains her composure. "Kess."

They have not said the names of the men who died at this meeting. They have called them by their titles. They have called them the victims, the dead.

But the girls?

They say our names aloud.

Nev, *our* Nev, has a look in her dark eyes as if for the first time in her life, she's gotten exactly what she wanted.

CHAPTER TWENTY

I SAY MY SISTERS' NAMES, EVEN KESS'S.

And the town sucks in a gasp as if they cannot quite believe it. A gasp, and then rumors, spreading out like a wave across the room.

In the row beside me, Merrick's brow is furrowed in concern. Roan wears a twin expression of worry, Maraam nudges Priya and whispers something to her that I cannot hear.

"What does the mayor have to say about all this?" someone shouts from the back.

It's just a representative of the mayor's office here, someone on one of his cabinets. He has still not made an appearance—

And neither has his son.

I shiver as I take my seat between Roan and Merrick again.

I have not said their names in so many, many years.

I cannot talk about Kess, not now.

Maybe not ever.

Just the feel of her name in my mouth tonight was almost enough to undo me.

But Eva.

Oh Eva, with her red lipstick and her dark curls and her fury.

She was so angry we thought spite might be enough to keep her alive—and it should have, strong as she was. She always loved a chance to argue—debate team and mock trial and regular arguments with her favorite teachers—and she never, ever backed down. Sometimes at dinner, Eva and Jeza would go rounds arguing about anything from socialism to online fandom culture to a new song that one liked and the other didn't.

Most of all, Eva was so angry that no one was surprised when she was the fourth girl to go missing.

And tonight, my body cannot hold the weight of it.

I want a different world, one where we can survive even without our rage and our determination and our goddamn *will* not to die.

I want a different world.

I want a different world.

When Merrick heads for his truck, I follow Roan to her car, and I find myself reaching out to hold on to her arm, just barely gripping the half-sleeve of her neatly pressed shirt, as if she will slip away from me, into the dark forest and leave me here alone.

"Are we going?" I ask. "To Sister's Place?"

"It's late," Roan says once we've reached the parking lot.

"Yeah." My voice cracks. "But I—I miss them."

Beneath the dim yellow glow of the streetlight, Roan looks at me intently.

I scuff my boot against the uneven pavement of the parking lot. "I mean, I guess we shouldn't go tonight," I say finally. "Right? We—we shouldn't. Since it's so late."

Roan draws in a long breath, lets it out. "Tomorrow morning, then? Sister's Place? And then we should really talk about when you want to head home. And I do think it should be soon, okay?"

Johnstown isn't home, and I still have no intention of letting Roan drag me away from Avan Island until I've finished what I started, until I've fucking *found* them. But for tonight I let Roan have her peace.

"Do you have a key to Sister's Place?" I ask as I climb into the car. "For tomorrow?"

She tilts her head down to look at me from the driver's seat. "Do you need one?" There's the smallest of smirks on her face.

I shake my head.

The car rattles just a little bit as we head out of town toward the motel, the sound reminiscent of a dying man's cough.

"Did you tell Jeza and Priya and Maraam?" I ask. *Will they come with?* I want to ask her, but I don't. I can't demand that from any of them.

"Yes," Roan answers. "Are you okay?"

"Yes," I tell her, because I am alive.

Because I am here.

Because much as I want a different world, this is the one we have, and in this one, being the only girl not to die is the only fucking victory I know.

• • •

Roan has work that calls her back into town, but she waits until I am inside my motel room. When I flick on the light and peer out of the curtainless window, she is still in the lot.

Only when she sees me inside my motel room does she start her car, the rattling only louder.

My phone lights up.

Don't forget to lock your door.

I roll my eyes, which I'm sure she can feel even though she's not in the room with me. *Okay dad*, I text her back.

She leaves me on read.

I wait, just long enough until I'm sure she hasn't circled back to anxiously check on me or to tell me that she wants me to stay in her room where she can keep an eye on me, actually.

And then I grab my own keys, shove Roan's long knife into my boot, and reach for—the book.

I told Roan I couldn't go to Sister's Place at night.

But that's not true.

I couldn't go there with her. Not after I said the names of all our sisters and saw the pain and the fury weighing down her body like they would drown her.

No.

No, this I have to do myself.

The duffel I packed has about as much in it as the black trash bag I arrived with years ago did—a few variations of the black jeans I'm wearing, a few T-shirts, some threadbare bras and a few pairs of underwear and socks. And then the book I stole from the church earlier today. The group home had two copies of the book of rhymes, something that had been left over from a church rummage sale, in all likelihood.

I run my index finger along the faded title—*Blaisely's Treasury of Rhymes*—and then tuck the book under my arm and walk back down to my car.

It is not far from the motel, this place I used to call home. One right turn, and then a few miles on a road that turns from pavement to gravel to dirt somewhere along the way. Shorter if you walk.

Sister's Place is at the end of the dirt road, just outside of town.

The last house before Sister's Place on this road is Mayor Portman's, his property stretching for miles and miles along the riverfront, jacketed with thick forested land. It is just him and his son, the golden boy. Are they there now, avoiding the town hall and the names of my sisters?

Or is *he* closer, taking the path the deer know, looking for me?

Night is falling, heavy around us, when I arrive at Sister's Place.

I scrape my hand over my scalp and suppress the urge in me to cry.

I want a different world.

They are all here—Zara dressed in daisies, Cezanne with her headphones, Saem with her cello and her daring, Eva with her rage. They stand, one in each of the windows, and the other three—Lily and Jordan and—

If only I could unlock the door.

"Nev? *Nev.*" Lily is laughing and holding out her hands. "Hey, Nev, wake up. Do you wanna come in?" She hesitates, and she is still smiling, but she won't leave me out here all alone. None of them will, and that thought is the only thing holding me together.

It is the only thing I have at all.

I look up, and the girls are gone from the windows.

Come find us, they might be whispering, but their whispers are useless, because I know.

I know exactly where they are, the place burned into my memory, if I could only remember how to *get* there.

"I'm coming," I say to no one.

I jimmy the lock, the sound of my penknife loud in the stillness.

When I step inside, the noise of the first crickets of spring stops as if someone has turned the volume down.

The front porch is empty, its only occupants spiders spinning their tired webs, the entrance hall dark with the same dust and disuse.

The staircase leads up to my left, and the living room to my right with the kitchen and laundry room just beyond.

And then Lily is beside me, and I forget how to breathe.

• • •

I am twelve, and even after four disappearances no police have come.

Girls like that, they lie.

Girls like that, they don't come back.

Runaways, lost girls, nothing tethering them to this town.

Nothing tethering them to this world at all.

Lily is fourteen, and I think it is laughter holding her here. Laughter and sunlight. She is loud beneath the trees, talking to the birds and to all of us, but especially to me. Is that why he took her? Because she was loud and no one could make her be quiet?

Or was it just because, like every other girl he took, she was there?

One morning, we are scolded for burning the oatmeal, but as soon as the group home attendant has gone upstairs to wake the older girls for breakfast, Lily turns to me and she is laughing.

"The only way to get pancakes for breakfast is to burn the oatmeal first," she tells me, and then she throws back her head in the sunlit front room and spins, as if joy is a living thing and she is dancing with it.

I hate her for making us do extra work.

I hate her for wearing all the light of the sky in her eyes.

I hate her for believing adults could keep her safe, and I hate her because it scares me, the jubilance that held her together when everything else was falling apart.

I hate her for dying instead of me.

And worst of all, sometimes I don't hate her at all.

• • •

"I miss you," I say in the dark house.

She doesn't say anything. Just smiles at me and dances away, flits through the house up the stairs, her hand light on the banister. She still takes the steps two at a time.

The stairs do not creak, and I know if I open my eyes I will see the empty house and the cobwebs and nothing else at all.

"I'm coming," I whisper again, and I don't know who I'm telling.

My sisters, who I abandoned. Or myself, that secret locked room in my mind that knows how to find the way through the forest.

And perhaps I could not bring Roan tonight because I do not know how to tell her this in a house full of nightmares and ghosts:

I cannot remember why I ever left in the first place.

• • •

The house is still furnished the way it must have been when we lived here, if only I could remember. It haunts me more than the fact that they are missing, more than the fact that this place was shut down because of it—it is the echo of their lives, here in this place, that haunts me more than anything.

There is a dusty couch in the living room and one tall bookshelf. The books on it are old—I catch titles like *McGuffey's Eclectic Reader*, Volume I and *First Catechism*.

It looks as if, once the choice was made to close this home, they simply shut the doors and never looked back. Did they take Jeza and Roan and Maraam and Priya away as fast as they took me, then? Did they drive them to Johnstown and tell them to forget?

But we're still here, I want to tell them. *Why did you shut the doors? We're here. We exist. We exist.*

There are four bedrooms, one a primary bedroom with its own bathroom, and a second bathroom in the hallway. A bathroom shared by twelve of us once.

If I open the door, I'll see the lineup of toothbrushes—Zara's the color of strawberries, Priya's with the worn image of a boy band I don't recognize, Cezanne's bubble-gum pink toothbrush. Mine was always between Jeza's and Cezanne's, and Saem would get pissed if anyone rearranged the order.

Why do I even try to keep us neat? she would sigh, but her eyes would always, always stay soft, and she'd ruffle my long hair with one hand.

I think Roan must know what I see. *Who* I see.

I hide it all so well from everyone else, but here in the dark all the pain in me radiates through, and if she were here beside me, I think it would drown us both.

I don't know how much Roan remembers, or how much she has forgotten, but I know, I know:

The body always remembers.

I clutch the book to myself.

It is the only thing keeping me here. I sit down at the top of the stairs, where the sun used to hit midmorning. It feels warm against my shoulders.

I open the book.

Jordan did not speak, but she would read to me here, read in her hoarse, whispering voice. She would read these rhymes, over and over, and it would soothe me when nothing else could.

One for sorrow, she says.

Two for mirth.

Three for a wedding.

Four for a birth.

Five for silver

And six for gold

And seven—

Her voice would always cut off here, tapping seven fingers against the pages of the book.

I cradle the book close to me, run my fingers over the pages, worn at all the edges.

This was my copy.

I do not realize I am crying until the first tear drips onto the pages of the book and smears the word *sorrow.*

It was carved into the body at the morgue.

Sorrow.

Something that is maybe a scream, or maybe a sob rips out of my throat for all I have lost and all I do not understand.

Jordan, I call. *Jordan Jordan Jordan.*

I call her name, and then Lily's, and then Zara and Saem and Eva and Cezanne and Kess, over and over again until my throat is hoarse with it.

But I do not find the answers, and I do not find my sisters, and the words on the page haunt me the way the words carved into the bodies haunt me.

Sorrow.

Five for silver, six for gold, and seven for—

Seven for—

I slam the book shut.

• • •

I do not remember locking the door behind me, or hauling my duffel bag up those stairs, or pulling back sheets on a bed that has not been slept in for five years. I am the hollow gaps between memories. I am smeared words on a page.

I am nothing at all.

But I remember this:

I pace my old bedroom until dawn, and I say it over and over again, the words of the poem.

I do not say it aloud, no.

I whisper it like Jordan did, eyes to the ceiling, fingers tapping, hoarse voice whispering, and whispering and whispering.

One for sorrow as I walk a path in the worn floorboards and Chuck's bloated hand clutches his badge.

Two for mirth in the dark dark dark empty bedroom as Dr. Goodwin chokes on poisonous air.

Three for a wedding as the floor creaks beneath me and Jake Norryc's skull comes apart.

Four for a birth as everyone else in the motel falls asleep and the corpses lie silent in the morgue, Ramsey quiet at last.

Five for silver as I hold the book to myself and Pastor Williams's office door slams shut.

Six for gold as the sun starts to unspool across the sky outside my window and where is he, where is he, *where is he*?

And seven for—

I do not know the rest.

CHAPTER TWENTY-ONE

I WAKE WITH MY HEAD PILLOWED ON MY DUFFEL, THE midmorning sun spilling through my window. The duvet is still a faded pink, used even when they first put it on the bed years ago. Kess's bedspread has cobwebs, which I brush off gently. There is a fine layer of dust on it all, illuminated by sun streaming in the windows.

The book is open beside me, and I slam it shut again.

There are a handful of missed texts from Roan, a missed FaceTime, too.

I text her *slept in sorry* and then flop onto my duffel. My head pounds, and when I sit up, the room swims around me for a moment before I steady myself.

Answer your phone, she texts back.

I do, but with video off. No one needs to know I'm home.

And that's when she tells me: There's been another murder.

• • •

The fifth body is Pastor Theodore Williams's, found in the wide-open green space on the east side of town, when the day is still young and the sun is still bright.

This is what I know: He died with a knife in his stomach and a word carved in his gut and a scream on his lips.

I do not want to tell the rest.

SISTERS

WE WILL LOSE NEV TO THE FOREST.

We can see it in her eyes, the way she stares right through Roan, right through all of them. And when they bring in the most recent body—the pastor—we know she's not with them at all.

We want to hold fast to her—hand on her shoulder, pulling her back—but we do not know if we can. We do not know if it's too late.

LOCAL POLICE CAPTAIN DEAD, FBI TO TAKE OVER INVESTIGATION

By Roan Ellison

The death toll in the Avan Island murders rises to five as two more members of the now-infamous Sister's Place board of directors were found dead, one of them the head of local law enforcement.

The death of police captain Arnold Ramsey sent shock waves through Avan Island. Detective Jason Edwards, the highest-ranking member of law enforcement remaining, has stepped in temporarily to fill his role. He was unable to comment at the time of this article.

A local clergyman, Theodore Williams, was found stabbed to death shortly after the police captain's brutal murder.

While law enforcement has yet to publicly state the connections between these murders, one fact is clear: Each man was connected to Sister's Place.

The only surviving member of the board is Graham Portman, mayor of Avan Island. Local police have set up a twenty-four-hour watch outside the home he shares with his son, fearing a potential attempt on his life. Neither the mayor nor his son, Calhoun Portman, a former volunteer at the group home, could be reached for comment.

An FBI task force comprising both CID (Criminal Investigative Division) and VCAC (Violent Crimes Against Children) members, is set to arrive in Avan Island to take over the investigation within the week.

CHAPTER TWENTY-TWO

THE DAY PASSES IN A BLUR—ROAN AND JEZA AND PRIYA and Maraam hard at work, me tagging along with Roan when she allows it, and, more often than not, hanging out in the park with Merrick, who has stopped arguing with Roan and seems content to chill with me and talk about windowsill plants and martial arts and his sister, Lucy, who is starting college this fall.

On the morning after Pastor Williams is found murdered with the word *silver* carved into his stomach, Roan calls to tell me she is in town already but coming back to pick me up from the motel, that we're visiting Sister's Place together, and then we're leaving. Me and her.

She doesn't know that I will never leave, not now. She doesn't know that I have moved back into Sister's Place, that I crawled between dusty pink sheets in a narrow twin bed, that I still fit there. I packed my clothes back into the drawers, next to Lily's sundresses that used to be too big for me but now I have outgrown.

It's discordant. I can only remember Lily as taller than me.

I unpacked my sweatshirts next to Zara's hand-me-down shorts and Jordan's books and Kess's sweaters.

I tell Roan I need half an hour, that she can pick me up outside of the motel. My motel room is empty, everything cleared out, no evidence I ever lived there except for the cash I paid the manager.

But I'm not ready to tell Roan that, so I go back to the motel to wait for her.

About half an hour later, the crunch of tires on loose gravel announces Roan's arrival.

I tuck the book into my backpack, just—just because, and wave to Roan.

She holds out a bag of takeout from the diner. "You sleep okay?"

One for sorrow.

I nod my head. "Yeah. Slept fine."

Roan tilts her head, considering me. "Jeza and the rest are at the funeral home. Maraam was able to get some new data off the crime scenes and out of the phones."

"Fuck." My head snaps up. "What did she find out?"

Roan pinches the bridge of her nose. "Just that they were all texting one another," she says. "All these men. They tried to use Snapchat for some of it. They were . . . well, there's enough to suggest they were all working to cover something else up before they started killing each other off. It's not just detectives coming, anymore. The FBI is sending people, and my boss wants me to stay. Merrick's boss definitely wants him to stay, and I wouldn't be surprised if a few more news vans rolled into town."

"That's the kind of story that can make your whole fucking career,"

I say slowly. “So that’s good, right? That your boss is letting you stay on this?”

Roan looks as if she’s about to cry. “None of this is good, Nev,” she says softly.

“Why are you telling me about it?” I sip from the latte she brought me.

Roan shoves her hands into her pockets. “Because you deserve to know that someone is finally looking into everything,” she says. “Before you go home.”

“Roan,” I say. “I don’t exactly have a place to go? In Johnstown?”

She curses under her breath. “God damn it, Nev,” she says. “What did you do?”

“I didn’t renew my lease,” I tell her. “Or . . . or tell my social worker where I was going.”

Roan’s eyes meet mine, the look on her face intense. “Shit,” she says. “You . . . you’re a runaway.”

I flinch, but nod.

She squares her shoulders. “All right,” she says. “All right. I’ll help you figure it out.”

It is more than I deserve, but that seems to be the story of Roan and me.

After all that has happened, and Avan Island is finally right about me. A runaway, the kind nobody goes looking for because I did it on purpose.

Roan tips her head back, looks at the sky as if begging some deity for patience. “Okay,” she says finally. “All right. Give me your social worker’s number, okay? We’ll sort this out all together. But this morning we’ll go and visit Sister’s Place.”

I get into the car with her.

We are silent as Roan drives, and I shove down the questions I have, about the marks carved into the men, about the book and the poems and all of the answers and questions tangled in my head.

Five for silver, and six for gold—

"Nev."

We are parked in front of Sister's Place. It is so lovely in the sunlight that I can scarcely remember all the fear and grief of the last few nights.

It is spring, the sharp edge of chill still reluctant to move on as summer comes closer, but it is almost planting time. In the summer there will be peonies on the south side of the house near the woodshed, and watermelons in the garden.

Saem will pick one of the watermelons we are supposed to be saving for the county fair or the church dinners—they call them Love Feasts—and we will all sit on the stumps and rocks on the riverbank and eat watermelon and dangle our toes in the water and we will not dream of bones in the forest, never once.

There will be watermelon and peonies.

Our feet swish softly through the overgrown brown grass of last year. Beneath it, this year's green is beginning to struggle to the surface.

When we reach the door, Roan looks at me. "I can get the lock if you want," she says.

"I got it."

The older girls were the ones who taught me, initially. But I took to it fast: Busting locks so we could get to communion wine. Jimmying the lock on a bedroom door when an adult had locked someone away as punishment.

I shove open the porch door again, grateful that I am not doing this for the first time with Roan here to see me come apart.

Roan steps inside, floorboards creaking as she does. It is how I know she is real, here with me and not one of the sisters I've lost to the forest. She looks around reverently. The bench where we used to sit to lace up shoes or shove our feet into boots—that is dusty now, though still here.

Everything here is paused, waiting for us to come back home.

In the long rays of sunlight, particles of dust dance.

A tear tracks down Roan's face. Drips off her jaw.

There isn't anything to say, nothing at all, so I reach out and take her hand.

It is a more peaceful walk than the other night, when my sisters flitted around me, laughing and dancing and living while I crouched on the stairs and wept over a book of rhymes. With Roan with me, we walk the halls.

The kitchen where we fought over last servings and the halls we raced down to be first to the bathroom to get ready or have the last hot water for a shower. The living room where Lily danced. Is dancing.

She is there—just there—and she is listening to Cezanne's favorite, "Le onde." She is there—spinning, twirling. She slipped from one aesthetic to the next, despite the limitations of our wardrobes, from sundresses to what she is wearing now, her high-waisted blue jeans and her skinny little T-shirts and her natural makeup looks and her soft golden hair in waves down her back.

I thought she would live, just because of that. Because she laughed like nobody could steal the joy from her.

"Nev." Roan calls me back to now, but I don't want to come.

I want to stay in the version of this house where we are all alive.

I want to stay here with Lily, but I can't, I can't, Roan is calling me back.

"I'm sorry," she says, and then she is holding me tightly and I am hugging her back.

"Do you want to go upstairs?" she asks me when she finally steps back. "I don't—I don't know if I can look at the bedrooms."

She shared a room with Jeza and Saem and Zara. She and Jeza had the top bunks. Saem and Zara had the bottom bunks.

"No."

No, not until tonight, when I slip between those covers and dream of being a child again. Will I find it here, the answer to that question of *where*? Will I find my way home, sleeping in these beds and waking here alone?

"Okay," she says finally. "Okay, Nev. I'm going to take you home."

I follow Roan out to her car, through the creaking door and dusty porch and swishing grass.

We are quiet as we drive back to the motel.

When we pull up out front, Roan clears her throat. "I'll find you a place to stay," she tells me. "In Johnstown. I have a studio, but you can stay there while I'm on Avan Island, or I can get you a hotel or something. Here . . . shit is only going to get worse before it gets better. And when I'm back in Johnstown after this is done, I'll help you find something permanent, all right?"

"Roan," I say, my throat tightening until I can barely speak. "Roan, you know that I can't."

Her hand clenches over the steering wheel. "You *can*," she says. "You have to. You have to be safe."

Safety is a fucking illusion.

"Roan, I want to *know*," I tell her. "I want to understand what's happening. I'll stay out of your way. I will. But I have to know. I have to—"

"Nev." Roan has tears cutting sharp lines down her face now. "Nev, *please*."

"I'm sorry," I tell her.

I am, I am.

I am sorry for it all.

For scratching a boy and pushing a house of mirrors down. For refusing to apologize. For being small, for being weak, for being alone.

For loving them as fiercely as I did, for not dying beside them when I was meant to.

"All I ever wanted was for you to be safe," Roan whispers.

"I wanted *all* of us to be safe," I tell Roan. "And we weren't. Nobody could keep us safe then."

"But I can keep you safe now," Roan says. "If you let me."

But how can I? How can either of us ever even know where to start?

I shake my head, and the look she gives me has the weight of all the years and the loss in it.

"I'm staying, Roan," I tell her. "I'm sorry."

For better or worse, I am going to see this through.

CHAPTER TWENTY-THREE

I AM TWELVE, AND I AM ALIVE.

I am still alive.

I have faced the eyes in the dark and stared the loss of my sisters in the face, and I am alive.

But I am lost, and I will never be found again.

I am on a path in the woods, and I am faster than the devil himself. I am teeth and nails and fury. My hair catches on a branch, and I rip myself free and keep running.

When at last I am sure no footsteps echo behind me, when at last I am sure that the darkness cannot take me, I run to a place in the forest only I know.

There are no hands reaching for me, no eyes searching for me, and I climb.

I climb and I climb and I climb to the tallest tree, and ominous and all-seeing as they are, the tree holds me safe in its arms.

I am just another missing girl, and the only person who cares to come looking is *him*.

It beats like a drum in my chest, hollowing out a space in my rib cage where my heart used to be.

My sisters.

My sisters.

My sisters are gone.

When you are a foster kid, you can't hold on to anyone, because everyone leaves. But if you're small and lost and angry and sad, like me, you can't help it. You can't help loving them all.

You can't help it, and on the day you turn twelve all that love twists inside of you because all of a sudden *love* is just *loss.*

And you know, you know—

You will keep loving until the day it finally kills you.

• • •

I stick close to Roan the rest of the day. She moves across town like a wildfire, filming clips to send to her boss, stopping by with coffee and bagels for Jeza and Priya and Maraam who have had to process so much horror in so few days, waiting outside Mayor Portman's office for a few hours for a statement or interview he keeps dodging, and finally stopping by with takeout for all of us to eat together when Jeza is finished for the day at the morgue.

At the end of a day like that, it would be cruel to ask her for more. I can't, but I tell her I am going back to Sister's Place tonight.

The cruel part is that I hope she goes with me. I don't want to be the only girl left alive. I want us all to be there. I want to be the youngest again, looked after in a world that has never cared if I was okay.

"Will it bring you peace?" Roan asks.

I hesitate, and then, finally, nod. "Yes," I say. "I think so."

Peace seems so foreign, but the idea of finding the path behind the house, the path through the forest—finding my sisters at the end of it all? That seems like the closest I will ever be able to come.

Why you? I ask Lily again. *Why you, why me, why us?*

And she never answers.

"Then I'll take you," she says. "But we won't stay long, all right? I don't want to get stuck out there with no service after dark."

• • •

There's another town hall meeting tonight, because the worried townsfolk of Avan Island demanded it after their pastor was found in the field, though I don't listen to most of it—and it's as dull as Pastor Williams's church services used to be. Well, not quite that dull. But close.

The town gasps and ask questions when Detective Edwards talks about the FBI sending a small team, and the metal folding chairs squeak and scrape, and outside the wind and the trees and the girls whisper.

Home, they are saying.

And I tell them *Almost*.

When it is done, finally, the sun is still up, though it is slipping toward the horizon.

Roan glances at the skyline, at the tree line and the gap between them. "Not long," she tells me.

"We'll meet you back at the motel," she tells the others, and explains no further.

We drive in silence, my copy of the book of rhymes clutched in my hand.

"You've held on to that," she says softly when we pull up in front of Sister's Place. "I've seen you carrying it around the past few days."

The setting sun slants its long bright-gold rays over the faded white paint of the farmhouse, casting long shadows behind it.

"It's mine," I say.

Roan waits, the car idling.

"It's important?" I add hesitantly.

"Yeah," she says. "Okay. I recognize it, too. You ready to go inside?"

"Not inside," I tell her.

She stiffens. "I don't want to be out in the open."

"I know," I tell her. "But not long? I promise, not long. I just—There's a path. There's a path behind the barn. Next to the woodshed. A footpath. I haven't been—I haven't been able to find it. But I have to."

Roan nods. "At the *slightest* sound of trouble, you run," she orders. "You understand me? Can you do that for me?"

I ran for my life in these woods once, and I was fast enough to escape. I was. I will be again, but if *he* finds us here, I would never run and leave Roan behind.

Still, I give her the smallest of nods, and then I lead the way, my boots crushing last year's long grass, the occasional crack of twigs beneath my feet gunshot loud.

The barn roof is sagging at the middle, and the windows are boarded up, but otherwise it is the same. I can imagine what it is like inside—sweet-smelling timothy hay and sawdust and the faded scent of the cows housed there before our day. Beside it, the woodshed is small, the roof barely higher than my head, narrow as two girls sent out to gather the wood late.

The shudder wracks my body before I can stop it, and Roan pauses.

"We don't have to do this," she says carefully. "Nev. *You* don't have to do this."

I run my hand over my scalp, the bristles of my shaved hair poking at my palm. "I want to do this," I tell her.

Behind the woodshed is a path.

It is not much to look at. A small, narrow footpath, a bare indent where feet once walked, the brown grass parted for a trail I never wanted to follow. It leads into the forest, a place for deer and raccoons to wander.

A place to be dragged by your long hair, side by side with your sister, by a boy who thought all the world belonged to him, but you most of all.

I walk the path, my body trembling. I duck under a tree, its long fingerlike branch trailing across the back of my head, and I shudder, again, because the last time—the last time my hair caught on this branch and was yanked free.

"That's enough," Roan says. Her hand closes over my arm. "Nev, that's far enough."

I want to argue, to tell her I have to walk this path, I *can* walk this path, but the sun is getting lower and Roan is exhausted, and this would not be fair to her. So instead I follow her back out of the forest, up the hill past the barn, and into the car.

"I can do it," I tell her once we are safely inside, doors locked behind us. "I'm fine."

Roan turns to me, tears shining in her eyes. "Why are you saying that?" she asks. "Why are you telling me you're fine when I saw you?"

"Roan?"

"Nev," she says softly. "Nev, you were sobbing. You were sobbing with every step that you took."

CHAPTER TWENTY-FOUR

I DO NOT KNOW HOW LONG WE SIT THERE TOGETHER. Roan says words that are soothing, soothing and gentle and I will never remember later what they are. With one hand I rub back and forth over my shaved scalp, back and forth and back and forth, and with the other I hold the book tightly to my chest. *One for sorrow, one for* sorrow—

And she waits with me, waits until I am back in my body.

It is dark by now, all the way dark, a sliver of moon peering through the trees at us, witness to the pain.

"We should join the others," Roan says finally, when my breath is even.

"I'm going to try again," I tell her.

I have to find them.

I *can* find them.

One day I will go to the path behind the barn at Sister's Place. I will walk the path into the forest and I will find—I will find all of it. I will find all of them.

Then, and only then, will I be able to go home.

The silence between Roan and me is long, heavy.

"I know," she says finally. "I know, Nev."

She turns the key in the ignition and—

Nothing.

The engine is dead. Not a spark of life.

"Nev." She turns to me. "Does your phone have service?"

My eyes are wide in the dark. "No," I say shakily, my hand scraping frantically back and forth across my scalp. "One bar? I can try to call Jeza."

"Okay," Roan says. "I want you to listen to me. You are going to *stay in the car.* No matter what, you will not leave this car. Do you hear me?"

That cannot be a whimper in my throat. It cannot.

"I hear you."

"I'm going to get out of the car now, Nev," she tells me. "I'm going to see if I can find the problem. Nev. No matter what, stay in the car. *No matter what.*"

"I know more about cars than you," I tell Roan. Or, at least, I know something about cars, and the Roan I knew had no interest whenever Cezanne rambled about the pros and cons of different types of vehicles. When she doesn't argue that point with me now, I know I'm right. "We both get out, I look at the car. Or we—"

I had opened my mouth to say *We stay here for the night*, but Roan wouldn't want to, of course she wouldn't want to. I know how it would sound, to say we should stay here. I know how it would look, if she sees the imprint of me in my old bed alongside the dust and spiders.

So I don't say it.

She looks as if she's about to say more, but then her gaze flickers past me. "Nev," she says. "There's someone upstairs."

My body turns to lead. "No," I tell her. "No, I locked it when I left."

"Fuck," she says. "Nev, there's a man in one of the bedrooms upstairs."

I hear her yelling at me to *stay here*, but I'm already out of the car and running for the house.

This is my fucking home.

Mine.

I broke a boy's collarbone just for touching me. I clawed and I fought my way out of the worst the world could do to me. I won't fucking let someone in my space. I won't let *him*.

I throw open the door to the building and take the stairs to the second floor two at a time. There is a crash and a clatter and the sound of doors slamming, and I catch a glimpse of a man in a hoodie and jeans disappearing down the stairs toward the back door.

Roan catches me, her lean wiry body slamming into mine. "What the *fuck* are you doing?" she snarls. "Let *me* chase after the fucking psychopath who broke into this house. *Stay where it's safe.*"

I shove Roan, hard, my hands making contact with her chest. *"Fuck you."* I shove her again, and again. "Fuck. *You.*"

"You should have stayed in the car." She is furious, seething. "*I* could have gone after him."

I shove past her and stalk back up the dusty stairs toward my bedroom. The bathroom door is shut firmly, the doors to Jeza and Saem and Roan and Zara's old bedroom, too. Eva and Priya and Cezanne and Maraam's room, that's shut, too.

But mine stands open. The sheets are thrown off the bed, the contents of my duffel scattered across the room.

Roan grabs my arm and yanks me back. Her other hand is on her Taser. "I go first," she says tersely.

I huff but let her go past me.

The drawers were emptied, Kess's and Lily's and Jordan's clothes mixed with mine, looking so much smaller than I remember, and it isn't fair, it isn't fair, their clothes should still be hand-me-downs that fit me, I shouldn't have grown bigger than they ever got the chance to.

And besides that, there is the particular vulnerability and shame and rage of having my personal belongings scattered about after someone fucking *touched* them.

It takes Roan a few minutes to understand exactly what she is seeing, to realize that it's my duffel, my clothes *now* scattered across the floor.

"Nev," she breathes. "Nev, *no*. No, no, no."

"Roan." Her name catches in my throat. I hold my hands out, palms up, because what do I have to say, really? "Roan, I—"

Roan lets out a sound that is part fury, part sob. *"No,"* she says again.

And then she sends a message, cursing under her breath at the cell towers.

"They're coming home," she says a moment later.

And I know who she means.

Roan waits with me here, and when I start to fold Kess's sleep T-shirts and shorts, Roan sits down on the floor and joins me, her hands gentle and slow. She sorts them without me having to help—she knows, like me, which are Jordan's and which are Kess's and which are Lily's.

"We burned the oatmeal on purpose," I tell Roan as we fold and sort, fold and sort. "So we could have pancakes."

It's a detail without a shred of context, because she can't see Lily dancing through the living room, hair swinging down to her hips, catching sunlight in every inch of her and reflecting it back while she laughs. Can't taste the blueberry pancakes doused in margarine and the fake, not-quite-maple breakfast syrup.

Roan leans forward, brushing a tear off my cheek with her thumb. "I'm so sorry," she says softly. "I'm so sorry, sweetheart, but I cannot let you stay here. You'll stay with me tonight. I wish I'd been able to get you safely home before this ever happened."

But I am, I am, I *am* home.

And I should be furious in this moment, furious at the intruder.

But instead tears are pricking my eyes. "What did he want?" I ask her, my voice shakier than I want it to be. "Roan, *why*? And which of these assholes was in my room?"

Was it golden hair I saw when he ran tonight, or was it just the memory of golden hair?

I am ten, and no room belongs to me.

I am twelve, and the room smells like him, even though he hasn't ever been here, not that I know.

I am seventeen, and he is standing in my room. He is running from me into the forest.

"I shouldn't have let you be in that room," Roan says softly. "*Fuck*. I should have kept you farther away from this—"

"No," I whisper. "No. Roan, they were never going to let me rest. No matter where I was."

"Is that why you didn't answer?" Roan stares away from me, out the window into the gathering dark. "All those years?"

"Partly," I answer. "Because I thought he'd kill me. Because I thought he'd kill you. Because I had to put the memories away."

I take a breath.

It's like diving to the bottom of the river, water closing over my head, sinking down so far I can only barely see the sun. But I force myself down, down into the silt where the memories wait. And then I say it.

"It's Cal, isn't it? Doing this?"

It feels good to say his name, to let it out like a breath I've been holding.

We can say it now, can't we? That we know who's running around this town, carving up all the men who knew his secret and silencing anyone who he thinks might know something—but not just that. Who might know something *and* might be listened to.

"They don't know anything," Roan says, but her voice is shaky, too, her chest rising and falling fast as if she cannot quite catch her breath. "The cops. They don't know who to look at for this, and they don't know enough to look at Cal or his dad. But *you* aren't part of this. God *damn* it."

There's a screech of tires, and Roan sighs.

"They're here," she says softly. "They're home."

My sisters descend on this place like a storm, spilling out of one car—Jeza's, I think.

They look out of place in the darkness of the front yard, Jeza and Priya and Maraam. They cluster together, eyes peering into the night, waiting, because we alone have heeded the warning that has hung over this place for the last five years.

I scoop my clothes back into my duffel, because I cannot bear it if anyone else sees what little there is to my life, upended. "Roan," I say. "Roan? I can't— I don't want them to see."

Her face softens. "Yeah," she says. "Yeah, of course. Come on. We'll meet them down there."

They surround me a moment later, Jeza gruffly asking if I'm okay, Priya cupping my face and looking me over for injuries, Maraam taking my hand.

Merrick arrived in his own truck, and now he stands a little apart from the group, staring at us as if he is just now realizing some things. I wonder, again, how much or how little Roan has explained to him, or if she has explained things to him in the wandering, unmoored way I explain things—

We burned the oatmeal on purpose.

My sisters are still here.

This was my home, the longest one I ever had, except it wasn't.

This was the only home I was ever sure of, and it ate me alive.

This is her sweater, and she's still here, even though she's gone.

Merrick looks both overwhelmed and confused and then—when Roan tells him what happened—furious.

"Who do you think it was?" he asks her, but his eyes are sweeping the house, the doors, the exits. He is taking me seriously. He is not asking if I am sure, or if I imagined it, or if perhaps I am making it up.

Girls like that, they lie.

But that's not what Merrick sees.

"The fucking mayor," I say. "Or Cal. Or Cal's best friend, Brett. The rest of them are dead, or I'd suspect them, too."

Now that I have begun saying his name, it falls freely, the word bold in my mouth. I will not return to silence. I will *not*.

All eyes turn to me. Jeza's and Roan's, guarded. Maraam's, unsurprised. Priya's, thoughtful.

"The *mayor*," Merrick says. "Well, shit. No wonder he's avoiding interviews and town halls."

He looks from me to Roan.

I stiffen, shoulders tensing, hands curling shut.

"I believe you," he says, before I have the chance to pick the fight I so desperately want. "All right. Roan? Do we call the cops?"

She hesitates before she shakes her head, exchanges one of those long looks with Jeza that no one else will ever be able to decipher.

"If it's him," Jeza says softly, "do not let me close to him."

Merrick is the only one who looks troubled by this. "I . . . I don't think I realized it was all of you," he says finally. "I knew you were friends from before. But you . . . you're all friends from *here*."

"It doesn't matter," Roan says. "It doesn't matter who we are. But if you think the cops will listen to you, be my guest."

Merrick nods once, very slowly as if mulling it over in his mind, and then he looks at me. "I'm sorry," he tells me. "Are you okay?"

"I'm fucking peachy." I step back, away from all of them.

What was it Cal Portman thought I knew? What was it he was looking for, and why me, *again*? Why not Roan, who is writing scathing articles about this town that go more and more viral as more bodies drop? Why not Jeza, the medical examiner who searches the bodies and finds answers there he does not want? Why not Priya, who takes pictures of the evidence left behind, or Maraam, gathering more traces of him at each scene?

Why *me*?

Merrick nods and steps past me. "I'm going to the precinct now," he says. "I'll talk to the officer in charge, ask him if he can comment on the involvement of the mayor and his son. Do you need me to drive any of you back to the motel first?"

Roan shakes her head, telling him that Jeza will jump her car, and when he's gone, she turns to Jeza, her face set. "I know," she says, before Jeza can speak.

"I don't like it either," Jeza says. "But she is safest closest to us."

Finally, Roan nods, and they walk out of our home together, fingertips just brushing.

"Did you get any of that?" I ask Priya. "They had a whole conversation and somehow barely said anything."

"They do that," Maraam answers for her. "But they *also* had a conversation, a whole one, out loud, before Roan came to get you this morning." She looks at Priya again. "They were revisiting that just now."

"And," Priya adds, "Jeza said you would probably be in danger no matter where you are, because what is happening here on Avan is . . . well, people are starting to think you know something."

I nod in understanding, because there is nothing else to say. Because I came looking for answers and a path in the forest and a little bit of revenge, and what does it matter, really, if I don't get to leave when all this is done?

I never planned a way home.

I walk past them, push the creaking door open, and step into the darkness, the sleepy grassy lot.

Roan doesn't look at me. "You'll stay with us in my motel room," she says. She is staring past me, past Jeza, straight into the heart of the forest as if she can see something beyond the spring buds and twisting branches and deadened leaves of last year. "You don't go anywhere alone, and you don't go anywhere near the morgue again. Is that clear?"

I scoff at this last one, the laugh ripping from my mouth like a violent thing. "They called me in every other month to look at the dead," I tell her. "Every fucking time a dead girl washed up, they asked me to look at her and tell them if she was one of mine."

Roan's face twists in pain. "I know," she says softly. "I'm sorry I could not stop them."

"What's one more body?" I ask her. "Or two more, or five more, or—or seven."

One for sorrow, two for mirth, three for—

"Enough," Jeza says softly, and that settles it. "No more bodies. No more of this. We cannot protect you from everything. We know that. But we will protect you from this, if we can."

"Fine," I say. "And you both and Priya and Maraam? Are you keeping them close, too? What if they're also targets?"

"Anyone who was here five years ago could be a target," Jeza answers finally. "Which is all of us. We've told Merrick that as well. Anyone from the group home could be a target, and any of the people who ran it could be targets as well."

"So Brett or Mayor Portman might die?" I ask.

"Yes," Jeza says.

"Good," I say.

As one, they all freeze, as if I have said something earth-shattering and not something similar to my usual furious bullshit.

"Is it?" Jeza asks carefully.

What do you remember? Jeza asked me. So many have asked me that now, both my sisters and their killer wondering which parts I remember. And which parts I have lost.

Five for silver, six for gold, and seven for—

There is something I am supposed to remember now. Something just at the tip of my tongue, slipping away again even as I reach for it.

I am coming out of the forest—

I am trembling—

I am asking—

"Let's go," Roan says, and turns away quickly, before I can see the expression on her face. "Jeza's going to jump my car, and then we'll get to the motel together."

"Why don't you sit with us for a bit?" Maraam asks. She pulls me away, and we gather by the front door of the home that raised us. Maraam sits on the step, braiding Lily's hair.

Priya leans against the rail, talking to Saem about music school.

Jeza and Zara are laughing, Zara the only person who could ever pull a smile like that one to Jeza's face. Jordan leans her head against Maraam's shoulder.

Eva and Cezanne are helping Roan with the car, Cezanne's perfectly smooth hands greasy with engine oil and Eva laughing at them both.

And I'm here with Kess, and she's holding my hand so tightly, and the moon slips behind a cloud, and everything is darker and perfect and none of us have ever left at all.

SISTERS

WE ARE AFRAID, TERRIFIED FOR THEM ALL.

Nev sees us, and it is the joy in her face when she sees us that nearly breaks them. But they should not be here, our girls. They should not, and neither should we.

We want to tell Roan, especially: *You are not alone.*

But the trees are whispering our warning for us, and there is nothing but the yawning mouth of darkness above them, the stars forcing themselves through the skin of night like wounds.

We see him move in the dark, and we scream but Roan cannot hear us.

She does not have the time to lift the hood of the car.

She does not have the time to think or breathe or hope or listen to the warning that has always been in this forest, that has hung over this abandoned farmhouse for five long empty years.

He strikes the back of her head, and she does not have any time at all.

CHAPTER TWENTY-FIVE

ROAN FOLDS AGAINST THE CAR LIKE SHE IS A RAG DOLL, and I do not see who is behind her, I do not see who is with us in the dark, I do not see anything at all, but I am moving, I am moving, I am moving.

I am sorry, Roan, I am sorry, I cannot do what you ask.

I cannot stay safe.

I cannot let you become another girl lost in the wood.

I am sprinting away from the step into pitch-blackness, and there are hands reaching for me, but it does not matter this time, because there is not enough left of me to feel fear.

He is running.

He has golden hair and a beautiful face and expensive running shoes. He has strong corded muscle in his arms and a bright, promising future. He runs from me, and I pursue.

My sisters are behind me, screaming for me to stop.

I enter the forest.

I pursue the boy.

His hair catches on a branch. It is not as long as mine, but it is long enough to be dragged by, to the shack—to the saw—to the dark—

I strike, a closed fist straight forward, the bones in my arms perfectly aligned so that when I make contact, there is an unmistakable *crack.*

Because don't they know, don't they know?

Don't fight a girl like me in the dark.

I am made from it, I was born in it, I died in it five years ago, I am a part of it now.

It is all that is left of me.

I don't need to see and I don't need to feel because I know how to break.

Cal crumbles, he crumbles, this man in the dark.

The hands are reaching, large hands, pale hands, two hands that would have taken everything from me if they had robbed me of Roan tonight.

He runs, his face broken, blood streaming from his nose. *I see you,* I want to tell him. *I know you.*

I will find you again.

And then Roan catches up with me and grabs my hand, and my sisters surround me, Jeza and Priya and Maraam, and they are crying and cursing and breaking, but I take their hands. I take their hands, and we are running, sisters hand in hand in a forest full of monsters, and the words pound in my head, words from five years ago that I have worn like guilt all this time.

Find the shortcut, the one only you know.

Find the path, and run and run and run.

Don't look back.

Don't ever look back.

There is nothing left.

Our attacker's footsteps are thunder behind us, but by the time we reach the edge of the trees I know without looking that there are seven girls between us and this man who wants us to die.

Zara and Saem, Cezanne and Eva, Jordan and Lily and—

Kess.

The footsteps fade behind us, and I am dragging Roan, and the rest are around us, and Roan is trying to say something.

"I'm sorry," she is saying. "I'm so sorry."

"Shut up," I gasp. "Shut up and run."

Every crack of a twig, every murmur of newly budding leaves, every single noise in this impenetrable forest is a knife in the dark and hands that will always take what they have wanted. Somewhere above us, a crow screams as we disturb its rest.

We reach the motel, breathless and alone and alive.

The word sings in my rib cage. *Alive, alive, alive.*

I rip the key from Roan's shaking hands, open the motel door, and then slam it behind us.

I am trembling from head to toe, and I deadbolt the door, then pull the curtains shut, tight. "Please," I say, and I don't know what I'm asking. I don't know who I'm begging.

Please, no more. Please, let this be all tonight.

Roan lowers herself onto the bed, one hand on her head. "Call Merrick," she says. "Call the police. Did you see him, Nev? Are you okay?"

"Are you bleeding?" I ask her.

Priya does as she asks, makes the call to Merrick, while Maraam calls the police and tells them to come.

"I'm fine," Roan says, but she closes her eyes and sways.

"Lie down, Roan," I tell her, and when she does what I tell her I know it must be bad. "I'm getting you Advil and an icepack."

"Mmm," she says.

Her eyes are still closed, her gaunt face pale, and I make another promise:

I will not leave another sister behind.

I will not let Roan die.

I move slowly, carefully so she doesn't hear me, to take her knife from the boot she kicked aside a moment ago. I straighten, facing the door, facing the forest, facing the night that tried to swallow us.

Because don't they know, don't they know?

Don't fight a girl like me in the dark.

• • •

I will not let him take another sister.

The ache in my head is a thunderstorm, and I can barely see straight, but Roan is worse. Roan is still dizzy and tired and when she tries to sit up, I push her gently back down onto the bed.

"It's okay, it's okay," I promise her. "We're okay. Stay here. Rest."

"You called Merrick?" she asks weakly. "Someone called Merrick?"

Jeza, spine made of steel and hands strong enough to hold us up. Jeza is here, and all will be well. It was like when we were little—if it was emotions, you took them to Zara or Lily. But if it was a true crisis, it was Jeza we came to. Jeza, strongest, angriest. Unlike the rest of us, Jeza has never been an easy target.

"Yes," I say firmly. "Close your eyes, Roan. Everything is okay."

Close your eyes, Roan.

Her lips are moving, though no sound is coming out, as if there is something she is trying to say, something she is trying to remember. Trying so hard to say it just might kill her.

"Nev," she whispers finally.

I tuck a blanket around her, and her eyes focus and then unfocus. She must see me just barely, a shadow girl in the dark. I see her eyes, stones made of night, but there is a flame in them now and it flickers so softly.

The words are there, finally, the only ones she's been looking for.

"I'm sorry," she whispers. "I wanted to keep you safe."

My hands are gentle, and I push back her dark waves of hair.

"I know," I say. "You do."

But I see in her eyes: It echoes in her head all the same.

I'm sorry.

I'm sorry for what you have had to become.

I cannot change for her what has been, or what it has made me. I cannot, I cannot, so I take her hand in mine and wait until her breathing slows.

Close your eyes, Roan.

Close your eyes.

• • •

Roan reminds me of the sixth girl to go missing.

My Jordan.

We hardly knew her, in the grand scheme of things. We are haunted by her nonetheless.

I am ten, and Zara and I are hanging laundry when the van pulls up in front of our little farmhouse. It is summer, and the sun is bright.

I recognize Mayor Portman's van, and his son, Cal, is in the front seat. Cal Portman, who he has raised like a young king.

Cal Portman, the boy in the house of mirrors, the boy in the forest.

There's a girl in the back of the van.

How kind of you to pick her up in Johnstown, someone is saying, but Zara is frozen.

Zara ducks her head, and I grab on to her hand, because in all my naivete I think somehow by doing this I can save her.

That somehow I can keep her beside me.

"Come, girls," one of the group attendants says, and we do as we are told because we know the cost if we do not obey. "Say hello to the new girl."

The girl in the van is not like us.

I know this immediately, as soon as Cal Portman opens the door.

She is wearing dark jeans, and her hair curls down to her shoulders, but her eyes. Her eyes. They are so very, very far from here, and I think if I could ask her just the right question, I could go there, too, wherever she is.

"This is Jordan," Mayor Portman says.

Cal Portman reaches in and unbuckles her seat belt when she does not move, and then he puts one hand in hers and one hand on her waist as he guides her out of the van.

Something flashes in Jordan's distant, aching brown eyes, but she does not look at him or at any of us. She will look like that every time she returns from those tutoring lessons in the little church office late at night.

She looks at the sky, and Cal Portman looks at her like he is hungry, and I feel like I might vomit right there in the sun-soaked front yard of Sister's Place.

Please, I think, but I do not know how to finish the plea. I do not know who I am begging or what I am begging for.

Maraam and Roan stand side by side, Saem next to them. But Zara crosses the grass in her daisy-strewn shirt—so small on her now that it is almost a crop top—and takes Jordan's hand. Zara pulls her from Cal Portman's cold, clammy hands, and I think I knew then that Zara would die first.

Jordan never did speak to us, except when she sat with me on the staircase and whispered the poems. Or when she sang.

Teachers would say all sorts of things about her, but we knew better.

She did not speak, but *oh*, how she sang.

She made flower crowns for us all, and even Eva with all her fury bowed her head and let Jordan place a crown upon her.

We were queens for a day, queens of flowers and grief, queens until one by one they killed us.

Jordan was the sixth girl to go missing, and it is this one that makes rage twist in me like something alive, a serpent in my belly that wants me to *strike.*

I knew, I knew that she would die.

I knew, I knew, because here is what happened on the Tuesday after she arrived:

They made a bet.

The boys in the parking lot behind the school, after school was done and they lingered to talk. It was the boys, Cal Portman and Jake Norryc among them, and they said, *What are the odds that you can get in the pants of the—*

But I won't say what they called her, I won't, I won't.

She won't tell, they say through their laughter, because we are jokes to them, and sometimes, sometimes the laughter is all we remember.

We hardly knew her, this girl who wove crowns and whispered poetry and sang like she could see god.

But I remember her.

I remember her kindness, and I see it in Roan.

Close your eyes, Roan.

I hope when he found Jordan, that she saw the whole sky. That she thought of her flowers. That she was not aware of what was being taken from her.

I hope she closed her eyes.

I hope she dreamed.

CHAPTER TWENTY-SIX

MERRICK REACHES THE MOTEL BEFORE THE COPS, AND I know even before the headlights of the truck pierce the darkness of the lot that he is driving fast. He's out of his truck and running, and I greet him just outside the door.

"Roan," he says.

"She's okay," I tell him because his eyes are wide and his chest is heaving.

He nods, squeezes my shoulder, and then guides me back inside as he rushes to Roan.

She sits up, presses a hand to her head, opens her mouth to offer reassurances.

Merrick's panic is gone, smoothed over so he can be steady and calm for Roan, and I recognize this because she does it for *me*.

I should do the decent thing and give Roan a moment to lean on Merrick and Merrick a moment to make sure Roan is okay, go back to my own room, but I can still see the blond hair and reaching hands of the man who attacked us, so instead I hunch over, as close to Roan and Merrick as I can bear. As far from Roan and Merrick as I can bear.

The cop arrives another fifteen minutes later, a uniformed officer who has been promoted in the wake of Chuck's and Ramsey's deaths. I go outside first, followed by Roan, leaning on Merrick's arm. He doesn't insist, but he offers, and for once Roan takes the offer of help.

Jeza follows, eyes sweeping the dark past the ring of cars, waiting for the same thing I am. She looks down at me, and then wraps her arm over my shoulders.

Priya follows, hand on Jeza's arm.

Maraam after her, her eyes on us. Where Jeza scans the perimeter for threats, Maraam scans us, over and over again.

I recognize that, too: If you cannot see your sisters, cannot touch them, they will be taken from you so fast it leaves you breathless.

The uniformed officer introduces himself as Detective Edwards, and then his first question is not if Roan is okay, but is—

"Why were you out there?"

"We're from there," I say sharply.

Roan and Merrick move closer, Roan squinting painfully against the brightness of the lights. Merrick sets a hand on my shoulder, but I don't snarl or shove him away. Panic doesn't eat at me, not when it's him.

"You— You're *from* there?"

Detective Edwards was still in the academy when the girls went missing, so I can't blame him, not entirely, for not knowing.

I was one of the missing girls, I want to say, but he won't understand, and it won't help.

"We were paying our respects," Roan says. "All of the women here were raised in that group home, and we went to pay our respects to our missing friends, since they don't have graves. We went before dark"—he snaps his mouth shut, clearly the next question he had answered for him already—"but someone tampered with my car and it was dead. I was attacked while attempting to fix it, and Nev saved my life."

We were all there, together. We all fought for Roan.

But I don't argue with her, because whatever story your sister tells a cop, you say, *Yes, yes, yes that's what happened*, no matter what you do or do not understand about it.

"Hmm." Detective Edwards peers at the other women, all gathered around us. "Do you all want to give a statement?" he asks, pinching the bridge of his nose. "Together?"

Many people look at us this way: as if they are trying to see what we are to one another, what we are capable of together, and why the bond between us remains so tight. But what we have survived is unthinkable, so people can rarely make sense of us. How do you begin to understand the unspeakable?

"Yes," Jeza tells the detective flatly.

All of us, five stories of the same brutality, with one as well-spoken as Roan's, and they will have to listen to us. We are not little girls anymore. We are not so easily dismissed.

Medical examiner, crime scene photographer, lab tech, journalist. They have power now they did not have before.

"Did you recognize your attacker?" Detective Edwards looks at me, and the forest holds its breath.

"He had blond hair and blue eyes and was wearing a nice sweater," I say slowly. It unspools before me, memory then, memory now. The attacker in the woods. "He's older than when I knew him. When I knew him, he was a teenager. A valedictorian. He tutored us."

We read the rhymes.

He liked the rhymes, the symmetry, the strangeness.

He wanted each of us to play a part in his story. His rhyme.

"And?" Detective Edwards's voice leans snappish. "Why is that relevant?"

Roan and Merrick close ranks around me, their shoulders nearly blocking me, until Detective Edwards puts his hands up in apology.

"Cal," I say.

Tell them, tell them, my sisters are begging. *Tell them what was done to us.*

"Cal Portman," I repeat his name. "I saw him in the woods, and he attacked me. He attacked Roan."

He attacked us all.

Detective Edwards's face reflects a hundred different things: surprise, disbelief, anger. But the disbelief shifts when Roan tells her story, identifies him just as clearly, and sounds well-educated and sure of herself.

And then they all tell the same story: Jeza and Priya and Maraam and even Merrick.

He has been named twice before.

First by Saem, standing in church all alone, pushing back when Pastor Williams said we were runaways.

And then by me, in front of the entire board of directors. But despite the fact that a police captain and a detective were in that room, Cal's name remained out of the records.

But tonight this changes.

Cal Portman, attacker. Cal Portman, the golden boy, his name written in a police report at last.

• • •

I do not have much to say about Kess, except this:

I am twelve, and she is thirteen, my first best friend. Red hair and green eyes and freckled hands. A girl who would have stayed at my side forever, in a different world.

I recognize that hair when I find her in the forest.

Because here is the ugliest truth I have found in my memories yet:

On that last night, he took two girls, instead of one.

Dragged them by the hair through the forest.

Did what he did with every girl he had dragged here. But the ugly part is this:

I run, through a shortcut in the forest only I know. Only God knows.

And I leave Kess behind.

• • •

It is still dark when I wake, only a few hours later, to sobbing. My own.

The women stayed—all of them—and some of them are curled up in bed with me, safety and warmth. This is the safest place I know. All of us are here, but I was dreaming all the same, dreaming of hands and hair and soil and I know:

My hair is long, it's too long, and when I run through the forest with my sisters, someone might catch it, might drag me away. It will snag on the branch, and he will rip it free. *One for sorrow, one for sorrow*, his hand is on my *knee*, his fingers are twined in my hair—

Before I realize it, I am crouched beside the mirror, the lamp turned on low, and there is a razor in my hand and blood pouring down the side of my head, and I am sobbing as if my heart has been ripped from my chest. Because it has, it has. I left it in the forest, covered in daisies—

Roan scrambles out of the bed, stumbling over Maraam and then Jeza, and then she is beside me. "Nev, Nev, what is it?" She wraps her arm around me, her eyes on my head, trying to find the source of all the blood.

I'm bleeding. We are bleeding, I should tell her. *We've been bleeding for five years.*

"My hair," I sob, gasping as if the air has been torn from my lungs. "My hair."

Slowly, slowly, she takes the razor from my hand.

"Your hair, precious girl?" she whispers. "What's wrong with your hair?"

"Too—long—" I gasp. "*Please*, Roan. Please. I need it to be gone. He could grab it." I am getting tears all over the front of her shirt. "Please, Roan, please please please—"

"Okay," she murmurs. "Shh, shh, okay. I got you. Enough, Nev. Enough."

I sag against her, spent.

"I will cut it for you," she promises. "But first let me take care of the bleeding."

I tear away from her, scramble to my feet. "No," I snarl. "No."

It doesn't matter if I bleed—as long as I'm free, as long as I can get away.

Roan raises her hand, palm up. "Okay," she says softly. "Okay, Nev. I'll cut your hair first."

She's gentle, her hands sure despite her recent head injury, when she shaves my head in the wee hours of the morning in this cursed town.

The hair falls around us, remnants of a girl who can save her friends and escape the monsters of the woods but who cannot, cannot sleep.

"There," she says finally. "There. It's done." And I fall against her again, limp with exhaustion.

They are around us in a moment, these women. Jeza with a cloth to clean the blood from my razor-wound. Priya with a bandage and a water bottle she holds to my lips. Maraam to brush bits of fallen hair from my face.

They lift me, Jeza and Priya, and carry me back to bed, and then they surround me, all of us on this queen bed, until I fall asleep in the heart of our little circle.

My hair is shorn again, and there is warmth around me, and I know—

He cannot reach me here.

CHAPTER TWENTY-SEVEN

I SLEEP THE REST OF THE NIGHT.

When I wake, my sisters are not beside me, and panic jolts through me. Both of my hands snap to my head, raking furiously across my buzzed scalp.

Zara is not here to hold my hand, Saem is not here to kiss the worry from her face, Cezanne is not here, dancing, Eva is not here with her stories and her dreams for the future and her rage, Lily is not here to pull me into mischief, Jordan is not here with her ever-blooming flowers, Kess is not here beside me, breathing—

I do not scream.

I do not scream.

I do not scream.

I have not woken without them, not in all the years since I saw them last in the forest.

These other sisters are beside me instead, Priya and Maraam on either side, my body wrapped in their warmth.

Roan paces, her hands twisting. Jeza is still in Roan's place on the bed, her hair spread across Roan's pillow, but her eyes are open and she is watching Roan pace.

Roan catches sight of me, eyes open, and then she looks to Jeza. "All right," she says loudly enough that the women on either side of me stir. "Time to get moving."

She was waiting for me to wake, damn her.

"You could have woken me," I tell her irritably, and she sighs.

"Just get dressed," Roan says. "We're going to Priya's for some breakfast."

"No," I say. "Not to the breakfast part. The getting dressed part."

The sweatpants I'm wearing are comfortable—Priya's, maybe?—even if I have to roll them up and even if I have to pull the string so far through to tighten them that I might as well wrap it around twice. But when you wear loose, baggy clothes, no one can see the parts of you that curve softly.

There are fewer man grabbing you, fewer men calling for you no matter how bitchy you keep your expression and no matter how short you keep your hair.

"You can wear whatever you need," Roan says patiently. "I—"

"I don't need you to give me permission," I snap, and then bite down hard on my lip, because this isn't fair, I'm not being fair, I'm cruel and vicious and falling apart and Roan shouldn't have to deal with that, but she's *here*.

I woke up without my sisters today, I want to tell Roan, but how can I tell her that they are the first thing I hear when I wake and the last thing I hear before I sleep? I am surrounded by sisters I love, and I am still longing for ghosts.

I wanted it to be all of us here. Not five of us. Twelve.

All of us here. All of us whole.

"Nev." Jeza catches my attention. She is sitting up, a goddess even in her sleep shorts, eyeing me with warning in her face. "Are you ready to go?"

I roll my eyes. "Yeah," I say. "I'm ready."

Priya and Maraam exchange a look over my head, and I push myself away from them.

Come back, I want to say. To reach out for the girls I am always seeing, close my eyes until they return for me.

"What do we have to do today?" I ask, the edge still in my voice.

Roan's look is guarded, hesitant. "Nev," she says. "We're all sticking together today. They put out an APB on Cal Portman, and the mayor has police guarding his house around the clock now."

"They're not arresting the mayor?" I say. "Are you fucking serious? You don't think *he'll* start hunting us, just like his fucking son? Just like—"

Just like last time.

"There isn't anything I can do about that," Roan says softly.

"You could have fucking *tried*," I snarl, which is unfair, brutally so, because all Roan has ever done is *try*.

"Nev," Jeza repeats my name. She stands, towering over me. "If you need space—"

"You can't have it," Roan interrupts. "And I'm sorry, but you can't. You stay with us, even if it pisses you off. Even if it isn't the option you like."

"I think," Priya interrupts before I can shout at Roan, "that we could all use some breakfast."

"Fine," I say. I turn away so I don't have to look at Roan.

Maraam stands, holding out a pin. "Can you help me with my

hijab? I injured my arm on—well, it makes pinning it alone a little more tricky."

I take the pins, nodding quickly. It's an out, and she's indulging me to offer it, but I need this. I need to be part of this circle of sisters, and I need it all the more desperately after waking without Kess and the others at my side.

Kess.

Her name thrums in my chest.

"I miss you," I say, and Maraam's hand pauses beside mine, hovering with a pin in her grasp as if it is frozen there.

"Nev." Roan is at my shoulder. "Do you . . . see them?"

"No," I snarl and shove her hand away.

Shock registers in her face, and then something else behind the anger that I have never seen before, that I cannot bear.

Disappointment.

"I'll meet you all at the vehicles," Roan says, but her eyes are still fixed on me. She might as well have shouted *everyone out*, because the others finish pinning the hijab and are gone within moments.

As soon as the door shuts, her hands snake out and grab my wrists.

"You will not do this," she says, her voice gentle and fierce as the wind in the trees. "You will not try to get rid of everyone who loves you. I will not let you. Not again."

I had expected a scolding for pushing her, a lecture about the attitude, maybe even a nagging reminder about naming cadavers when we're in public or running away or going back to Johnstown or whatever the fuck else.

But this—

This is immeasurably worse.

"That's *not true*," I shout at her. "You're full of shit. You're full of shit like all of them, like you always have been. None of you are going to stay, and none of you are going to make it, *none of us are going to make it—*"

It ends in a sob.

Of course it fucking does.

"Get the fuck away from me," I manage, but it's just a sob, that's all it is. I shove her again, because it hurts, it *hurts*—

And then she lets out a noise, low in her throat. Pain, suppressed.

I remember her head injury too late, realize that the jarring motion of being shoved must have made the pain spike, and then someone's arms wrap tight around me from behind, lift me from my feet and pull me backward.

"That's enough." It is Merrick, stern and quiet, and he must have heard me screaming and entered and that makes everything about this worse, that he heard me, that he thought I was bad enough Roan needed backup, that—

The breath leaves me entirely.

Merrick lets me have my feet beneath me again and he holds me gently, but he keeps my arms pinned in place, immobile.

I should be raging and panicking in his grip, but instead I am just crying, I am *crying* in front of both of them for the hundredth damn time.

"Are you okay?" he asks Roan.

She nods, and for a moment I think she will demand that Merrick release me.

I don't want her to.

I want someone to hold my hands in place, to make sure they don't hurt anyone ever again. I want someone to stop me.

I want someone to stop me.

"You're okay," Merrick tells me softly. "Roan's okay. And you're okay."

I collapse against him. He releases my arms, but I can hardly stand, and then Roan reaches for me.

This is not how it was supposed to be.

But I let them hold me, and I hate myself for it, for letting them love me even when I hurt them. Even when I know I will hurt them again.

I am falling apart.

But as soon as we leave the motel room, I stand straight and tall, refusing to lean on either of them, even if it is all still there inside me, crashing over me like a wave.

Self-loathing and longing all in one, needing them and fighting them and loving them.

"Breakfast," Priya says pleasantly, taking my hand. "What do you want to eat?"

I know they all heard me shouting a few moments ago, saw Merrick go through that door to help, but they are kind to us all and they say nothing.

When Roan climbs into Merrick's truck, he gives me a hand up, too. I let him.

I hesitate, and then I settle in beside her. I do not look at her, but I buckle and then sit upright, so still and rigid that I do not so much as brush against her.

"Nev," she says firmly. "I forgive you."

The words shock me enough that I look at her, dare to meet her tired, angry, kind eyes.

"So forgive yourself."

• • •

I do not speak throughout the long, quiet ride to Priya's house. Priya lives on the opposite edge of town, near the wide-open field where Pastor Williams died and where he once made me apologize to a monster.

Could she see him from there?

We can hear the river from Priya's place, the rush of the water swollen by spring melting and recent rains. Strong enough to carry a body all the way from Avan to Johnstown.

Despite the fact that it's light out, albeit dimmed by the ever-present fog that lingers near the river, we move as one across Priya's lawn, Roan and Jeza and Merrick flanking our little group.

Priya deadbolts the door behind us while Merrick and Jeza sweep the house, just in case. When they call that everything is clear, Priya ushers us all into her living room and gestures to the couch and easy chairs.

Her space is cozy, woven blankets thrown over the back of most of the chairs, and a long fleece throw bunched at one end of the couch.

How did you stay? I want to ask Priya. *How did you stay when so many of us left? How could you bear it here, just the two of you?*

"I'll make breakfast," Maraam says, squeezing my shoulder as she passes.

"I can," Merrick volunteers. "Tell me what to do, and then you can rest."

She smiles gratefully. "Thank you."

"Pancakes," Jeza says imperiously. "That's what we all need this morning."

Priya looks down at me, her dark brown eyes shining a little. "Burn the oatmeal on purpose, right?" she says softly.

It takes my breath away, to know others who have carried on the work of remembering our sisters. That it's not just me and my ghosts after all.

Maybe we can put a plate of pancakes out for Lily, just in case.

Merrick turns toward the kitchen. "Nev," he says firmly, "you can help me." He does not wait to see if I listen but walks away as if he *expects* me to.

I surprise everyone, including myself, when I follow him.

Roan moves to a chair nearest the open door, where she can still see me.

I don't look at either Merrick or Priya as we assemble ingredients, and when Priya rejoins the others, I hear the words she says to Roan.

"I can't tell if the kid is sulking," Priya says to her in a low voice, "or enjoying being the center of attention."

I curl my fist shut to avoid flipping the bird.

What kind of monster treats them this way, when I know, I *know* how quickly I can lose them? When they are my *sisters*?

"I don't care if she's sulking as long as she's safe." Jeza's voice is next, but it is softened by emotion I rarely hear from her.

"I don't care if she sulks every day for the rest of her life as long as we don't lose her again," Roan says softly, and then I have to step away, farther into the kitchen, because I cannot hear this.

Cannot face that they lost *me*, too, when they lost all our sisters. And that meant something to them.

Merrick hands me a measuring cup, and I take it without meeting his eyes.

"Nev." His voice is unbearably soft.

I do not look at him, because I do not trust men and if I look at this one right now, this one whose hands have never moved to hurt me, that might change.

He reaches out one hand—massive hands, calloused hands, hands that should scare me but don't—and tilts my chin up.

Any other man, and I'd contemplate biting a finger off, but instead I just stare back at Merrick.

"You okay?" he asks me, and I remember what he said: that his little sister and I would get along. Would Lucy snarl at the people who love her? The people she loves? Would she shove them away with everything she had?

I shake my head, unsure whether I'm saying yes or no, and he sighs quietly.

"Okay," he says. "Blueberry or banana pancakes?"

"Blueberry," I say, but my voice is quiet, as if I speak too loud I might shatter something. And today, today, just for a moment, I don't want to be the girl who shatters everything.

He stirs the pancake mix, and I lean forward to add the blueberries, and then I just stay there, leaning ever so slightly against Merrick's shoulder and breathing.

I hear their laughter in the other room—Roan's first, rare and swift and golden. "Do you remember?" she asks. "Do you remember what she was like?"

"Damn skinny and knobby-kneed and pissed as hell," Jeza answers, and I look over my shoulder at her. "Do you remember when she cut that boy's hair in gym class because he was rude to Lily?"

Roan snorts. "And that time Brett broke up with Cezanne so Nev threw cow shit into the back of his truck?"

"Vengeful little thing." Maraam laughs, the words said with affection that is almost unbearable to hear.

Merrick glances down at me. "They've all spent a lot of time together since they've been back. Every second they get, they're off together, just the four of them," he says softly. "And they really, really love you."

I flinch, step away from Merrick as he adds batter to the pan.

"You can join them," he says.

"I wasn't waiting for permission," I tell him sharply, and he smiles slightly.

"I know," he says.

"Is this when you tell me Lucy is just like me for real?" I ask.

To my surprise, his look is pained. "No," he says. "No, Lucy was a firebrand, but she asked permission a lot more often than you do."

Something about his words, his expression, pulls me up short. "Was?" I ask softly.

He nods, his look distant. "Yeah," he says. "I don't talk about it much."

"Does Roan know?" If anyone would understand the loss of a little sister, it's Roan.

It hits me in that moment, that Roan's loss is different than mine. I lost my protectors, the girls I admired and looked up to. Is it worse, to lose a little sister you felt you had to protect?

I reach out and set my hand on Merrick's arm. "I'm sorry," I say.

"Thank you." He clears his throat. "I—I understand how they feel about you," he says. "And I know this is hard for you to accept, but it *is* okay if people look out for you. Keep you safe."

His eyes flick to Roan, the grief shifting to admiration as he looks at her.

I elbow him this time. "You look at her like that a lot," I say.

The faintest blush colors his cheeks. "All right," he says, ignoring my comment. "Pancakes will be ready in a few. I'll call you when it's time to fill your plate."

I rejoin the others, taking one last look back at Merrick as I go.

Jeza has her notebook open; she and Maraam pouring over it together while Priya and Roan discuss something in a low voice near the door.

Roan pauses her conversation and reaches for me, tilts my head so she can see the bandage from last night, her hands featherlight. "This feel any better today?"

I nod. Outside, a single crow rustles and takes flight.

One for sorrow, two for mirth, three for—

Merrick enters with a tray of pancakes and some plates Priya has gathered, and then we sit together in a circle, Jeza on the floor beside Merrick, Roan on the love seat because they both demand she sit somewhere comfortable, and Priya and Maraam next to me on the couch.

They are all so gentle with me. So protective. So kind.

But I am not a girl who needs those things. I am not a girl made for gentleness.

I am a girl who broke a boy for touching her. I am a girl who rescued her sister, who fought the man in the dark, who *lived*.

And I will find the truth I am looking for.

When Merrick settles onto the floor with his pancakes, I set my fork down and look at him.

"Merrick," I say. "Can I tell you about Cal Portman?"

My sisters wear near-identical startled looks, because this is *me* offering information, because telling a man about what happened to us used to be unthinkable.

"Yeah," he says quietly, because he is Lucy's brother and he will believe me. "Of course."

• • •

He is just a boy.

A nice boy, a good boy, a golden boy with beautiful blue eyes and a round face and a doting father and mother who shower him with everything he could ever want. The mayor's son, sunlit and perfect.

There is no hint that there is anything wrong with him, nothing at all.

He is a nice child, but for one thing.

He has a strange greediness to him, this son of the most powerful man in a town that doesn't matter. He is used to getting his way but is still a nice child. He is talkative from an early age, reading by the time he has finished preschool. He collects things, things he takes from the other children—a hair clip, a small stuffed animal, a bracelet, a picture.

It is innocent, of course. A child seeing something shiny and wanting it for his own.

He is good at getting what he wants from adults, and they smile indulgently and talk about how strong, how smart he is. He lives with his father and his mother and no other siblings, and they all say it—how he will be a man just like his father.

Born for influence, born for leadership.

A man with a world carved out just for him.

His mother dies in an accidental drowning while boating with him. He is only thirteen, then, and everyone grieves her. A kind woman, a powerful woman, a dead woman.

Everyone feels for Cal Portman. Everyone showers him with gifts, sweet and smart and a little bit tragic, this boy at the center of every story the town tells themselves.

Oh, how they love him in the little church at the heart of the town. They ask for his opinion, they offer him leadership roles as a teenager. They love him at school, class president, varsity athlete, student of the month.

When they suggest opening a group home in honor of his mother, Cal expresses interest in volunteer work. He can help the board with administrative tasks, with tutoring the girls once they arrive.

He is everything to the board: precocious, well-spoken, highly educated. They speak of law school, a place as an elder in the church when he returns, a place on the town council, a place anywhere he may want to be.

While still in high school, he does coursework at an Ivy League school. It does not matter which one, for they are all made for him.

Perhaps he even believes he has earned it.

When he is seventeen, the girls begin to arrive, one by one.

Cal Portman and his father are kind, welcoming. They pick each girl up from Johnstown and drive them to the little farmhouse they are calling Sister's Place.

And every Sunday, they drive their van to the farmhouse to take the girls for church. The girls all fit in the back of the mayor's vehicle, their narrow shoulders pressed together, their faces solemn as a morgue.

The local newspaper takes pictures, praises their generosity.

Tireless stewards of community, they call them.

Until one day, Cal Portman enters the house of mirrors at the same time as the youngest child, a dark-eyed little girl with long black hair and a thin, frail body.

She scratches him, leaves long lines down his face that mark him, and when they tell her to apologize, she stares at him with ceaseless rage in her eyes and stands, unbending, until together they manage to break her.

But it is the first hint, the first shadow that has ever been cast on him in his sunlit life. The first time anyone has dared question why Cal always has had exactly what he wanted.

He shows nothing, this son who belongs to this whole town. This son of their hearts.

But inside—

inside, rage begins to build.

• • •

When I finish, my missing sisters rush in like water. I have lost time again. They are all sitting quietly together, listening to me, my sisters. Eva leans her head against Jeza's shoulder. Lily plays with Priya's hair.

I am so relieved they have returned that I almost cry right there, in front of Merrick and all my sisters.

Merrick's dark eyes are on me. He is cross-legged on the floor, leaning his chin on his folded hands as he listens. "This boy," he says. "He's the one who attacked you. And you think—you think he was involved five years ago, in all the disappearances?"

I shift, looking to Roan.

"Are you going to print it?" she asks. "If we say yes?"

It seems a cruel question, because this is not the man Merrick is. I know this in the same way that I know Zara would have never run away and left us. I know this in the same way that I know Priya has loved Maraam since they were fourteen and that they love each other still.

"No," he says, eyes still fixed on me. "Not if you don't want me to. This story doesn't belong to me."

"He hurt us," I manage. "Long before any of us went missing. But the board didn't listen to us. When I said—when I told them I thought someone hurt us, they said we lied, we were behavior kids, we were wrong, we were bad. But I think—"

I don't know how to untangle the rest of the words. I survived.

I lived.

And that scared Cal, maybe enough that he told his father, then. I know Mayor Portman well enough to know that he would never let his son go to prison, not even for something like this. And if he told his father—maybe Mayor Portman told the rest, at least some version of things. Maybe he asked Dr. Goodwin to make any bodies found look like an accidental death.

Maybe Chuck was asked not to search his property, Ramsey, too.

Maybe Cal told his friend Jake.

There are so many maybes, and so many whys, and all the wondering will never bring me the truth I can only find when I walk the path to my sisters' final resting place, if I can ever summon the courage to do it.

"You think?" Maraam prompts me gently.

My sisters have the same look on their faces: watchful, curious, waiting to see just how much I remember and how much I know.

"I think if they find Cal Portman, they'll find the truth," I say.

Though if I find Cal first, I am not certain anymore just what I will do—or where I will stop when I do it.

CHAPTER TWENTY-EIGHT

WE STAY AT PRIYA'S ALL MORNING, ROAN STRETCHED out on the couch with an arm flung across her face to block out the sun, Merrick tapping away on his work tablet, Jeza sorting through some of her notes while she and Maraam discuss their findings.

Priya sits down next to me on the window seat and places her hands over mine. "Nev," she says gently. "You know we have been trying—and failing—to keep you far away from the grimness of this case."

I stare back at her, those warm brown eyes that have always looked on me with such kindness. "I know," I whisper.

"Well," Priya says, "after we talked this morning—and after we made that report about last night's attack—we asked the police to check some of the DNA found at the scene against a DNA sample of the Portman men. They're working on a court order for that now."

I sit straight up, heart thundering louder than the river.

There is a memory tearing at me now, something about Priya—something about damp leaves beneath my bare feet—something about *all* of us, together—

There is a storm in that gap inside my rib cage where a heart used to beat.

There is nothing else.

Roan is beside me suddenly, which means I have lost time again. She looks worried, worried as always. "Hey," she says. "Hey, I'm here. We're here."

Priya is on the other side of me, still holding my hand.

Maraam sits at the floor at my feet, one hand on my knee.

Jeza stands behind her, stance wide as if she is both here to support and standing guard.

We are all so close, always, that I sometimes cannot tell where one of us begins and another ends.

Merrick is at the edge of the group, tablet closed, that steady calm on his face that he wears for Roan—and for me.

I nod, but she must see in my eyes the fury that shook loose when I spoke of Cal, the thing that snapped when he went through my room in Sister's Place and attacked Roan in the forest.

"I want to talk to them," I say. "*Both* of them."

The golden boy and the man who covered for him.

This is why I am here.

Find my sisters, my memories, my grave.

And find the man who killed us.

"Nev," Merrick says, but Roan holds up her hand.

"You have their numbers," I say. I square my shoulders. Chuck is in the river, staring up at me. Dr. Goodwin is stretched out on the table. Jake is a smear in the grass. Ramsey is bleeding in his truck, fear his last expression. Pastor Williams is crumpled in the field. I am running through the forest, and my shin is bleeding from Cal's knife.

"We do," Jeza says evenly. "But they don't answer, Nev."

"Give them to me anyway," I tell her. "Both of them."

For so long, I have waded through a sea of lost memories and clawed my way past fear that almost crushed me. But now I am *sure*, sure of this one thing.

I am going to find Cal and Graham Portman, and I am going to make them pay for everything they took from me.

• • •

My hands shake when I put both phone numbers into my phone, but I do not waver.

Cal does not answer, his phone going straight to voicemail.

"That's what happened every time we tried to call this week," Jeza tells me, exchanging a look with Roan. "Don't bother with him. But Graham Portman may take your call."

Merrick steps outside to his truck to make a call, but my sisters remain beside me as I call the Portman men.

It was the one thing Roan asked me not to do at the beginning of all this—but it is the one thing I need to do more than anything.

When he does not answer, I send them both a text.

Sister's Place. Meet me there. One hour.

I shove my phone into my pocket. "We're meeting them at Sister's Place," I tell them.

Roan's face crumples for a moment, but she nods. "We'll all be with you," she says.

Jeza nods. "I've already told the police not to expect us until the town hall meeting tonight," she says. "I said we needed time and space to recover from last night's vicious attack."

Merrick rejoins us, and nods to Roan. "I've taken myself off this story," he says without preamble.

I run a hand over my scalp rapidly. "What the hell?" I ask him.

He shakes his head, looking between Roan and me, and then around the circle at the rest of my sisters.

"I signed up to do a story about a small town and the death of a community leader," he says. "But this is—this is not my story to tell. This is *your* story, Roan. All of yours. And I don't think I can be both a good journalist and a good friend right now."

My sisters wear their feelings differently—Jeza's is just a shift in the look of her eyes, Roan's an expression that is almost a wince, almost pain, Maraam's a quick intake of breath. Priya's eyes fill, just briefly.

I step closer and walk into Merrick's hug. He squeezes me for a moment and then steps back.

"Right," he says. "What do you need?"

"Something you never would have agreed to as a journalist," Roan says wryly, but the look she gives him tells us all how much his choice means to her. "We've asked the mayor and his son to meet us for an interview. But this one won't be like the others. This one—"

"This one isn't just for a story," Merrick finishes for her. "This is for closure. Ask what you need to ask, Roan. Do whatever you need to do."

"We're talking to them." I look at Merrick, searching for something I can say to lighten this moment, pretend it is not as heavy as it is. But the sharpness and sarcasm I usually lean on have been stripped away by this forest. "At home."

It takes him a moment to realize I mean Sister's Place, but he doesn't argue. He just says, like my sisters—

"I'll go with you."

I don't say anything, but I walk out of the house and into the crushing light of day, and I know Roan and the rest will follow. She is a shadow, always at my side, as if she is afraid if I am left alone for a moment that someone will hurt me.

Or, perhaps, that this thing inside me will come uncaged and I will do the hurting.

They surround me before my living sisters do.

Zara and Saem, Cezanne and Eva, Lily and Jordan and Kess.

Sisters.

I say the word, and it calls them back to me.

I think it is Zara who takes my hand in hers. I think it is Eva leading the way, beckoning for me to follow. I think it is Lily who cups my chin, brushes hair back from my face.

Hair that I used to love.

Hair that I cut from me like I tried to cut out the evil that had been done to us all.

"Nev."

Roan's voice calls me back. She has my hand in hers, and she cups my face in her other hand.

They disappear, seven sisters, as if they were never there at all.

Come back.

Come back.

Come back to me.

I want a different world.

"Stay with me," Roan says, and my heart breaks.

Because what about the day I am no longer able to?

What if, at the end of all this, I join my sisters?

Where will that leave Roan, with her worry and regret and the aching memories that haunt her?

This town is a sin against us both.

I am following Roan and Merrick to his truck. My living sisters are saying something, but I do not hear.

I do not listen.

There is a gash down the side of my head from a razor. I can hardly remember where it came from.

There is a wound on the back of Roan's head. I can hardly remember who gave it to her.

Memory and grief, sisters and forests and blood.

It is a cacophony of loss in my head.

It is a tomb.

They surround me even if I cannot hear them, these sisters.

Jeza, who stands like Roan, strength in her shoulders and worry in the sharp set of her jaw. Maraam, with a voice like lavender, and the sound of it helps fear bleed away. Priya, eyes like the river, guiding me home.

And Roan, Roan at my shoulder, holding us all together with the sheer, unbreakable might of her will.

They are still around me, and I am safe in this circle of them.

And these sisters—

They do not disappear.

• • •

Girls like us are not meant to love one another.

They are meant to compete, to view the resources as finite and the competition for them as infinite. They are meant to be at one another's throats, fighting and furious until they destroy one another.

And perhaps that is why they killed us.

Because we did not adhere to the natural order of things. Because we loved, anyway.

Because the resources were finite and the competition for them was infinite, and we loved, we loved, we *loved* one another.

I am ten, and eleven, and twelve, and I am infinite.

I am eleven.

I feel new to the group home even now, but Zara and Saem are lifting me between them, swinging me so I fly far above the earth.

The green of the leaves flashes by me, dappled with sunlight. There is warmth here, and the world is alive, and Lily is laughing and running beside Maraam, and Jeza and Roan are lifting Kess between them, too, and Kess and I—

We are both flying.

One for sorrow, Lily says, singsong.

Two for mirth, Kess yells, and then she is shouting with laughter so uncontainable that I tip back my head and I laugh.

It is just us. Sisters in the forest, laughing and singing and unafraid.

It is just us, and we are infinite.

CHAPTER TWENTY-NINE

WHEN WE REACH SISTER'S PLACE, MERRICK AND JEZA sweep the house, the rest of us staying in the vehicles until they wave us inside.

There is crime scene tape around the house—evidence that the cops finally listened, that they checked out the house sometime today.

We ignore it and duck underneath it.

Maraam pauses by the bookshelf in the living room, running her hands over the titles, pausing at the gaps where books have been removed.

One for sorrow, I want to tell her, because I can almost remember something important.

Two for mirth, I want to tell her, but the knife is digging into my shin and I cannot say anything at all.

Three for—

There is a knock at the door.

My sisters and Merrick draw close to me.

I am the one who opens the door, the way I often did when people came to call. A woman, a nurse from the medical center, who brought tomatoes and peaches from her garden. Dr. Goodwin stopping by because this is the kind of small town that still had physician home visits. Pastor Williams coming to consult on *spiritual health.* Captain Ramsey, stopping by on his rounds, sometimes to tell the group home attendants that one of us had gotten into some trouble again. Jake, picking up Jeza and returning her to us bruised.

Cal Portman, here to pick up a girl for tutoring.

Cal Portman, always in this fucking house.

But it isn't Cal today.

It's just him. Graham Portman.

His hair is more gray than blond, but he has the same build as Cal, similar clothing.

His blue eyes are wide, but there is no other evidence of fear or discomfort. He is bruised, though, purple ringing one eye, his nose a little more crooked than I remember.

I point to the long wooden table. The group home attendants sat at the head and the foot of the table, all of us crammed along the benches on either side. I was usually between Saem and Eva, so close Saem's black braids always brushed my shoulder when she moved. Today I sit at the head, fold my hands on the dusty tabletop.

Roan sits on one side, Zara beside her. Jeza sits down opposite, Eva sliding into her place next to her, and then Saem, and then Priya. Maraam joins Roan on the other side, Lily following. Jordan lingers away from us, and it is Kess and Cezanne who convince her to join. Merrick sits at the end, between my sisters and Graham Portman.

"Sit down," I tell Graham.

"What do you want?" Graham asks. "What do *all* of you want?"

"Who hit you?" I ask, gesturing to his bruise.

He looks confused, running one hand nervously down the front of his Patagonia jacket.

When he answers finally, his tone is halting, uncertain. "I—I was attacked on my way home last night," he says finally. "I've already talked to the police. They have extra protection stationed at my house right now."

Around the table, my sisters and Merrick wear looks that mirror his.

I come to the conclusion last, after all of them:

That it was Graham Portman's face I smashed last night, not Cal's.

But that's not right.

I saw Cal. I *saw* him. His eyes were cold the way they always were. His hands were reaching in the dark. I *saw* him.

Didn't I?

Same height, same build, similar face.

But it was *him*.

So maybe they were both out there, then. Maybe I saw one, and then the other.

And if they were both out there, then Cal is still out there now, somewhere in that fucking forest, still waiting for his turn. Waiting to finish what he started.

One for sorrow, one for sorrow—

"Nev." Roan pulls me back. "Did you have questions for Graham?"

Graham Portman is waiting for me to ask my questions, his fingers drumming on the long wooden table.

His eyes dart to Roan, and then Jeza.

"I've told the police everything I know," Graham answers. "Why did you want to meet here, Nev?"

"Where is *he*?"

That's the only other question that matters now, when it comes down to it.

Because we always met here, didn't we?

It always comes back to this.

• • •

I am eleven, and the mayor visits before his reelection. His son has just graduated high school. He is interning on the campaign, a PR specialist here to take our pictures.

We could take pictures that are a little more fun, he says to Jordan, because Jordan doesn't speak, so Jordan won't, can't tell.

But I hear, and I glare at him.

I shove him with two small hands.

I get in trouble, and Jordan hides her face in her hands, and it all ends too soon.

He does not get pictures for the mayor's campaign, and for this, the mayor is upset. Not because of what Cal said, though.

Never because of that.

• • •

"Tell me about Cal," I say. "Tell me what you *knew*."

Graham squares his shoulders. "My son is away on a hunting trip," he says finally. "I am sure he will be devastated to hear about all this when he returns."

"Is he off-grid?" I ask. "You haven't heard from him?"

Is he—is he in the place I remember him best, pale fingers clenched around the knife he used on me?

My shin aches with the half-memory. Eyes in the dark. The knife and the saw and the door swinging shut behind me.

I look down the table at my sisters.

Beside Cezanne, I catch a glimpse of—

Someone else, someone smaller. She is tiny, her brown eyes sunken, her hair long and black and easy to drag her by.

I cannot look at her, and because I cannot, I cannot find the memory I need.

I look at Graham instead.

It is easier to face him than it is to face—

"Nev," Roan prompts again, endlessly patient.

"He does an off-grid hunting trip annually," Graham says defensively. "He left around the time Charles did."

If I were spinning a story, I would ask him if they left together. I would wonder about the details, if Cal killed Chuck first and has been picking off the other board members since. If some said they would tell, or if he just feared they would.

One for sorrow—

"Did you believe us?" I ask. "Did you believe us and cover it up anyway? Or did you really not know?"

"I don't know what you're talking about." Graham Portman's face reddens as my sisters and I lean closer. "Did I believe *what*?"

• • •

I am twelve, and six of us are gone.

We are gathered in the pastor's office. In a conference room at town hall. At the precinct. In the group home. The memory slips and shifts and I do not know, anymore, which of all the haunted places I am standing in.

But I know this.

"Someone is taking us," I am saying. My hair is so long.

Cal's fingers brush against it as he passes.

He is invited, because he is the mayor's son, because he volunteered as our tutor, because he knew us well, he said. Beside him is Jake, because he has something to tell the board—something Jeza told him in confidence, now being used against us all.

Their friend Brett waits outside for them.

I say it again. "Someone is taking us."

"That's absurd," Dr. Goodwin says.

"Jake says the girls have all been planning to run away." Cal's voice is louder than mine, powerful, sure.

"It's true," Jake confirms. "Jeza said the girls wanted to leave, couldn't wait to get out."

"There's no evidence of a struggle or foul play," Captain Ramsey says, looking to Detective Aisley for backup.

"None at all," Detective Aisley says.

"It's a tragedy, of course," Pastor Williams says. "But we did the best we could."

Cal looks down at me. Blue eyes in the mirror. Blue eyes in the forest.

He sets a hand on my arm, fingers splayed across my skin.

My shin aches before his knife ever pushes deep into skin and tendons.

Across the room, Mayor Portman looks at Cal, at me, at the placement of his son's hand.

The other men look sure of themselves and the story they have been fed, too satisfied with their own power to look any further—but the mayor, his look wavers.

"Please," I am saying, surging forward toward him. "Please believe me. *Someone is taking us.*"

I am twelve, and six of us are gone.

"It's him—" I say, pointing my finger back at Cal. "I think it's *him*."

I am only *twelve*.

I have no evidence.

And Mayor Portman makes sure that nobody believes me.

I am twelve, and I will go missing next.

• • •

"His name is in the police report," I tell Graham. It is such a small victory, but it is victory all the same.

Maraam leans forward. "Last night," she confirms. "After he attacked us."

Jeza nods coldly.

Graham Portman's face had been flushed bright red, but now he turns pale as snow. "I'm sure it was a misunderstanding," he says. "My son isn't even on Avan Island right now."

"They are looking for DNA matches from the other murder victims," Roan tells him softly. "And if he killed those board members, do you know what case they will reopen next?"

Roan's eyes are flickering dangerously when she looks at Graham. She is no longer pretending that she is only here for work. She is here because it is personal.

When Graham says nothing, Roan slams her hand on the table in front of us. Portman flinches, but my sisters remain calm.

"Tell me, Mr. Portman," she spits the words. "If they find his DNA and send dogs to *your* land, what will they find?"

Merrick glances at her, brow furrowing.

This is not journalism. This is not how it is done.

But he has decided to leave the journalist behind for now, so he remains silent, lets her ask her questions.

Roan is here for something else, and I understand the way it beats within her chest, the way she would do anything, give anything, even her job, to bring us all home.

Across the table, Graham Portman is small and pale and he looks very, very tired.

"It's all a horrible misunderstanding," he says, voice more fragile than I have ever heard it. "But I think it's time my side of the story is told."

• • •

I watch her take the king apart in front of me.

He is made of power and silence and he has held on to his throne for longer than I have been alive, but today—today he is afraid.

She is young, and she is sure, and she has come for him.

The girls, in the forest. The girls, all around us.

They lean close, closer.

Graham Portman begins to tremble.

All this time, the girls, they have been whispering: *We are coming for you.*

Today, today, they whisper:

We're here.

• • •

"My boy has always been a leader," Graham begins. "Even when he was young. And after the tragic loss of his mother—he was there, you know, when she died, and he tried to swim out and save her but couldn't. That kind of loss is so hard for a young boy—"

"I have lost more," I interrupt him. "And more again. Skip that part."

Graham presses one hand to the bruise on his face. "If you want to hear what I have to say," he attempts, "you can at least show respect—"

Roan half-rises from her seat, and his words trail off.

He clears his throat. "I don't know what went wrong," he admits, looking back at me. "But my son was *smart*, a good son and a good leader. When those girls started running away, it was tragic, but—"

"Did you believe us?" I ask again.

"I—"

The pause is enough to tell me.

That after six girls had gone missing, he *did* believe us. Or he at least knew *something* was wrong.

"Of course not," he amends, but it is too late for Graham Portman. It has been too late for Graham Portman for a long time now. "It was a preposterous story. But now I—I have to admit—maybe some of the board members knew something else was going on. Jake was always a little difficult, you remember, Jeza, he—"

A snarl rips from my throat.

"Nev," Jeza says softly. "It's all right."

She is the picture of calm, despite this. Calling Jake *difficult*, when he left bruises in places he could always deny?

But in the end, I suppose, Jeza outlasted him. The bruises have healed, and she lived long enough for Jake to be just one more body on the autopsy table.

"I began to wonder if Jake might have done something," Graham says. "Maybe he hurt some of the girls, so they ran away. Of course I wasn't *sure*. I've told the police my theory now."

It is scarcely an impressive feat, to lie about a dead man.

Jake hurt Jeza often. Hurt all of us when he claimed we had been planning to run away.

But it was not Jake with the private tutoring lessons.

It was not Jake's eyes in the dark, or his hands on the saw.

"Dr. Goodwin claimed—" Graham begins again.

"Other DNA was found on Dr. Goodwin's note," Maraam interrupts him.

My head snaps up. This is news to me, that the police suspect someone other than Dr. Goodwin was involved in his own death—and by extension, Chuck's.

"Let's not lean too far into the conspiracy theories," Graham says with a little laugh, but he is outnumbered here, his eyes darting from one girl to the next.

I cannot follow his gaze, because *she* is still there, the little girl with the long dark hair, begging for me to look at her.

"Do you have other questions?" I ask Roan. "Because all I wanted to know was if he knew and covered it up. I don't care about the rest."

I don't care if Cal killed Chuck and framed Dr. Goodwin. I don't care if Cal killed all of them. I don't care if Graham helped him do it.

Roan nods and begins asking questions about when Cal left, about each of the dead men, all of it.

But I lean back in my chair at the head of the table and close my eyes.

The girls around us whisper to me. Even Kess.

• • •

After the interview, Graham leaves first, looking relieved to be released from our hold.

Once we are outside, Merrick sags against his truck. "Jesus, Roan," he says. "I don't know how all of you keep going. It's fucking superhuman."

Beside us, Roan looks gaunt now, frail. As if she has given more than she could afford just now.

She rubs at the injury on the back of her head, fingers trembling. She has a small gash from the attack, a bandage one of my sisters must have put on it.

"I'll get you a new bandage," I tell her softly.

"Shit," Merrick says, his gaze falling on Roan with concern.

She waves him off.

I pass Jeza on her way out, car keys in her hand. "The police have asked us to come in early," she tells me. "The FBI asked them to expedite some of the DNA testing, and they have some updates to share. We'll see you tonight at the town hall, okay? Don't go anywhere without Roan or Merrick."

Maraam and Priya follow her to the car.

When I rejoin Roan and Merrick with the dusty first aid kit from inside the house—still in its old place under the kitchen sink—I pause on the other side of the truck.

Merrick is crouched beside Roan. They are so close they are practically touching, and she lets him like she only ever lets Jeza. I should not be here, I think suddenly. I should let them have—this. A moment.

"I—I needed to tell you," Merrick is saying. "When the FBI gets here and asks us all a hundred questions, I can tell them that the kid stayed here out of trouble and harm's way. That we were here for journalism, and nothing more. I will stick by your story. I will always stick by your story."

"No," Roan protests. "I will face the consequences of endangering Nev. I owe her that much. And—and I'm sorry you didn't get to finish your story here. I owe you, too."

I'm trembling, trembling so hard I can hardly stand. I want her to know: *It was never your job to keep me safe.*

No one can keep me safe.

There is sadness in Merrick, deeper than the Patuxent. Deeper than the Chesapeake. He wears it like a heavy coat around his broad shoulders. "When the time comes, Roan," he says, "and you have done everything you must, I hope you remember to save yourself, too."

I make a sound, my boot crunching against the gravel, and Roan jumps, startled by my presence.

I hold the first aid kit out, and Merrick takes it.

When he turns back to Roan, she tries to suppress her wince.

"Shit, Roan." Merrick examines the injury briefly. "Can I rebandage it for you?" He leaves it a question, because, as always, he is trying not to push his way into power in the spaces she inhabits. And I think it might be for this reason alone that she allows him to touch her.

He adjusts the bandage on her head just slightly.

"You're allowed to feel pain," he murmurs. "You're allowed to show that you do."

Her eyes water, and she turns her face away, her cheek just touching his shoulder. He moves fractionally closer, enough so that now she is leaning on him as he adjusts her bandage.

"I'm going to put the new one on," he says. "It might hurt. *Let* it, Roan."

It does.

She does.

But she buries the sharp intake of breath, the only evidence she feels any pain at all, buries it in his shoulder.

It is strange to see Roan let anyone so close, let alone a man like Merrick. He's about their age, young enough to have been one of the boys in this town.

If he had been, would anything have been different? Would he have been pulled into Cal's golden orbit like everyone else?

I settle into the middle seat between Roan and Merrick as we leave my home, a strange finality settling over me like a heavy blanket. *Goodbye*, I want to say, to this place, but especially the little dark-haired girl in the window.

I turn away from her again, not quite ready.

When we reach town, we drive down Main Street past the empty church, which is dark with disuse, its tall windows like yawning mouths that tried and failed to swallow us.

Merrick parks outside the funeral home, where Jeza greets us in the parking lot.

"It's him," she says.

Roan's shoulders drop as if a weight has slipped from them. "They confirmed it?" she asks. "How?"

I reach for Roan's hand. Cling to her tightly when she takes mine.

"They subpoenaed an ancestry test he did a few months back," Jeza tells us. "And the FBI wanted results ASAP, so a lab in Johnstown did the rest."

"Shit," Merrick says.

"They've formally reopened the investigation into the Sister's Place disappearances," Jeza continues. "And the FBI is sending a team tomorrow."

Kess, I tell her, *they are going to find us now.*

But when I turn to find her, it is the other girl waiting for me, shadowing me wherever I go, so I turn sharply back to Merrick and my sisters.

Merrick is the only one who looks unsettled by this news, sick to his stomach at the thought of Cal and all he has done.

Roan and Jeza and me? We look like we have finally gotten what we wanted.

"Roan?" I ask her. "Does the mayor get to speak at the town hall tonight?"

Jeza looks at me, suspicion tinged with warmth. "Why? Are you planning something, little troublemaker?" Her voice is equal parts rough and affectionate.

"Always," I tell her. "But nothing particularly for tonight. What are they going to do with the mayor?"

"The cops haven't decided if they'll keep him here to avoid any more dead men," Jeza says bluntly. "Or set him loose and follow him."

Set him loose, that thing inside me says.

Because if they did, *I* could follow him. I could follow him, and I know he would lead me through the forest. He would lead me to my sisters, and the boy who killed them.

For now, though, I hold my peace.

Outside, the trees lean closer.

It is almost, *almost* time.

Merrick brings more takeout from the diner, and we eat in the lobby of the funeral home while Jeza prepares her notes and Roan helps her, Priya and Maraam joining us as soon as they're done in the lab. I sit on the floor, takeout box in hand, and I listen to the noise and warmth and *life* of them.

In another world, we would be a family nobody could separate, belong to one another on paper.

In another world, I would be ten and I would never get into a van with a gray-headed mayor and his hungry son and drive to a small town in the heart of the forest that will take everything from me. In another world, I imagine that women like Roan and Jeza drive me home instead, and that home is a place with sisters who do not disappear. He would be there, too, I imagine, a man like Merrick with an ocean of kindness in his eyes and hands that bring takeout and offer help and ask for nothing in return.

It is a world that does not exist. This world is sitting on cold tile, eating takeout from a shitty diner while the only people you love try and fail to mend one another. This world is one that cannot be mended.

The world I long for was never anything but a dream.

I miss it all the same.

SISTERS

WE ARE PROUD OF MARAAM, AND WE ARE SORRY.

She has been so brave for so long, and she is in so much pain, but she stands tall at the front of Avan Island anyway. She stands there for us.

At the town hall, the front row is the faces we love—Priya and Jeza, Roan and Nev.

Merrick sits beside Roan.

The cop speaks first, slow and shaky.

But the town is here to see Maraam, the small-town lab tech who collected the DNA evidence that damned him at last. We are all here to see Maraam.

"Good evening, everyone," Maraam addresses the gathered people. Their nervous hum is louder, more desperate than it was a few nights ago. Fear they have never felt in their comfortable lives is now a living presence among them, feeding off their anxiety and growing larger, looming over them.

They are almost lost to this forest of fear, these good people in their safe town.

They are almost, almost ours.

"Evidence from each recent homicide has been collected by police and lab techs here," Maraam tells them. "We have worked with a lab in Johnstown to expedite testing, and preliminary results suggest that DNA evidence at these crimes scenes belongs to Cal Portman. Additionally, initial forensics suggest the note was not created on Dr. Goodwin's computer."

Yes, we whisper to her. *Say his fucking name.*

We need these people to know that a boy they worshipped has done unthinkable things.

There is a collective gasp. Collective horror.

"Please know Cal is considered armed and extremely dangerous," Detective Edwards adds. "If you see him, do not approach. Call 911 immediately and let us handle it."

Maraam's voice almost trembles when she speaks of us. The truth of her grief is there in her body, but she will not let them see.

A shudder, a ripple of rage, runs through this crowd. This, *this* is not the truth they wanted to hear. This is an ugliness, a blight they thought had been long buried.

When Maraam speaks Cal's name, sure and slow and confident, like she has been waiting to utter this truth to these sleeping people for years.

They are jolted awake, all of them.

This is not the truth they wanted either, but it is the only truth we have to give.

They are choking on their fear, all of them, and they are ours now, *ours*.

"He is wanted in connection with multiple homicides," the detective tells them when the shock has passed over them like a wave in the Patuxent, carrying them all toward the Chesapeake, toward the sea. "Because the men shared an association as members of the Sister's Place group home, we have formally reopened the investigation into the disappearances. Preliminary results in both investigations suggest that this is the work of a serial killer, and as such we have requested reinforcements from the FBI."

If *Cal Portman* were the words to wake them up, *serial killer* are the words that destroy them.

SUSPECT NAMED IN THE AVAN ISLAND KILLINGS

By Roan Ellison

Calhoun "Cal" Portman, a young man from Avan Island, Maryland, has been named a suspect in the recent string of homicides that have rocked the community. While police have not yet been able to locate Portman, they have coordinated with local labs to fast-track the process of compiling and testing DNA evidence, and have found Portman's DNA at the scene of each homicide.

Additionally, witnesses have come forward to share stories of inappropriate relationships Portman had with the young residents of Sister's Place five years ago.

Portman's father, the mayor of Avan Island, Graham Portman, is being held in protective custody. A detective who agreed to speak off the record has suggested that Cal Portman may be trying to silence anyone with knowledge of the whereabouts of the missing girls.

The FBI task force in charge of the case has also named Cal Portman as a person of interest in the Sister's Place disappearances, and will coordinate the reopening of the investigation into the seven girls who went missing.

CHAPTER THIRTY

THIS TOWN HAS NO MORE FIGHT IN IT WHEN MARAAM finishes with them—and I find that neither do I.

I sway, biting my lip so hard I bleed. Beside me, Roan's hands are trembling just slightly as she finishes up some details on her most recent article.

"I'll drive." Jeza reaches into Roan's pocket unceremoniously and takes her keys, but her hand is gentle when it brushes Roan's. "We're all going back to the motel. Now, Roan. And we're all going the hell to sleep."

"What did they end up doing with the mayor?" I ask them.

The silence is heavy.

"They're keeping a police car stationed outside his house," Roan answers me. "Twenty-four/seven."

"Let's hope the surveillance leads them to his son," Merrick adds.

Or that it fails, and his son gets to him.

I have been angry at all the men who did not listen. But Graham

Portman—he *knew*. I am not sure how much, or when. But he knew, and he covered it up anyway.

"Roan? Do you want me to pick up any more food?" Merrick asks as we reach the vehicles.

Roan shakes her head, too tired for this.

Priya grabs my hand. "I grabbed snacks before the grocer left today," she says. "Maraam and I walked there together this afternoon."

"You *walked*?" Roan cuts in. "Through Avan? Without backup?"

Priya smiles sadly at us both. "I was with Maraam. Now come on. Let's go get some sleep."

We finally reach the motel after a long, silent drive, and we move as one huddle toward the door. Merrick and Roan flank the group, me between them. Jeza walks at the front, and Priya and Maraam bring up the rear.

We crowd into one room, all these women and me. I hesitate, and then I pull Merrick in after us.

Merrick draws the shade down and then sits down on the floor beneath the window. "Priya," he says. "Did you say there were snacks?"

And this is how we end up together—Merrick and Roan and Jeza and me, Priya and Maraam, six of us crammed into one small room, desperate for the safety we find in one another.

"Cal Portman is finally fucking *done*," Jeza says, stretching out on Roan's bed and reaching for the bag of chips in Priya's hand. She closes her eyes, and Roan looks over at her as if all she wants is to crawl into bed beside her.

"Now the whole town knows he's a piece of shit," I say. I squeeze between Priya and Maraam, who both look down at me with such fierce affection in their eyes that I want to stay here beside them forever. "The whole town knows his name in a way they can never un-know."

"You know what?" Merrick looks at me and then at Jeza. "We could all use a break from these assholes and their crimes. Maybe we can—"

"A break?" I stare at him, incredulous.

"Yeah," he says. "Case updates can wait until the morning. For now, I brought something to play—" He hesitates, eyes on me. "You may laugh. You seem like you would."

"Yes." I grin. "Mercilessly."

He clears his throat, not meeting my eyes—or any of ours. "Uno," he says finally. "I brought Uno."

"You brought Uno," I repeat. "The *card game*? To your grown-up job where you write about murders?"

He reddens only slightly, but he digs through his bag until he finds it. "To be fair," he says. "It was never supposed to be a story like this one."

Someday, I will ask him if Lucy also liked playing Uno. I won't ask him what happened to her, unless he wants to say. I'll ask what her laugh sounded like, and what she would have thought of the new Ludovico album, and what her favorite comfort foods were, and what he does when he feels like he misses her so much it's like there's a black hole in his chest.

But for now, we play Uno together.

Priya and Maraam join us in a circle on the floor, and Merrick deals. Priya amasses cards and snacks at the same rate, but Roan and Maraam are cutthroat with their skips and reverses and draw twos. They're so immersed in competing with each other that none of them notice when I'm down to my last card.

From the bed, Jeza complains to Roan about "loud, childish games during a criminal investigation" while Roan laughs at her, and I'm giggling now, a buoyancy in my chest.

"The only crime here is that Merrick is about to get *killed* in Uno," I tell her, and Merrick's head snaps to me as I lay down my final card, a draw-four.

He groans dramatically and clutches one hand to his chest as if I've physically injured him. "Roan," he complains. "You didn't tell me your kid sister was a competitive Uno champion."

I lean back against the bed behind me and close my eyes.

This, I think, is what I want, what I told Merrick about, or at least part of it. The room of my own, the plants on the windowsill—but maybe people, too, people who make you feel this thing called *peace* in your chest.

I must have drifted off at some point, because I hear Merrick's low grumble of a voice.

"Roan?" he's saying. "I can lift her."

And then his arms are carrying me and Roan's hands—Maraam's, too—maybe Eva's—maybe Zara's—are tucking blankets over me.

"Tomorrow," Merrick is saying, and I drag my eyes open.

"Tomorrow," Roan repeats wearily. She rises from the chair she had dropped into, sways on her feet.

Merrick catches Roan, and he does not let her go.

"Tomorrow," Roan says quietly, turning to Merrick. "If that detective will listen, we could suggest a search party go through the woods, especially near the Portman property, to see if we can find a trace of where Cal went. Or even—the girls . . . where the girls might be."

The blood rushes from my face, and a memory tugs at me, something deep and dark that I've tried to find for so long, or perhaps I have tried to keep secret from myself. "I think," I whisper. "I think we won't need a search party."

I have known that forest since I was a child. It was a safe haven, when school was impossible and the expectations of the adults around me weighed more than I could bear. I knew it like the back of my hand—

And so did *he*.

And now, I remember more of the path I found for Roan away from Sister's Place, my feet sure in the underbrush as I helped us escape the man in the dark and find our way back to the grim safety of the motel. I remember. I remember more and I have to speak before I lose it again.

The branches pull at my long hair, and his hands are so, so heavy on me.

"The last time," I whisper. "The time I got away. I think—I think if you went with me I could find my way back."

It is not, after all, hard work or suffering or forcing myself to continue that shakes this memory loose. It is not dragging myself to the home that haunts me. It is not torturing myself with the forest.

It is warmth and playing Uno between Roan and Merrick, and being treated as if I was something precious, not something to throw away. It is that, it is being surrounded by love I had forgotten was possible, that lets the splinter of this memory work its way to the surface.

• • •

The morning comes, and the memory is still there, so close to the surface it will tear me apart.

I tried to walk this path with Roan before, right after we first returned to Avan Island, and I could not bear it then. In so many ways, I have been trying and failing to walk that path for so many years.

All my sisters come with me, and Merrick, too. They bring Detective Edwards, tell him that we might find Cal and we might find evidence and that it is time, at last, to listen to one of the girls Cal hurt. So Detective Edwards comes with, because he must bear witness. He is white with fear. He is afraid of this. He was still in the academy in Johnstown when we were stolen, but he can see it in my face. He can feel it in the air in this place.

I tell them to drive to Sister's Place, and we do. We start there, behind the little woodshed and the barn, and this time I do not sob when I take my first step into the forest.

I wait for a moment for all my sisters, the living and the dead, to join me.

And then, finally, I wait for the girl who is not quite either.

She darts down the path ahead of me, hair catching on the branches at times. My fingers trail those branches as I follow her, the little girl only I can see. My hands are as gentle as Roan's as I untangle the bits of hair caught on sharp twigs.

The path is narrow, steep in some places, muddy in others.

The others follow me behind the Portman property, and I think, briefly, of the men in the morgue who wanted this truth buried—or at least wanted it not to be true at all. Bodies, bloated and decaying, men who were always too cowardly to stand up for the innocent.

They are nothing now but names.

Nothing now but victims.

Chuck, sorrow.

Dr. Goodwin, mirth.

Jake Norryc, wedding.

Captain Ramsey, birth.

Pastor Williams, silver.

Their names echo in our footsteps.

Above us, a storm petrel startles from its nest.

Crows call in the distance, their voices high and loud, carrying their mourning through the trees.

"Once," I say, but I am not speaking to them, not really, "I clawed myself free and I ran on this path, the path he did not know."

Roan is at my shoulder, her hand brushing my arm. "Can you tell us more?" she asks softly, but I shake my head.

They are strange things, memory and voice. Sometimes the two are severed. Sometimes you are locked in your aching head with your memories, and they belong to you alone. Or you belong to them.

Sometimes memories are so bloody you cannot speak them, not even if you summoned all the courage you can.

Sometimes you cannot even speak them to the people who love you best. The people *you* love.

Merrick and Jeza and Priya and Maraam say nothing. Priya and Maraam are here in their official capacity, Merrick and Jeza and Roan because I told Detective Edwards I needed their support.

Though we will need a medical examiner, too, if we find what we think we might.

What we hope and dread we might.

But that is not why they are here.

They are here because they love me. They love *us*. Because they lost us to this forest, and they have been looking for us for all these years.

We find nothing, not for almost three miles, not until the path winds farther into the woods on Mayor Portman's property, far from his house, out of sight from any road, and I begin to scream.

Roan catches me, and they surround me, my sisters, and Merrick shields me with his body, his eyes sweeping the trees, the land, suspicious of everything from soil below to birds above us.

I catch my breath, but barely.

It was here, I want to tell them. *It always happened here.*

"Nev?" Roan whispers.

Merrick looks down at me. "My god. Nev, what is it?"

"He dragged me here," I whisper, and the words set a part of myself free that I did not know had been waiting so long for this. "Cal Portman dragged me here."

Merrick swears, the look in his brown eyes haunted.

"Just there," I say—

And then we round a tree, and we are here.

The shack in the forest, where we all see faces in the dark.

The shack with the saw and the secrets.

The shack where once I went to die.

SISTERS

WE WALK WITH THEM THROUGH THE FOREST BECAUSE we love them.

Because we are afraid for them.

Because we need them to remember us.

We need to know we existed.

The place they find, it makes us weep. It is a small shed with a sagging roof and shattered windows. The wind whistles through them, mourning for us all these years and years.

We want to hold Nev close and never let her go.

She is not screaming anymore, at least for now, but each breath she draws is a ragged gasp. She looks around wildly, as if she is looking for something she knows is here. Something she is desperate to see.

Finally, she meets Roan's eyes. "Where are they?" she asks. "Where are all my sisters?"

And they have no answer for her.

"Nev," Roan says. "What are we going to find in the shed?"

"A saw," she answers. "A table."

Merrick steadies himself on an oak tree, one hand bracing there. "Will he be there?"

Nev shakes her head.

They stand there, trembling, all of them. The weight of evil hangs over this place, sagging on the roof, twisting in their stomachs, slicking their hands with sweat.

We breathe out, a whisper in the trees.

Thank you for bearing witness.

Roan takes a breath and looks at Nev, and for her, Roan steps forward.

For her, she opens the door.

A *creak*, a breath of stale air, a cobweb swinging above them, disturbed by their entrance. We have been here for so long, waiting for someone to open this door.

There is a long wooden table in the center of the room.

There is a saw.

And there is a stain. On the saw, on the table, on the floor beneath.

We do not want to tell the rest.

CHAPTER THIRTY-ONE

I AM TWELVE, AND KESS AND I ARE PICKING FLOWERS at the edge of the forest.

One of the attendants brought us with her to town while she ran errands—first the farm store, then the town hall, then the church.

The church stands beside the empty, open field that holds the county fair later in summer. Jordan loved this part of town, loved the silence and the wildflowers and the unimpeded sun.

We hear a whisper in the trees, wind and warning, and I jump.

Kess laughs at me, says that nothing there can hurt us, that I am too afraid of what I may find. She draws back a branch. *See?* she says. *Just a rabbit. Nothing to be scared of.*

We are not afraid of the forest then, at least not enough.

It is her courage, her daring, her foolishness that drives us forward later that night.

It is *my* chores we have to do. I forgot to bring in firewood from the shed behind Sister's Place, and Kess offers to help me, because Kess is my best friend.

I have long black hair that flows down almost to my waist. She tucks a strand behind my ear, and I reach for hers, for red hair that flames against the setting sun. We do not tell the attendant that we are going outside for firewood, because we are foster girls and she is an adult. We don't want to get in trouble, and foster girls don't trust adults.

We are small, at twelve and thirteen. So very, very small.

It is so easy for him to stifle our screams.

To hit me so that Kess doesn't scream again.

It is so easy for him to drag us. In one of his hands, the sunset. In the other, my hair, black as crows. Black as night.

When my hair catches on the branch, just as we duck onto the path, he yanks it free.

I sob then. I sob and sob and sob and it is like he does not hear us, like our pain means nothing to him except a piece of power for him to hold in those relentless hands.

He drags us to a shack in the woods, and I see—I see what he has here, everything blatant, everything exposed. He has not tried to cover what he did before, what he did to the other girls, and it is his arrogance that makes me despair.

He knows no one in this town will look at him. No one will search here. No one will question him.

No one.

No one.

No one.

There are few details after that: wood, splintered and stained, my cheek pressed against it. The blossom of pain and Kess clinging to my hand. The way the moon looked through the small window, trees so close outside they were touching it.

The sound of the river, thundering with rage that she cannot save us, either.

Golden hair, a halo in the light of his lantern. Strong fingers, curled around my locks.

All I have lost, and I must keep this memory, so that Kess will not be alone.

I will not say the rest. I will not say what he wanted from us, what he believed was his to take.

The rest of it is only this:

I ran.

Kess was on his table when I left.

• • •

Merrick vomits in the forest, but when he stands up and wipes his mouth there is something in his eyes I recognize.

Rage, dark as the river, dark as the discovery we just made.

"All of you stay out here," Maraam says. "Detective Edwards, will you call in backup? And when the officers give us the clearance, Priya and I... we need to document what we find. Process what we can. I'll see if we can find any DNA samples. Do a sweep for fingerprints."

The cop is outside, and he is weeping. He is on the phone with the FBI. He is telling them, but he cannot stand here beside us. He cannot bear witness.

"I can stay with Priya and Maraam," Jeza says to us. "You can all—"

"No," I say. "I can stay. I can do it."

"We know," Merrick says. "But, Nev, you don't have to."

"We don't split up," I insist. "I'm not leaving them alone in the woods." My voice rises a notch, verging on the hysteric. *"I'm not leaving them here."*

"Okay." Roan raises her hands, palms out. "We'll stay close by. But come away from the door. You don't need to see this place, not anymore. Not ever, ever, ever again."

I turn toward her, my back to the shed, and she stares over my shoulder at the gaping mouth of the wooden door that creaks and groans on its hinges.

My own memories are crawling up from the soil—hands in the dark, hands reaching. A hand on my knee. Eyes in the mirrors. My hair caught on a branch.

One for sorrow, one for sorrow.

I stop the rest.

I look back at the girls around me, Saem and Cezanne and Zara in daisies and bones, and I want to tear his heart from beneath his rib cage. I want to open him. I want to unmake him. When I find him, when I see him, it will be his turn.

"Roan," Merrick murmurs.

I look down.

Roan's hand is clenched into a fist, but at the sound of his voice, her fingers relax again.

When Priya and Maraam finish with their initial work—Priya taking pictures and Maraam sweeping for anything she can collect for the lab—they emerge with the ghosts still clinging to them. Above them, a crow circles, cries, and I stagger.

Roan reaches for me, but Merrick catches me first. He lifts me easily, holds me like a child, and then walks away from this cursed place without waiting to see if the others follow.

He carries me all the way, however many miles it is back to our vehicles, but he does not seem to tire and he does not falter—and I let him, my head leaning against his shoulder, my eyes open and empty, staring at the sky.

Looking for my sisters.

Looking for home.

I should be panicking at the touch of a man, but the truth is that I feel nothing at all—not his touch, not the stain of this place, not my own heartbeat.

When we reach the truck, Roan opens her mouth to give the orders she needs to, to hold us all together. To keep us moving forward.

It takes her a long moment to uncover her voice.

More officers arrive, and they talk to Maraam for a long time. They try to ask me questions, and Merrick and Roan slip in between. But I hear fragments of it—there are trophies inside the shed, there is DNA. There are pictures. *Pictures.*

I do not remember the pictures, though some must be of me.

And now they are looking for—

"A grave," I interrupt them when a voice catches, fades into grief. "Their grave."

• • •

That afternoon, my sisters keep me close beside them.

When they are working, Merrick tucks his coat over me and Roan pillows her jacket beneath my head.

I close my eyes, and though I do not expect to find sleep, it takes me within seconds.

• • •

I am twelve, and I creep through the woods when dawn finally comes. I am shivering, cold to my bones, and I am listening for him.

For any hint of him.

The house of mirrors, the church, the field, the shack, this haunted fucking forest, they all blur together.

I am twelve, and I am alone.

The truth is that I must do this alone.

I find the grave.

It is open, a pit he has not bothered to cover.

I recognize them all, and my heart splits open in the forest. I bleed to death from the pain of it.

And then they stand beside me, seven sisters who rise from the earth.

It is rage that brings us back.

It is rage that stitches me together again.

And now, it is rage that opens the door in my mind, the door where the last memory lies.

I wake up, and I remember where my sisters are.

I am dreaming, and I am awake. I hear the living, but I am among the dead, too.

"Zara," I say, and I stretch both hands up.

My eyes are still closed, and I am still sleeping.

"Cezanne," I whisper. "Saem." My hand flutters, and I reach. Reach. "Eva. Lily. Jordan." My body is trembling beneath Roan's jacket. *"Kess."*

And then I sit straight up and open my eyes.

CHAPTER THIRTY-TWO

I REMEMBER HOW GRAHAM PORTMAN DID IT NOW.

I am eleven, and he spins a story about how I had revealed something to him in the van on the way to Sister's Place. I had told him, he says, about a traumatizing experience.

Before I even have the chance to tell the truth, I am just a traumatized kid in their eyes, stuck in my memories, and that was probably why I had scratched Graham Portman's innocent son in that house of mirrors. Nothing more.

They nod sympathetically, the men and women on the committees, in the town hall, in the church, and it is a perfect cover story when his son finally finishes what he started.

The good people, they will look at me like I am a liar at worst, and at best just a traumatized girl who could not possibly be *sure* it was him.

How did you know, how did you know? they will demand. *We aren't going to ruin his life, not for a rumor.*

Because who could believe her, when she can't even string a sentence together? When she can't find her way to the place she said this happened? Who would believe a messed-up little kid over the mayor and his son?

Girls like that, we run away.

Zara showed us kindness.

Cezanne danced.

Saem demanded justice.

Eva was too strong.

Jordan did not speak.

Lily burned the oatmeal.

Kess goes with me so I will not be alone.

And no one has believed us this whole time.

No one ever believes us.

But when I wake that afternoon, memories ready to finally leave my mouth, Roan does not ask me if I am sure, does not ask me for the details my broken brain cannot piece together at once.

I tell her about the shallow grave in the heart of the forest, and the daisies, and who rests there, and she does not wonder or ask or even, really, look surprised.

Instead, she looks at me with eyes that know, the steady beat of her heart whispering *I understand* and *I believe you.*

I believe you.

I believe you.

And I tell her everything.

• • •

I tell her everything, and Roan goes to find Merrick and Jeza first. Jeza accepts it with that flicker in her eyes, grief and fury, but her face remains stoic. But when Roan tells Merrick—*Nev might remember where the grave is*—I watch the last fissure in his heart crack, watch him break apart.

I don't know if they tell the cop. Edwards. I assume they do, but he cannot bear this. I don't know if he'll survive the night, not with what he saw in the forest today. So many of us cannot survive this.

"Okay," Merrick says. "We'll go with her. But not tonight. We're almost out of daylight as it is, and she doesn't—she shouldn't have to be out there doing this in the dark. We'll go tomorrow, in the morning, and I don't give a fuck if that means she doesn't remember by that time. I know—I know how memory works for her. For kids . . . kids who've lived through the—the shit—"

He wipes the back of his hand across his eyes, and then he looks at me. "I'm sorry, Nev," Merrick murmurs.

I have no sorrow left for myself.

One for sorrow, one for sorrow—

But not for me.

"The FBI will be here by late tonight," Roan tells him. "So tomorrow, we ask Nev to lead us through the forest one more time, if that will bring her peace. And then, Merrick, we get out of here and take her the fuck home."

"I agree," Jeza says, and Merrick nods.

There's no talk of Roan's articles, not anymore, no talk of work. This is bigger than that, more personal than that.

"Do you live in the group home?" he asks me. "In Johnstown?"

"No," I say, shifting uncomfortably. "Well, not currently. But I'll probably be sent back there because I *was* emancipated and then I disappeared on my social worker and fucked around in a murder investigation and worked with an investigative reporter and shit. So. Yeah. I'll probably get un-emancipated and sent back there."

"You deserve better," Merrick says fiercely. He glances at Roan and Jeza, exchanging a look with them that I don't understand. "We should *do* better." He hesitates, and then he lets out a breath. "You don't have to answer this right now. But if you would feel safe with me," he says, "I could talk to your social worker. You could come stay with me instead. I have space at my place. You'd have—a room. With plants on the windowsill."

I can hardly breathe.

Roan's hand is on my shoulder, gentle, impossible. "She can choose," she says. "I was going to ask her social worker the same thing. If Nev could stay with me."

"Or me." Jeza's hand settles over Roan's.

The last time I was torn away from Avan Island, alone for so many years. But this time, when I leave Avan Island, it will be to—to go *home*, in a way I am not sure I have ever done before. The thought hits me so hard I can hardly stand. But if I fall—if I fall, they will catch me, so is falling really so bad?

"I don't . . ." I say. "I don't know. Also, my social worker is pretty pissed at me, I think. She thinks I'm a runaway. I guess I am, but—"

I can't finish.

"It's okay," Merrick says, "if you can't decide now. But whatever happens, when we go home—I'm here." He looks at Roan and Jeza. "We're here." And then, abruptly, he pulls me into a hug. Roan and Jeza fold in around us after a moment, and then it's just the four of us, and I'm safe. I'm *safe*.

Merrick releases me and steps back, and then Priya knocks to tell us they're ready, it's time for this evening's town hall, because Detective Edwards is holding them nightly, now.

Beyond Jeza and Merrick and Roan I see Eva and Jordan, hand in hand.

Eva is smiling, soft and sad, her usual fury tempered with grace.

Nev, she says, and she looks at Roan and Merrick and Jeza. *It's time to go home.*

SISTERS

WE GATHER THE TOWN OURSELVES, WE REAPERS OF the forest, who whisper the memory of our last fear in their ears. It is theirs now, this fear.

And they are ours.

This time, every last person in this godforsaken town is here.

In the front row, again, are the people we cherish. Priya and Maraam, Jeza and Roan and Nev at the very end. Merrick beside them. "Today, we issued a warrant for Cal Portman's arrest," the police officer announces finally, "for the recent homicides and for the murders of the seven girls who went missing five years ago."

"What evidence do you have?" someone calls from the audience.

Us, we shout back. *We are the evidence, and you didn't care.*

"A murder weapon," he answers. "And a disposal method."

It sounds so cold and clinical, describing it this way, but Roan and Jeza are here, our oldest living sisters, and they would not let them give gory, graphic details that will fascinate them. They will not do that to Nev. To us.

Nev, now, is older than most of us ever had the chance to be. Once our littlest sister, she is now a girl who would have protected us.

She protects us, even now.

“We also have evidence that Avan’s mayor and Cal’s father, Graham Portman, worked with his son to cover up the crimes,” the officer tells them. “The evidence we discovered was all on Mr. Portman’s property this afternoon and has been documented and sent to the state police, as well as the regional FBI office. We believe that the recent homicides have been an attempt to silence complicit members of the community who allowed the cover-up to happen. We are conducting a manhunt for both men, and anyone with information is urged to contact—”

“Graham Portman?” A woman in the middle stands up. Confusion is rife across her face. “I saw him tonight.”

“Portman? Where?” Both Jeza and Roan are focusing on her, and that is how it happens.

“Outside,” she says. “On my way in. I . . . I said hello to him.”

We ache, we ache with fear.

Not again, we beg.

Not one more, we demand.

Please.

Our eyes sweep over the crowd, but we stop because the seat at the end of the front row is empty.

Nev is gone.

CHAPTER THIRTY-THREE

THE FOREST FOLDS AROUND ME LIKE A FAMILIAR, WORN coat, and I breathe in.

Oak and soil and horror.

The sounds I have known so well surround me, birds calling, trees whispering. Cruelty and crows.

Two sets of footsteps, mine and Graham Portman's.

We are going to his son at the heart of the forest.

We are going home.

Five for silver, six for gold, and—

Oh, I know the rest.

Seven, seven, seven for a secret—

Never to be told.

SISTERS

"NEV," ROAN SAYS. *"NEV."*

Beside her, Merrick says something—though what he says, or to whom, is lost to her as it is lost to us.

Utterly lost.

She is running—through the side door Nev must have used to disappear, and the others are beside her.

We are running together, through the darkness, into the wide-open field toward the forest that has always been waiting for us.

Priya and Maraam, Jeza and Roan.

Merrick's footsteps thunder behind us, but he cannot catch up.

We are sisters, survivors, and wind—

And we know the way.

Four of them flying, footsteps like thunder, and Merrick's footsteps fade behind us. We imagine the despair on his face as he loses us to the forest and it breaks us, because we know, we *know* he cares for our littlest sister as we do—

But broken, we have only ever been stronger.

We do not scream Nev's name.

We do not beg the forest to give her up.

We know better.

But our feet, they know this path.

We follow Roan as we always have.

She is scarcely aware of the branches that tear long lines down her face, but we hurt for her. We want to scream.

We want to scream.

Nev.

Not Nev.

Please.

We go past the shack.

It stands empty, door swinging open, but we continue.

Because tonight, now, this is not where they have gone.

Portman and Nev, they traveled this path before us. Through the dark, past the gaping hole of the shack, and plunging into the heart of the wood.

Nev remembers.

Nev remembers where the grave is.

And somehow, Portman knows it.

CHAPTER THIRTY-FOUR

GRAHAM PORTMAN IS A SMALL, SMALL MAN.

I feared him once.

He silenced me once.

But it is fear I see in him tonight.

Because all these years of power and complicit silence have been coming to an end and he has fought it in all the dark, ugly ways he knows how.

Breaking into Sister's Place, terrified there might be evidence there of what his son had done. Hitting Roan in the dark.

Our feet slow.

We are beside the river, where the forest opens to swaying reeds and then swift, silent water. A current that could take you all the way to the sea, if you let it.

But beneath our feet is truth.

My sisters surround me—Zara and Saem, Cezanne and Eva, Lily

and Jordan. Kess stands beside me, eyes wide open. Her chest rises and falls.

Breathing.

I lift my head.

We're home.

SISTERS

WE ARE IN THE FOREST. WE ARE WITH OUR SISTERS. WE see it all.

We see the moment Nev runs from the town hall, into the darkness beyond the parking lot. We see the moment her hand closes around Graham Portman's arm, the terror in his eyes even as he holds a knife to her and tells her, *Come with me, then, if you won't leave me alone.*

And we see our four sisters running, following the path through the darkness.

We see Roan and Jeza, Priya and Maraam, strong from footraces with their sisters, running not for their lives, but for their sister's.

They are the kind of women who would have kept each one of us safe.

We sigh, breathe out, oak trees whispering to them as they go.

And we see Roan's face when she bursts through the trees and finds Graham and Nev.

Graham Portman has a knife to her throat at the heart of the forest, and we will kill him for this, he will die where he stands, but—

Nev is smiling.

We stop as one, the four of us, the living, the seven of us, the dead, our breath ragged, our hearts racing.

"Drop the knife," Roan shouts, and she has a gun, she has a gun, she is pointing it at his head. Has she had it all this time, this sister who would have done anything to save us?

You will die for this. You will die, you will die, you will die.

"You can't run from this." Roan steps forward. "You never could, Portman. Time's up."

He presses the knife closer, a bead of blood appearing on Nev's throat.

She sucks in her breath, and we, all of us, feel the phantom pain on our own necks. Beside Roan, our sisters flinch. They feel it, too.

This pain, we share it.

Roan raises her hands, palms above her head. "Put the knife on my throat, then," she says. "If you need a hostage. *Take me.*"

Take her, Portman.

So she can end you.

The knife trembles in his hand. "I never wanted this to happen," he says, and despite the fact that he is the one holding a knife to the throat of a kid, he makes it sound like begging. "This isn't what I wanted."

And when, Graham Portman, has the world not bent to give you what you want?

"What did you want?" she asks softly.

A step, a tiny step forward.

We will take you down, inch by goddamn inch.

"It wasn't much," he whimpers. "I just wanted my life back. I wanted to be mayor and have my son go to law school. I wanted it all to be the way it was."

We needed you to know just how irredeemable you were.

"You wanted this town on its knees." Jeza's voice is a snake, curling around his throat. "You wanted to do as you pleased and get away with it."

"And your son, he wanted that, too, didn't he?" It is Maraam who speaks, and the gentleness of her voice has long since been carried away by the river and the night and the years of grief. "He wanted to take and take and take—"

"They didn't understand him," Portman interrupts her, his face twisting. The knife presses deeper into Nev's neck. "*No one* understood him. He was brilliant. He was strong. He was a good man. I could not let this ruin his life!"

"Listen, please." Roan makes it sound like begging, and she ghosts closer to his throat. "She's just a kid. She doesn't deserve to die for all of this. You need a hostage. Take me."

Nev scoffs. "No one dies for me," she says. "Graham. Don't we have a lot to talk about?"

"Nev," Priya says. At some point in the run through the forest, Priya's waist-length black hair came loose and now it flows around her like a dark cloud. "Nev, please."

We hear the rest: *Please don't antagonize him. Please don't die in front of me.*

"I brought you here for a reason," Nev says, and surprise loosens Portman's hold on the knife, just for a moment.

Roan takes another step forward, and another. *Breath by breath.*

"*You* brought me here?" he scoffs. The point of his knife is no longer digging into her throat. "*I* pointed my knife at you and you did what I told you to. *I* wanted you here."

And in his hands, Nev begins to laugh.

CHAPTER THIRTY-FIVE

THE PIT OPENS INSIDE OF ME.

I am rage and loss and stolen sisters. I am twisted innocence and I am broken and I am *done.*

"No," I tell him. "I saw you in the dark, and I led you here to the grave. I was going to kill you, did you know that? I was going to kill you and leave you here, and then—oh. Then I *remembered.*"

I followed her, in the end. The little girl who remembered all of it, who carried it for me because I could not.

"Nev," Roan breathes.

How much do you remember? Jeza is asking me, careful and guarded.

Go home, Roan is telling me, over and over again.

We just wanted to protect you.

I did not understand how all of these men would have let Cal close enough once they knew he was coming for them.

And it could only be—

Because they did not kill one another.

We did.

• • •

"Did you know your son is dead?" I ask Portman. "Did you know the whole world knows he was a rapist and a murderer?"

I have waited for this for so long.

Oh, I have waited.

"He's *not*," Graham Portman says desperately. "I told you. He's alive, and he's safe, and he'll be back any day, but he's just being *framed*."

"The knife," I whisper. "In your hands."

Priya breathes out, soft as the wind. "You remember," she says gently. "Oh, Nev. Sweet, beloved girl. You remember."

He freezes, and I know his eyes flick to the knife, to the odd white knife left for him in Cal Portman's bedroom.

"We made this knife," I say. "From the shin bone of your son, after we killed him in the heart of the forest. Zara and Saem, Cezanne and Eva, Lily and Jordan and Kess. And me."

• • •

I am twelve, and I survive the night.

Roan is the first to see me as I walk up the hill, bloody and tattered and torn, and she screams my name. She cannot stop screaming it, until Jeza wraps me up in her arms.

He killed me, I tell them. *He killed us all.*

The board of directors would not have believed me.

Cops would not have believed me.

Girls like that, they lie.

The town would not have believed me.

But *they* do. My sisters, they believe me.

Jeza calls for Priya and Maraam. We are the only ones left.

Baby girl, she says to me. *No, no, no.*

I lead them to the shallow grave.

It is the last memory I will have of it for so long.

I will bury it soon, tuck it away inside myself to protect myself. To survive until I am ready to face the darkness. The little girl I left in the forest, she carries those memories.

He killed me, I tell my sisters.

You're still with us, they tell me over and over again as they weep in the heart of the forest. *We won't let you go. We won't let him take you.*

Promise me you will kill him, I tell them.

And then they are all around me, fierce and furious.

Yes, Jeza says. *Yes, yes, yes.*

And here is how—

So I tell them all of it.

I tell them how to kill Cal Portman. I tell them to use his saw and his shack. I told them he pressed the tip of his knife into my shin and said it was a fine little thing. I tell them about the shin bone knife he said he would make of me. I tell them *use his left leg*, and I show them the mark he left on mine before Kess—before Kess staggered from the table and hit him and bought me time.

One for sorrow, one for sorrow.

I tell them how to kill the monster.

We won't let him take you, they promise me, over and over again.

But when we return to Sister's Place together, a car is waiting for me. Graham Portman, mayor, father, liar, is white-faced and afraid. He is afraid of what his son told him last night. He is afraid I will speak. He is afraid I will be believed.

So he drives me away, while my sisters scream my name.

And I am left in Johnstown, alone, waiting for the day Cal Portman returns to finish what he began.

And while I am alone, while I make myself disappear, my sisters do the only thing they have left:

They plan.

• • •

I was not there when they killed Cal Portman, or there when they cut him up, but I know—I know what I asked them to do. And I know if we are here in the forest, Graham Portman holding the knife made from his son, that we are at the very end of that plan.

Graham Portman drops the knife, and I let out my breath.

I step away from him, and the look I give him is triumph and rage and grief.

"Who *are* you?" he asks, and he sounds afraid.

"The ones who lived." Priya is the first of us to answer. Her hair flows past her waist in waves, her face as serene as the forest around us.

"Nev was our youngest, and she escaped your son," Maraam answers. "And she knew that no one would believe her. That it would not matter what she said, because you have never cared about justice for her or for our sisters."

"You stole my sisters from me, one by one," Roan says softly.

"You will not steal again." Jeza's words carry across the clearing. "You will never again do what you did to Nev."

"Because when we heard what happened to Nev," Maraam says, "we began to plan."

"You—you killed them?" he asks me.

"No," Roan says. "No, do you think we would let her near this darkness? No. We hid her away. We kept her safe, as long as we could. Her memories—" She looks at me, eyes full of tenderness. "She did not keep all of them, precious girl. It was better that way. So no. *We* took our revenge. Her hands are clean."

Portman looks at me again, hands trembling like leaves in the wind.

"We killed your son first," Priya says softly. "Weeks ago. But we were not as messy as him. We wrapped him in plastic, we cleaned every bit of his blood from that shack. We left nothing of him behind."

As if he had never existed at all.

As if he was just a runaway.

"It was easy to kill Chuck," I say. The pieces slip into place as I consider it all from a different lens. "He was leaving town anyway. So my sisters made it look like an overdose, and then they made it look like a murder-suicide, and then they planted Cal's DNA. On Chuck, on Dr. Goodwin's note."

"Who better to help than a lab tech?" Maraam says. "I cut skin and nails from him, Graham. After we killed him and he was nothing but a body on the table."

Graham places his hands over his ears. "You didn't." Tears cut lines down his face. "*Please.* He was my *son.*"

"He hurt us," I say. "Because he thought we were his to take."

Another memory, one last one slipping from the silt and rising to the surface.

• • •

I am in the shack. I am on the table beside Kess.

Cal Portman is finishing his poem.

One for sorrow. He crosses off Zara's name.

Two for mirth. He is laughing as he crosses off Cezanne's.

He is looking at me. *Should we start a new poem?* he is asking. He is holding Jordan's copy of the book of rhymes.

The little girl with the long dark hair stares back at him.

And

she

says

no.

• • •

"We are not his," I tell Graham Portman. "We were *never* his."

"Why—why all the rest?" He is stalling now, I can see it, but I, too, need to understand.

"I came back to find my sisters," I tell him. "But I also came back because I wanted to know—I wanted to know if all those men *knew* the whole time. If they believed us, if they just didn't care."

"I *didn't* know," Graham says. "Not at first. Not until the end."

"It doesn't matter what you knew," Roan says coldly.

It might have, to me.

But not to my four vengeful sisters.

"You knew enough," Maraam says. "Detective Aisley agreed to back off the investigation. Captain Ramsey, too. And you made sure their department was well-funded."

Jeza nods, takes another step forward. "And Jake—" Her face twists as she says his name. "Jake said we were planning to run away, because Cal asked him to say it."

"Dr. Goodwin agreed to make any bodies found look like accidental deaths," Roan adds.

"Pastor Williams used his pulpit and his power to convince everyone we were nothing but troubled girls," Priya finishes.

"And you," I say. "You *knew* there was more to our disappearances."

"I thought—I thought Cal might have hurt some of them, and that was why they ran away," Graham admits finally. "But I didn't know until—until the night he took *you*."

I close my eyes, feel the wind against my skin, and my sisters all around me.

I have truth from his mouth. After all this time, an admittance of guilt.

"So eventually, we made sure the only people you had to turn to were *us*," Priya says. "Your crime scene photographer. Your only lab tech. And of course, when Dr. Goodwin died, they would send the newest assistant ME in the county to Avan Island as replacement."

My sisters surge forward.

We are furious, we are waiting, we are ready.

"He carved my sisters up." Jeza's voice hardens into fury. "So we used his fucking poem, and we sent a *message*. In each man that died. One for sorrow, and Charles Aisley found himself in Johnstown, waiting for Dr. Goodwin to examine him."

"Two for mirth, and Dr. Goodwin had no more air to breathe," Roan says. "Three for a wedding, and Jake Norryc found himself face down on the side of the road." She reaches for Jeza, her hand gentle where it brushes Jeza's fingers.

"Four for a birth, and Captain Ramsey died fleeing town," Priya continues.

"Five for silver, and Pastor Williams died where he made me apologize to your son," I add.

"Six for gold." Maraam points a finger at Portman.

"And seven for a secret, never to be told?" I reach down and lift the shin bone knife, tap the handle.

They are beside me, around me, five years ago is now and now is five years ago, blurring together. Sisters, forest, graves, power stolen, power stolen back. "We were all here five years ago. We stayed in the house at the edge of the forest. Jeza and Roan and Jordan. Zara and Priya and Cezanne. Maraam and Saem and Eva. Lily and Kess. And me. We just wanted to live. But your son, Cal Portman, he was a monster. He's dead, and we get to tell the story. And the story is that he is a serial killer who killed six men and seven girls."

Portman's whole body is trembling, a reed in the wind, and now he lets out a moan like a wounded animal.

He wobbles on his feet, and I could do it now, bury the knife hilt-deep like I have been waiting to do all these years. "I don't understand," he sobs. "I don't *understand*."

"You don't understand what? That we have been planning this since you let your son take our precious sisters from us?" Jeza demands. She has cold fury in her eyes, the kind she must have had after she and Maraam and Priya killed Jake Norryc by the side of the road. "We only waited this long because it took five years to gather what we needed—our qualifications, our jobs, our timing, all of it had to be perfect. Nev deserved that. *We* deserved that."

And I know she thinks the girls are gone, but she's wrong. They're here around me, whispering louder and louder. They're here to watch Graham Portman die.

"This—this can't be true," Portman says. "You aren't killers. You—" He points at me. "You were just a little girl. A child. You can't possibly *remember*—"

"My memory isn't perfect," I tell him softly. "I hid the worst ones away. I had to. But I found them again. I fought my way through the dark. And when I could not remember, my sisters carried us forward."

It sings in my chest, that I am not the only one who remembers.

I am not alone in the house of mirrors any longer. I am not alone in the wide-open field. I am not alone in the forest.

I have never been abandoned.

Portman has tears running down his face. "I thought . . . I thought it was *Cal* killing them all," he says. "He was trying to keep us both safe. We were going to survive this."

"You were never going to survive this," I tell him. "Not when you stole my sisters from me."

Portman swallows hard. "No," he whispers. *"No."*

I lift the shin bone knife, turn it over in my hands once. Twice.

He lets out a whimper.

I raise it to his throat, slowly, slowly. I have waited long for this. I can wait a moment more.

And then I trace a line, the knife not digging in, not yet, from his throat to his navel.

He'll bleed soon enough.

Soon, the forest and the dead whisper. Maraam is at my shoulder now, and Jeza just behind her, teeth bared.

"Did he cry when you killed him?" I ask my sisters, and my voice is the hiss of a sharp breeze in the trees. "Did he beg you for mercy?"

Portman staggers, gasps when it makes the knife dig deeper. He tries to say something, but his voice is a whisper.

We have stolen it from him.

We have silenced him.

"Mercy." Priya laughs, a soft sound.

I press the knife deeper until a drop of blood appears.

I am so close to Portman that I can see his dilated pupils, these gasps for air as if his lungs know they have so, so few left. The pinprick of blood is a river now, trickling down his throat, and something in me comes untethered at last.

I have been waiting for this man's blood for so many, many years. But I, I don't need Portman to know anymore. Just one thing.

"The saw he had for us. I made them promise they would use it on him," I tell Portman, and I watch him die before me now before I even plunge the knife in. I see it in his cold, cold eyes. My voice drops. I am wind and forest and lost girl. I am more than I was. "He said *you* bought that saw for him, and after he used it on us, we used it on him."

"But," he gasps. "So many of them. So many of my friends died. I didn't . . . I didn't *know*. I wasn't complicit—"

"Graham Portman," I say softly. "You were always complicit."

And then Roan steps forward and together all of us lift the shin bone knife, made from a monster. Made to end monsters.

CHAPTER THIRTY-SIX

WE KILL HIM IN THE FOREST, AND HIS BLOOD STAINS THE earth of this hallowed ground.

We stab him once. Each one of us, all of us and none of us.

It is Roan who always carves the note, her letters familiar in their neat curls, their sharp edges. I should have known the first time I saw the words of Jordan's poem cut into a man's corpse. I should have known it was her, carrying forward the vengeance when my own shattered memories could not piece themselves together.

The sixth line of the poem.

Gold, for all the wealth and power he piled around him all those years.

If they were to look under the earth beneath our feet, they would find my sisters.

Cal Portman, he will be harder to find, with so little of him left. And my sisters, they were smarter than he ever was. There was no shallow grave for him, his remains buried so many feet beneath the earth that even cadaver dogs would struggle to find him.

One for sorrow and two for mirth.

Graham dies last, this man who is the last of those who hurt us. The last of those who damned us by their silence.

Three for a wedding, four for a birth.

He dies, and we are free.

Five for silver, six for gold, and—

We stand together, one last time.

Seven for a secret, never to be told.

We are here. We are together, together at last.

We are still standing. Merrick will find us soon. Later, in a few hours maybe, the FBI will arrive.

We will tell them that Cal and Graham Portman dragged me here to finish what they started. That Cal turned on Portman and stabbed him. That he would have killed me next, but my sisters helped me escape.

There is no trace of his death in the shed, no, because unlike him, we were better at covering our tracks.

We will tell them, and they will believe us. They will believe the autopsy reports, the DNA evidence, and the shack in the forest that does not lie. *We* tell this story.

We are this story's end.

The forest around us sighs, letting out a breath of wind.

The police, the FBI, anyone who looks will realize the DNA collected at each scene is a match for Cal Portman, pieces of his hair and nails strewn at each scene, fragments of him collected before we killed him. They will ask a whole town, and they will find the same answer. Perhaps, the FBI will look for a man who is nothing but memory and evil and bones.

They will know him as a monster.

They will never find him.

"We should go," Roan tells me gently. "Back into town. Get you all cleaned up before the FBI arrives."

But there is one, one last thing to do.

I step away from Portman's body, an unimportant set piece, a nothing, garbage to throw away.

I kneel on the damp earth.

Beneath it are my sisters.

I love you, I tell them.

They are all around me, one last time.

Zara is here, fingers threaded through Saem's. *Live*, she tells me, oh so gently.

We will be with you, Saem promises.

They leave first, fade away into the forest.

They go to Baltimore, I think, to a little apartment with space for Saem's cello. She will play the songs she writes for Zara. I imagine that world for them. I bring it closer to us.

Cezanne is dancing to Ludovico, and I dance with her, one last time. "Le onde" plays on for her, and then finally fades. And fades. And fades.

I will dance for you, I promise her.

Eva is next. She cups my face in her hands. I ask her, *Did you find peace?* She nods to me, eyes sharp and bright as they were in life, and then she follows Zara and Saem into the dark.

Jordan is next, and she does not speak, and she does not make eye contact, because those were never things she wanted in life. But she does press her hand to my arm and she sings, she sings, she sings something like a lullaby or a poem, something she will sing in peace in another lifetime. I dream that world for her now, where she is safe no matter whose eyes she meets or doesn't, a world where she is allowed to—*be*.

Lily is next, and she is still laughing, and I will miss her laugh, I will miss it, but I clutch her hands and I promise her to burn the oatmeal so that we can make pancakes, and then I let her follow Jordan into the dark.

Kess. Oh, Kess.

My Kess.

I'll find you again, I promise her.

And now she speaks to me, one last time. *In the next lifetime*, she promises.

In every lifetime, I think, we will find each other. But in the next one, in the next one, I promise not to lose her.

They are gone, then.

Seven sisters.

But there is one more person to say goodbye to, and then I will open my eyes and stand up from the forest floor and allow Roan and Jeza and the rest to take me to safety.

This girl is the smallest of them all. She is tiny, so narrow and scared. She has long dark hair, torn from where it caught on branches. She looks so small to me now, this Nev who has waited for me, this piece of me that will always remain with my sisters.

This girl looks scared, above all. She will learn anger, later. She will learn survival and power and ferocity and she will become a woman whom men fear.

But now she is just scared, out here in the dark.

There is so much I could tell her, but only one thing she needs to hear now, so I pull her close and I say—

I believe you.

I believe you.

I believe you.

When she trembles, I tell her one more thing, the most important thing, the thing I thought I could never give her:

I forgive you.

When I open my eyes, they are gone, seven sisters and the shade of a survivor.

But the living remain, Priya and Maraam, Jeza and Roan and—me.

"It is time to go home," I tell them.

And we walk out of the forest, side by side.

AUTHOR'S NOTE

SEVEN FOR A SECRET DEALS WITH SOME EXTREMELY difficult content, including ableism, abuse, neglect, and assault. While Nev's story is not based on any particular case, many of her circumstances unfortunately mirror the lived experiences of so many girls, women, and people of all genders.

It is important to note that CSA (sexual assault that occurs during childhood/adolescence) is a painful, sometimes life-altering reality that many people (not just girls) experience. Something Nev often references is that she is not believed by those around her, and that nobody listens to "girls like her." Children in the foster care system often face additional barriers to reporting and being believed if they do report. If someone tells you about an experience like Nev's, please, please listen and offer what support you can.

If you are interested in learning more about the complex intersections of sexual violence and other gender-based violence, who is most often at risk of these types of violence, or what can be done about it, I have listed some resources below. If you are a survivor, many resources have hotlines or additional support.

www.rainn.org/resources

www.nsvrc.org

www.thehotline.org

www.niwrc.org

ACKNOWLEDGMENTS

NEV HAS BEEN WITH ME A LONG, LONG TIME. BY THE time *Seven for a Secret* reaches publication, it will be seven years (almost to the day) since I first sat down to write her story.

This story saw many, many different revisions and died on sub twice before the right agent and the right editor helped me bring this story into the world.

Claire: Thank you for never giving up on Nev. It means the world that I had the chance to tell her story.

Kelsey: Thank you for seeing Nev in all her rage and grief and knowing how much her story mattered.

Regan: Thank you for the thoughtful edits, for loving Nev, and for showing so much care and kindness with a story that matters so much to me.

A massive thank-you to Phil Buchanan for another stellar cover, and to Peter Strain for creating the gorgeous, haunting art that so perfectly captures Nev and her sisters.

Finally, a huge thank you to everyone at Disney who worked on this book, in design, marketing, publicity, and copyediting (special shout-out to the copy editor who made sure my characters were eating the takeout, not the containers, and who was patient with my continued inability to understand the difference between *toward* and *towards*).

I am grateful to the countless readers who read various versions of *Seven for a Secret* over the years, including J. Elle, Meryl Wilsner, Rachel Greenlaw, Katy Lapierre, Susan Wallach, Cyla Panin, Christina Jo, Megan Lynch, Meg Long, and J. Nicole. Thank you to Alaysia Jordan for thoughtful notes on so many projects and the beautiful graphic you made for me when I thought this book was not going to make it across the finish line. Thank you, especially, to Brit Wanstrath and Jenna Voris, for loving this book and me and for rooting for us both for so many years.

My Slack writing group: We never did decide on a cool group name, but we are the coolest group. I am so grateful for you all.

Emma: Thank you for being here through all the highs and lows.

Ana Franco: I will always miss you. Thank you for everything you were, and for loving Nev and me and every living thing that crossed your path so well. You are a light that will never go out.

Melissa Bowers: You wrote what is still one of the best books I have ever read. Thank you for reading mine, for being one of my favorite authors, for rooting for me, and for all the support over many years. I can't wait for your turn.

Thank you to the authors who have written furious survivor stories that have lit the way for a story like Nev's: Courtney Summers (*I'm the Girl*), Tiffany D. Jackson (*Grown*), and Ashley Herring Blake (*Girl Made of Stars*).

And thank you, always, to J. Elle, who has loved Nev as long as this story has existed. Nev and Rue will forever exist together in my heart.

To every bookseller who has been so endlessly supportive, kind, and excited: thank you, thank you, thank you. To the readers and book reviewers who have shared their kind words about *Better Left Buried* and advance copies of this book: I am so grateful for the hours of labor you spend making the book community what it is.

I could not do this work without my family.

To my hapkido family: Thank you for coming to book events, putting swag tattoos on (you know what you did), and being the most incredible community.

Thank you, especially, to KJN Corey for your help with ground defense when I wasn't sure of the path forward, and to Rooney for knowing I'd find it.

Grandma Jean: Thank you for reading my stories, sharing recipes, and always making time for your grandchildren. You are a gift.

Grandpa Jack: Your determination inspires me every time this path is difficult. We are lucky to be part of the Roach family.

Grandma Pat: I started this book in the blue room, eating blueberries you had picked up for me because you never forgot that. I wish you were here to see this.

Nicole: Your voice note review of *Better Left Buried* put wind back in my sails when I needed it most. Thank you for everything.

Paul, Kim, Molly, Megan, and Emily: Thank you for coming to book events, hyping me up, and always making me feel so welcome.

Mom: Thank you for coming to so many events and filling your shelves with my books. You are my favorite person to beat at Uno. (And now it's in a published book, so there is evidence of my continued victory. Missed.)

Dad: Thank you for the surprise in Boston, and for showing so much care for anything your kids are interested in (including the publishing industry). You made that event (and all of them) so much better.

John and JoJo: Thank you for coming to my first ever book launch, despite having to bring four very small, very active little guys along with you. I wrote this book when we all lived together, and I treasure those days, and you both, always.

Grace: There are too many things, so in this one I'll just say for the poem on Tumblr, for the 6K book, and for being the first person I hugged as a black belt. I want to be like you when I grow up.

Paul: Thank you for yellow vitamin C drops, making me laugh so hard in Portland (and always), and being the most committed to tomfoolery in every moment.

Daniel: Thank you for always taking the time to ask about publishing, to try to understand the work that I do (even though this industry really doesn't make sense), and for all the you-know-what kind of questions (it rhymes with loner).

For Arynn: Thank you for sticking by me through late-night revisions, impossible deadlines, and every disappointment, and for shutting the laptop when I've seen a review that made me sad. Thank you for getting Nev. You are my heart.

And finally, to every reader who sees themselves in Nev: Thank you for reading. I wish you nothing but peace.